THE
UNTOUCHED
CRIME

THE UNTOUCHED CRIME

ZIJIN CHEN

TRANSLATED BY
MICHELLE DEETER

Text copyright © 2014 Shanghai Insight Media Co., Ltd.
Translation copyright © 2016 Michelle Deeter

Previously published as 无证之罪 by Hunan People's Publishing House in Mainland China in 2014. Translated from Chinese by Michelle Deeter. First published in English by AmazonCrossing in 2016.

Published by AmazonCrossing, Seattle

www.apub.com

Amazon, the Amazon logo, and AmazonCrossing are trademarks of Amazon.com, Inc., or its affiliates.

ISBN-13: 9781503937390
ISBN-10: 1503937399

Cover design by Rex Bonomelli

Printed in the United States of America

PART 1
COME AND GET ME

Chapter 1

There were too many people at the scene. The five police cars could barely park.

Zhao Tiemin, captain of the Hangzhou Criminal Investigation Division, had just opened the car door when someone thrust a black microphone in his face.

"What is this?" he growled, rubbing his forehead as he stood. More cameras appeared, blocking his path, and several reporters all started asking questions at once.

"This is the fifth murder; do you think you can catch the serial killer this time?"

"The killer left another sign saying 'Come and get me' at the crime; do you have any comments?"

"Could you give us a brief rundown of the case?"

Captain Zhao did not respond, pressing his lips into a thin line to suppress his annoyance. He had raced to the scene to investigate, and already these reporters were getting in the way.

If he were still a rookie, he probably would have lost his patience and shouted something along the lines of "I haven't even arrived at the scene; what the hell do I know?" But an outburst would only land him on the evening news. As the highest-ranking officer on the scene, he knew that keeping up appearances was important.

Zhao Tiemin coughed loudly and clapped to get everyone's attention. "Ladies and gentlemen," he announced. "For further information on the case, please contact the publicity department of the Hangzhou Public Security Bureau. I'm afraid I am not in a position to comment."

He hated dealing with journalists. With a wave of his hand, he ordered his team to disperse the crowd. The onlookers parted like the Red Sea, and Zhao Tiemin and ten of his officers stepped under the crime scene tape. The representative of the district Public Security Bureau securing the scene hurried to greet them.

Zhao nodded in greeting, his face expressionless. "Has Old Chen arrived yet?"

"Yes, some time ago. Dr. Chen is examining the body right now."

"Right. Your men can hand things over to us—this case will be handled directly by the city PSB."

Zhao scanned the area from his spot on the grassy area next to Wenyi West Road. Just beyond, a pop-up canopy had been erected over a body on an expanse of concrete. Several officers milled about.

Zhao walked towards the canopy to get a closer look at the dead man, who had several labels affixed to his round body.

His eyes were bulging and bloodshot—the capillaries had ruptured. He was naked from the waist up, and his chest and arms were covered in tattoos. It was highly likely that he hung out with the seedier crowd in Hangzhou. His tongue lolled out of his mouth, and a cigarette was stuck between his plump lips.

"What do you know so far?" Zhao asked Dr. Chen, who was crouched next to the body.

Chen lifted the dead man's chin with his gloved hand and pointed to a long bruise on the man's neck. "This, combined with his red eyes and protruding tongue, lead me to believe that the victim was strangled by a rope from behind. The marks suggest that the killer's left hand was stronger than his right, probably a lefty. The time of death is somewhere between eleven and one. I can pinpoint a more exact time when we complete the autopsy. But we should hurry." He looked towards the September sun, now beating down on them. "At this temperature, the body starts to decompose almost immediately."

Zhao rubbed his nose. It had been an extremely hot summer. Though the man had only been dead for eight or nine hours, the stench was awful.

Chen delicately retrieved the cigarette and put it in a small plastic bag.

"Not again . . ." Zhao's eyebrows furrowed.

"A Liqun cigarette, yes." Chen shook his head and frowned. "Every detail is exactly the same as the last four cases. The weapon was found in the grass about five hundred yards away from the body. It was a jump rope, like those used for PE class. There were fingerprints on the wooden handles. The killer attacked from behind, strangling his victim with the rope. Once dead, he put a Liqun cigarette in the victim's mouth and left a white piece of paper with the words 'Come and get me' printed on it. We have already collected that evidence."

Zhao pressed his lips together again.

Typically the district Public Security Bureau would handle any homicide that occurred in its jurisdiction. But this case was immediately transferred to Zhao because the officers could tell it was the fifth case of the serial murders. As soon as they saw the "Come and get me" sign, the district officers reported to the higher-ups, who transferred the case to the city level.

The serial murders were famous—each new case brought a panicked uproar from the city.

When the first killing happened two years back, the provocative "Come and get me" sign left the police reeling. Every media outlet offered nonstop coverage, and both the provincial- and the city-level government officials were furious. The mayor had slammed his hand on his desk and ordered the police to catch the killer.

The province and the city formed a joint special task force to investigate. Half a year later, the force was disbanded because it had made zero progress.

But not long after the special task force was disbanded, a second murder was committed. The location had changed, but nearly every other detail was identical. As before, the task force assembled was eventually disbanded after no new evidence was found.

The task force had now been disbanded four times. Different officers must have made several thousand trips to the crime scenes in that period, but it amounted to nothing. During each investigation, the police collected as many fingerprints as possible from local residents, but to no avail. In every case, the crime was committed in a suburban area where there were few security cameras, and those in existence did not seem to record anything useful. A few suspicious types were rounded up, but after thorough investigation, each was eliminated from the suspects list.

The police supervisors raged, but the investigators didn't have the slightest idea of who the killer could be. At first the mayor kept pounding his desk with nothing to show for it. After a while, he didn't bother.

For this fifth case, Zhao had been selected to be the head of the newest special task force.

It looked exactly the same as the other four cases. The murder weapon was a simple jump rope, the victim was strangled from behind, and the rope was abandoned, seemingly carelessly, not far from the body. Fingerprints were found on the handles of the rope.

Even more baffling, the killer always left a Liqun, a local brand of cigarette, between the lips of his victims.

What did it mean?

Was he trying to convey that smoking was unhealthy, or was he endorsing Hangzhou's favorite cigarettes?

The special task forces had discussed it time and time again, but they never reached a satisfying conclusion.

Chen studied Zhao's distressed expression. The past four special task forces started out with plenty of power and momentum, but they couldn't crack the case. Now it was Zhao's turn. Could he solve it?

Chen coughed slightly. "This murder does have a few aspects that are different from the last four cases," he informed Zhao.

"What differences?" His eyes widened.

Chapter 2

Chen pointed at the ground, near the victim's right hand.

Zhao looked down. "There's writing! Do you think the killer did it?"

Chen shook his head. "From the looks of it, it was probably written by the victim while he struggled with the killer. I found a small rock in the victim's right hand."

Zhao stared at Chen, puzzled. "What does it mean? It looks like nonsense."

"It's not nonsense; the victim didn't have a chance to finish what he was writing. I think it might be 'local.'"

"Local?" Zhao looked at the letters for a long time before nodding. "Probably. Does that mean the victim was trying to tell us the killer is from Hangzhou?"

"That's what I think," Chen agreed. "We found an ID card. The victim's name was Sun Hongyun, from Shandong province. That's all we know at the moment. Shandong province is over five hundred miles from here, so 'local' must refer to the killer."

Zhao considered this. "Compared to the last four cases, this is a breakthrough. If we can confirm that the killer is a local and not a migrant, that would significantly reduce the number of possible suspects."

"Based on this clue, I think it's likely that the killer and the victim knew each other," Chen added.

"Not necessarily." Zhao shook his head. "For the last four cases, the likelihood that the killer and the victim were acquainted was almost none. If the victim wrote the word 'local,' that leaves us with two possibilities. Either the victim knew the killer, but not well enough to know his name—or, during the attack, the killer spoke some Hangzhou dialect."

"There is one other aspect that sets this case apart from the other four," Chen said. "The place where we found the body is not where the killer started his attack."

"Do you mean to say that the killer moved the body after the murder?" Zhao asked, looking around. If the body was moved, then the crime would involve two steps: killing the victim and moving the body. That could lead to more clues.

Chen shook his head. "He must have been killed here because just before he died, he wrote the word on the ground. Let me recreate the scene according to the existing clues. Somewhere between 11:00 p.m. and 1:00 a.m., the victim was walking along this road. He approached the grass to relieve himself. In that moment, the killer approached from behind and wrapped the rope securely around his neck. The killer pulled the victim this way until he reached this spot, where the victim ultimately died. We discovered urine in the grass and we're taking a sample back to the lab to see if it belonged to the victim, whose fly was down when we found him. But there's just one thing that doesn't check out. The killer pulled him here, crossing at least seventy-five feet of grass. There are drag marks, but strangely all we can find are footprints of the victim, not of the killer."

"What?" Zhao exclaimed. "You've got to be kidding. The killer pulled the victim all the way here without leaving a single footprint?"

Chen nodded. "I think it's crazy too, but we looked and looked and could only find the footprints of the victim. There were signs of a struggle, but we didn't find a single footprint for the killer."

Zhao sighed. The killer pulled the victim over seventy-five feet without leaving one print. Could he fly?

Zhao felt uneasy.

Chapter 3

It was September, but the brutal summer heat persisted.

Even at seven in the evening, the sky was still bright.

Guo Yu got off the bus, his whole body fatigued, and started walking to his apartment. He wore thick-rimmed glasses that hung heavy on the bridge of his nose. He was too thin and had a gloomy expression on his face—both results of working overtime on a regular basis.

He had gotten a job as a programmer at a private company straight out of college and had been working there for three years now.

He was just a low-level programmer, but his workload was heavy and demanded long hours. He consoled himself with the one good thing about his job—it provided him with a modest but steady income. Every month when the six thousand–odd yuan appeared in his bank account, he felt a little bit better.

It was hard to get by in this city. His tiny apartment, about four hundred square feet, still cost him fifteen hundred a month, and he often sent a couple thousand yuan to his parents, who still lived in the countryside. When he had been accepted into a local college, his family borrowed tens of thousands of yuan for his tuition. Then last year, his father was injured at work, and it wasn't covered by his insurance, setting the family back another twenty or thirty thousand yuan. His younger sister had a disability and needed constant care.

Basically, everything cost money and he struggled to make ends meet. He wanted to settle down, buy a house and a car. But that was just a fantasy.

Some people never have to worry about clothes or food their entire lives, while others face enormous pressure from the moment they are born.

He was grateful for the steady job. Sure, the overtime was exhausting, but there was not much he could do about it. Even getting a job at a bigger company was a far-fetched dream.

He turned onto a smaller road towards his neighborhood and saw that two young men had tied up a mutt with wire for no reason at all. The puppy, no more than five months old, had his legs bound to his body and couldn't breathe properly. The two thugs dragged the dog up and down the street, laughing.

The dog's snout and legs were being rubbed raw, and he yelped and whined. Guo Yu could see the fear in his eyes.

The scene quickly attracted a crowd of onlookers, and people shouted disapprovingly.

One of the thugs answered scornfully, "It's my fucking dog; I can do what I want with him!" The front of his fauxhawk was dyed yellow, which everyone thought looked foolish.

Guo Yu frequently came across these jerks. They were locals—rumor had it that they lived with their families in a rural part of the province until their house was demolished a few years back. The families now lived in multiple apartments, and the young people had too much time on their hands. They stirred up trouble every day. Even though local police locked them up once in a while, they never committed serious crimes, so they were never severely punished.

Guo Yu had grown up in a small village. His family had dogs when he was a kid, and he loved them. Whenever he came across a stray and had food, he would share it with the dog. Watching those thugs drag the poor dog around enraged him. But he was timid and generally avoided confrontation. Besides, he was an outsider and these guys were locals. He stood in the crowd, quietly seething and watching it unfold.

Finally an old man from the area bellowed, "Stop! Nobody treats dogs like that! Hey! You're Zhang's boy, aren't you? Do you want me to go and get your father?"

Despite the fact that they were in their twenties, the young men were unemployed and completely dependent on their parents. Watching the crowd grow, they put the wire down and began to walk away—but not before kicking the dog and cursing to save face.

A twenty-something girl rushed forward to help the dog, who still couldn't breathe. She removed the wire and examined his injuries. Some other people also stepped forward to help.

Guo Yu recognized the girl. She and her older brother had a little noodle shop in the neighborhood, and Guo Yu ate there almost every day. Seeing her face was always a highlight, but he never told her that he liked her because he thought he should wait until he earned enough to support a girlfriend. Still, some days he managed to make a little conversation. That was enough.

Down the road, not far from the shop, the thug with the dyed fauxhawk said, "That bitch keeps prying in our business. I'm going to go to her shop today and teach her a lesson."

"You gonna do it? With her?" his friend said, egging him on.

His lips curled into a demonic smile. "Oh yeah, sooner or later. Last time I asked her she said no. But damn, she is hot! Daddy won't take no for an answer."

Chapter 4

The evening was still very bright, as if the sun couldn't bear to set. The scorching late-afternoon heat cooled down slowly.

A few retired folks sat on a bench, enjoying the cool air along a small river in the west side of the city. A young couple walked their poodle at a leisurely pace. A preschooler ran towards a dog. Her mother shouted after her to stop. Over by the bus stop, a college-aged couple seemed in the midst of an argument.

As night fell, the pace of the city slowed.

Luo Wen walked straight ahead at his usual pace with his head down, wearing his cross-body bag. He didn't look at anyone around him, not even a striking young woman in a miniskirt who was laughing with her friends. Nothing could break his focus.

Luo lived in the suburbs, in a neighborhood called the Village in the City. It was a residential district where the rent was very reasonable and attracted a lot of young professionals.

Just outside of the district was a row of storefronts, mostly restaurants and shops selling fresh fruit.

As was his custom, he walked into a place called Chongqing Noodles and ordered a bowl of *pian'er chuan*, noodles with bamboo shoots and pork.

The noodle shop was owned by Zhu Fulai, a thin man from Chongqing, and his younger sister. He had a bad leg, so he didn't interact with the customers much, just prepared the food. His sister was called Zhu Huiru. Her parents named her Huiru, *hui* meaning "intelligent" and *ru* meaning "one who is like," in the hopes that she would grow up to be very clever. Huiru lived up to her name. She ran the front of the house, greeting customers and making deliveries.

While he waited for his food, Luo Wen fished his wallet out of his pocket and reached for a well-worn photograph. It showed a much younger-looking Luo, standing next to his wife. She was a little plain, but Luo loved her deeply. In front, there was a pouting four-year-old girl unaware that the picture was being taken.

Luo smiled briefly and put his wallet away, his eyes blank.

They had been missing for eight years. His daughter would be in the sixth grade by now. Were they still alive?

For eight years, he had investigated every possible lead. He had quit his job as the director of the Forensic Science and Material Evidence departments. By resigning, he gave up his title as Zhejiang Public Security Bureau forensics expert, but he needed to do so in order to devote more time to finding answers.

Three years ago, the fragmentary evidence took him from Ningbo all the way to Hangzhou. He had no idea how long he would keep living like this. Even though there was only a tiny glimmer of hope, he felt like he had to keep searching. But what would he do when there was no hope left?

A voice behind him called, "Fulai, this dog was being abused. Can we keep him?"

Huiru carried a small, quivering dog whose straw-colored fur was covered in blood.

In the kitchen, Fulai looked at the dog disapprovingly. "What are you doing bringing that in here? Can't you see how dirty he is? Get rid of him. Now."

"No!" Huiru cried, though she seemed to have expected this answer. "Those thugs almost killed the poor thing."

"Thugs? Don't go looking for trouble, Sis." Fulai shot her a worried look. "I wouldn't provoke them if I were you."

"But I didn't provoke them," she said. "They were going to kill the dog. Everybody thought it was cruel!"

Guo Yu came in and asked for a bowl of noodles but shut up when he saw they were in the middle of a fight.

Fulai carried a bowl of noodles to Luo's table. He turned and frowned at the dog. "Just get rid of the dog and don't talk to those guys again!" he said more forcefully.

"I couldn't just stand there, could I? Besides, if we get rid of him now, he'll die in the street. Let's at least wait until he's a little bigger before we give him away."

"Why did nobody else step in? Why did it have to be you?"

"Somebody had to take care of him."

"You can't take care of him!" Fulai shouted. He returned to the kitchen and started on the next orders. Still angry, Huiru put the dog gently back on the floor. The dog tried to stand and immediately collapsed. With great effort, he crawled towards Luo's table and hid, eyes filled with fear.

Luo leaned down. It was a mutt, not particularly special, with grayish-yellow fur and a white spot in the middle of his forehead like a third eye.

Luo was startled by a sudden flood of memories.

Eight years ago, he had come home from work to find that there was a new guest in his house—a little mutt. He wasn't much of an animal lover, so he pulled his daughter aside, explaining that the dog was dirty and she shouldn't play with him and that they would have to get rid of him. His daughter started to cry loudly and his wife stepped in, refusing to abandon the dog. They had found him on the side of the road, where he had been hit by a car. His wife and daughter decided to bring him home, at least until his wounds healed. His daughter had clearly fallen in love with the dog. She had never had a pet before. Luo had no choice but to give in to her pleas. He even used his background in medicine to help heal the dog's wounds.

Just a few months later, his wife and daughter went missing, and the dog with them.

He remembered the golden mutt quite clearly. He had a white spot just like the dog quivering in front of him.

Luo's heart constricted just looking into the dog's little eyes. He picked a slice of meat out of his bowl with his chopsticks, leaned towards the dog, and put the meat in front of him. After hesitating for a few moments, the dog gobbled it up.

Luo smiled. He turned to Huiru. "Would you mind if I took the dog?"

Huiru recognized Luo as a frequent customer who rarely spoke to her or her brother. "You want to keep him?" She sounded uncertain.

Luo nodded. "I could nurse him back to health. I promise to take good care of him."

Before Huiru could respond, Fulai shouted from the kitchen, "Fantastic! Huiru, give this gentleman a box so he can take the dog home."

Huiru hesitated, but eventually went back to the kitchen to get a nice box for the dog.

Almost immediately, Luo regretted his decision. He needed to concentrate; he didn't have time for a dog. But when he looked into the eyes of the little mutt still crouching in the corner, he smiled again. If his daughter were here, she would have wanted him to keep him.

Luo had just finished paying and was about to pick up the box with the mutt when the two thugs burst into the noodle shop. The leader with the fauxhawk, disdainfully nicknamed Yellow Head by local residents, looked at Huiru menacingly and said, "What did you do with my dog?" Then he looked down at the box and smiled.

As Yellow Head bent down, Luo used his foot to pull the box closer. "What do you think you're doing?" Yellow Head said aggressively.

"Is this dog yours?" Luo asked calmly.

"Yeah! Give it back!"

"I see. Would you be interested in selling him to me?"

"Sell him to you?" The thug quickly took stock of Luo. He didn't want to be too rash, since he could tell Luo was older and not the kind of person who could be easily bullied. He finally said, "OK, three hundred yuan. We have been feeding this dog for several months, ever since he was born. He's going to be really strong—"

Luo interrupted him. "Three hundred? No problem." He reached for his wallet and took out three pink notes.

Yellow Head was surprised to find that Luo was so eager to spend three hundred yuan on a mutt, and after accepting the money, regretted not asking for more. Maybe the idiot would have paid five hundred without batting an eye. But after earning three hundred yuan for nothing, he sat with his friend at the next table and shouted, "Two bowls of *bao shan mian!*"

"No way," Huiru said angrily. "You still haven't paid for the last five bowls of noodles you ordered."

"For fuck's sake . . ." Yellow Head complained.

Worried for his sister, Fulai limped to the table. "It's fine, it's fine. Huiru! Go to the kitchen." He turned back to the thugs. "I'll make it right now."

"No!" Huiru cried. "Why would you let them eat for free? They've done this so many times already! Last time when I delivered their food, they didn't pay, and they . . ." She faltered.

"We what? That was just petting. You've been touched by a man before, haven't you?" Yellow Head broke into a wily smile.

Fulai had a look of helplessness on his face. He had suffered from his lame leg ever since he was a kid and was used to being bullied. He had learned to swallow his anger instead of fighting back. Now, Fulai gritted his teeth and gently pulled his sister's hand to stop her from saying anything else.

Sitting at the next table, Guo Yu couldn't take it—humiliating Huiru was the last straw. He smacked his chopsticks down on the table. Staring at the thugs, he tried to look as menacing as possible.

Hearing the sound of the chopsticks on the table, Yellow Head turned and saw Guo Yu glaring at him. He immediately stood up.

"What are you looking at, shrimp?" He stepped towards Guo Yu's table and pointed in his face. "You trying to protect the noodle girl? I don't fucking believe this."

Guo Yu, only briefly carried away by his emotions, became frightened. His cowardly side took control, and he lowered his head submissively.

"If you don't have the balls, then don't fucking stare at people, got it?" Yellow Head saw that this was someone who was easy to bully. He smacked the back of Guo Yu's head and swaggered back to his seat.

Huiru gave the thugs a hateful look, which they ignored, and quickly went to Guo Yu's table. "Are you OK?"

Guo Yu tried not to blush. He leaned his head forward. "I'm— I'm fine."

Luo watched the entire episode from start to finish without a word. He stared at Yellow Head and his friend for a few seconds, shook his head, and laughed it off before picking up the box and leaving.

Chapter 5

The key members of the homicide special task force sat in a conference room at the Hangzhou Public Security Bureau.

Investigator Yang Xuejun reported the latest developments of the investigation. "According to Dr. Chen, the time of death was confirmed to be between 11:00 p.m. and 12:00 a.m. The victim's details are as follows. Name: Sun Hongyun. Age: forty-five. Place of birth: Shandong. He has a criminal record; he served four years in Shandong for theft at the age of nineteen, then seven years for intentional assault when he was twenty-five. A year later he was released from prison, and he moved to Hangzhou to live for ten years. He began to sell stolen property and got involved in the freight business in west Hangzhou with a number of partners. Over several years, he managed to corner the steel market by threatening people and repeatedly breaking the law. Last year he fought with a truck driver and seriously injured him. He just got out of prison last year and was known to be vicious."

Yang looked up to make sure everyone was listening and continued. "He had two mistresses in Hangzhou. According to our investigation, neither of them knew what happened last night. We interrogated some of his assistants, who claimed that his schedule was irregular. Last night he was in west Hangzhou, eating street food with friends. They walked home together until they reached Wenyi West Road, at which point he continued by himself. When he reached the grassy area, he apparently decided to relieve himself and was attacked by the killer. He was pulled to the concrete area of the greenbelt and died of strangulation. The lab results confirmed urine found at the crime scene belonged to Mr. Sun. None of the people who were with him last night noticed anything out of the ordinary in his behavior. Still, we are going to interrogate each one to see if any of them should be included as suspects."

"Did anyone else know that he would be walking home alone on Wenyi West Road?" Captain Zhao asked.

Investigator Yang shook his head. "We asked Mr. Sun's friends, and they said that going for street food that night was a spur-of-the-moment decision. Nobody could have predicted what time they would finish eating, whether or not he would walk home alone, or what street he would take to get there."

"That means the killer followed him all the way to Wenyi West instead of waiting for him in the grassy area," Captain Zhao said, nodding.

"That's what I thought," Investigator Yang said. "But when we asked the victim's friends, they said they didn't have the feeling that they were being followed. It seems the killer must have been extremely careful. There aren't a lot of surveillance cameras in that area, but I contacted the traffic police, and we are looking at the available footage to see if there are any suspicious types worth investigating."

"In the last four cases, the footage did not provide any suspects. Besides, the cameras around Wenyi West Road are all pointed towards the street. They do not cover sidewalks or grass, leaving plenty of blind spots. I'm not expecting any breakthroughs. But we still have to check," Captain Zhao said.

He turned to Chen. "Old Chen, you checked the entire crime scene. Did you find any prints?"

"Footprints generally aren't preserved on concrete, and it looks like the killer deliberately cleared the area of any traces. The footprints on the greenbelt are well preserved, but we didn't find a single footprint that matched the killer."

Captain Zhao pressed his lips into his characteristic thin line and looked around. "So the killer pulled the victim over seventy-five feet but didn't leave a footprint. Any ideas, guys?"

Everyone was at a loss. It seemed impossible, unless the killer could fly. Zhao scratched his chin.

They all sat in silence and thought. Finally Zhao said, "Please remember that this part of the case is strictly confidential. Make sure to tell everyone in the special task force that the lack of footprint evidence is not to be leaked."

Noticing the clear confusion on his team's faces, he explained. "If it gets out that the killer pulled the victim that far and didn't leave a footprint, the rumor mill will kick into high gear. If the media give the killer some exaggerated nickname, it would drive the city into a panic. That will only put more pressure on us to solve the case."

Everyone nodded. Most of them had been in the force for a long time and believed in evidence above all else. They knew the killer couldn't fly; he had simply devised a way to make it look like he didn't walk on the grass. Unfortunately the average resident in Hangzhou did not think so rationally. Once a rumor got started, it wreaked havoc for the police.

As captain of his division, Zhao oversaw several hundred officers. If he couldn't crack the case, he wouldn't be reprimanded, but he would lose a little face. Still, he was desperate for a promotion to deputy chief of the Zhejiang Public Security Bureau, and pressure from the public would not help.

Zhao went on. "Let's put this aside. When you leave this room, you can think about possible ways to not leave footprints. But right now I would like to summarize the similarities between the five cases. First, all of the victims were ex-convicts, and their crimes were moderate to severe: rape, theft, and intentional assault."

One of the more experienced officers spoke up. "Captain Zhao, do you think the killer could be taking the law into his own hands?"

"The killings we typically deal with are cases of manslaughter. It is obvious that the five cases were not accidents. The two most common motives for murder are theft and revenge. The victims were still in possession of all of their property when they were found, so that leaves us with revenge. However, our investigation of the previous cases shows that there is no relation between the victims. So the revenge motive doesn't hold up. When we eliminate the three most common motives and consider that all of the victims had criminal records, I think it's very likely that the killer wanted to kill in the name of righteousness."

"I've looked at the records of the five victims," Yang said. "Their punishments were reasonable. None of them got off easy."

"Perhaps the killer thought that they deserved the death penalty," Zhao answered.

A criminal psychologist nodded. "I would venture that the killer thinks he is working in the name of justice or even in the name of God. He has no respect for the judgment given by the law."

One of the older officers shook his head. "One of the victims was just a thief. The killer would be crazy to think that theft warrants the death penalty!"

Zhao paused. The old officer had a point. "Let's put aside the question of motive," Zhao said. "It won't help us learn anything about the characteristics of the killer. Let's move to the second characteristic present in all five cases. After committing the crime, the killer always leaves his weapon close to the victim. And why does the killer always use a jump rope instead of a knife? A jump rope isn't foolproof. The killer might fail to carry out his plan if the victim puts up a good fight."

Zhao's assistants all shook their heads and shrugged. If someone wanted to commit a murder, a knife was the easiest and most reliable way to do it, since guns were all but impossible to obtain. Why would the killer make the job more difficult by using a jump rope?

"The third characteristic is that the jump rope is always the same, with wooden handles," Zhao continued. "In every case, the killer left clear fingerprints on the handles. He doesn't seem to be the least bit worried that those fingerprints could incriminate him. Why?"

Yang ventured a guess. "Maybe he didn't realize that leaving his fingerprints would be risky?"

"I don't think that's it," Zhao said firmly. "We barely have the slightest grasp on this killer even though he has committed five murders. It's clear that this person is very good at covering his tracks. There is no way that he was unaware of the risk those fingerprints would pose."

"He was probably less experienced for his first murder," someone suggested. "After he killed his victim, he panicked and left the murder weapon. Then in subsequent attacks, he knew that the police already had his fingerprints, so there was no need to hide them. It's just another way of taunting us, like the notes."

"That's possible," Zhao answered. "But in the past few cases we collected the fingerprints of thousands of residents in the area and never found a match."

"It's impossible to collect the fingerprints of everyone in the area," the officer pointed out. "It would be very easy for the killer to go unnoticed, especially if they don't even live near the crime scenes."

"I think the killer lives somewhere in west Hangzhou, because all five cases happened there at night," Zhao said. "If the killer had to travel to scope out the location and wait for the moment to attack, it would be much harder to coordinate."

"People move around a lot nowadays. If the killer wanted to avoid the police when they were collecting fingerprints, it would be easy to just pick up and leave."

Zhao nodded. "The fourth characteristic is the note found at the scene of every crime. He is clearly taunting us. And those Liqun cigarettes in the victims' mouths—I don't know what to make of that."

"Maybe the killer wanted to leave a few red herrings to put us on the wrong track," Yang said.

Another officer nodded. "That's the only explanation; otherwise it doesn't make any sense."

"So what do we do now?" Yang asked.

"We're going to split up into groups," Zhao said. "Yang, your group is responsible for investigating the surveillance tapes and making inquiries about the friends and enemies of the victim. Song, you'll lead a second group to find out which local stores carry this kind of jump rope. I also want you to ask the forensics experts to check the ink and the paper on that note to see if we can learn anything new there. I want a third group with as many people as possible to interview as many residents near Wenyi West as possible. Ask if they saw anything out of the ordinary last night, and see if anyone has been acting suspiciously over the past few days. I hope you can bring me some good news. Otherwise we will have to go back to gathering fingerprints. In this case the victim wrote the word 'local,' so pay attention to local residents."

Just as the meeting ended and Zhao was preparing to return to his office, an officer burst into the room. "We just got an important clue, sir," he said to Zhao. "The West Hangzhou Police Station got a report from a woman last night. She works at a bar downtown and claims that a man in his forties grabbed her while she was on the way home from work. The man pulled her onto a grassy area near Wenyi West Road and sexually assaulted her."

The time and place of the assault coincided closely with the homicide. It was about two hundred feet away from the concrete area, with just a few shrubs and trees between the two.

Captain Zhao squinted. It looked like he would need to investigate the sexual-assault case before continuing on the homicide.

Chapter 6

The next morning when Zhao arrived at the station, Investigator Yang followed him to his office.

"Here are the files from the district Public Security Bureau. Apparently the suspect has been grabbing and assaulting women for several months now. He finds a girl walking home alone, pulls her violently to the grass, threatens her with a knife, and then sexually assaults her. When he finishes he makes a couple more threats and then walks away with the confidence that he won't be reported. News stations have picked up the story several times."

"Then why haven't they caught him?" Zhao asked, incredulous.

"The guy always crouches on a quiet stretch of road, waiting for the perfect opportunity so he won't be caught. The district bureau opened a case after the first report but didn't prioritize it, because he didn't go so far as to rape the victims. But in the past few weeks, the assaults increased to one every few days. By the time eight victims had come forward, the district bureau increased their night patrols and found a suspect on the surveillance cameras, though he always wears a baseball cap to hide his face. But as they checked other cameras in the area, they discovered that he has a strange habit."

Zhao was immediately curious. "What strange habit?"

Yang hesitated awkwardly. "The camera footage shows that he occasionally defecates in elevators near the park."

Zhao rubbed his chin in bewilderment. "He goes into elevators and defecates?"

Yang nodded. "He goes into the elevator wearing that cap and takes off his pants right in front of the camera. He doesn't wipe, just zips up and leaves."

What the hell? Zhao thought it was all very strange. This guy was clearly a pervert, but was he the serial killer as well?

Zhao took the report and scanned the pages briefly. He thought for a moment before asking, "Have you contacted the woman who reported the assault last night?"

"I arranged an interview with her in her apartment in an hour."

"OK. Where does she live?"

"Just north of Wenyi West Road, in an apartment building southwest of Zhejiang University."

"Zhejiang University?" That caught his attention. He had an old friend at the university who might have an explanation for why the killer never left footprints. "I'm coming with you."

"Are you sure?" Yang asked. He knew it was rare for the captain to personally investigate such a low-profile case—for any captain to go in the field, really. Yang and the other investigators of the Hangzhou Bureau were responsible for menial fieldwork. Captain Zhao headed the Criminal Investigation Division; most of their time was spent providing strategic advice and authorizing others to take action.

"Yes, we'll go together." Zhao nodded.

An hour later, Zhao and Yang knocked on the victim's door. Her name was Ms. Liu and she was from northern China. Zhao saw that she was beautiful even without makeup. She had a great figure too.

The woman told them that she was a waitress in a bar and she worked nights. She usually came home late, around midnight. She was so unsettled by the assault that she had asked for the next day off. Zhao didn't pry. Whether she was a waitress or earned money doing other work was irrelevant to the case.

After asking some preliminary questions, Zhao finally asked, "Could you please give us a detailed account of what happened to you the night before last, Ms. Liu?"

"Do you think you can catch that pervert?" She gave him a worried look.

Investigator Yang was surprised. Police officers did their best not to make any promises, and he and Zhao needed to think of the best response. Before Yang even opened his mouth, Zhao said, "Definitely. But in order to do so we need more information. The statement you gave at the police station is not thorough enough."

"OK." Ms. Liu nodded. "The night before last, before midnight, I got off the bus, and I started walking on Wenyi West Road towards my apartment. I didn't see anyone else on the street."

"How far do you think you went?" Zhao asked.

"I just walked from the bus stop to that open space. I don't know, three to five hundred feet?"

"Right. Continue." Zhao took note of the distance.

"A man in his forties wearing glasses started walking towards me. He looked like . . . um . . . well, he just looked normal. He sort of had a long face, without any wrinkles. His hair wasn't too short or too long. He looked like a respectable guy."

Zhao interrupted her. "Was he wearing a hat?"

She shook her head. "No, but he was carrying a shoulder bag . . . like a leather Gucci bag. Basically I remember thinking he looked like he had a lot of money. I never would have expected him to do what he did. The police at the police station told me that the cameras show some guy wearing a hat, but I think he hid the hat in his bag or something, because if he had it on before, I would have been a little warier."

Captain Zhao nodded. Some of the victims remembered him wearing a jade bracelet. He seemed to give off an air of wealth. Nobody thought that a refined gentleman would turn around and pull a young woman onto the grass to sexually assault her.

Ms. Liu trembled as she continued her story. "We had walked a few steps past each other when I heard footsteps running towards me. I didn't even know what was happening. That monster grabbed my hair and pulled me toward him. He showed me his knife and dragged me all the way to the open space, threatening to kill me if I screamed."

"I know that you reported the incident to the local police station. But could you please tell me . . . how he assaulted you?" Zhao cleared his throat. "Did he force you to give him a hand job?"

The girl frowned, disgusted. She looked at her feet as she answered. "No, he threatened me with a knife and then made me watch him jerk off."

"He didn't make you do it? He did it himself?"

The girl nodded.

"How long did this last?"

"Oh, he came pretty quickly," she said, then blushed, shooting a glance at the officers. They waited. "It lasted one to two minutes," she said as delicately as possible.

Zhao felt uncomfortable, but he forced himself to keep asking questions. "Did he leave after that?"

"Yeah. He, he finished his business, looked nervous, and ran off. I was *terrified*. I waited a long time before getting up, and then ran to my building to report it to the security guard. Then I went to the police."

Zhao listened closely but felt that something was not quite right with her story. He just couldn't put his finger on it. Once again, he confirmed the location of the crime, just 150 feet from the murder. The two cases were only separated by grass and a copse of trees.

When they finished the interview, Zhao asked Yang to take him to Zhejiang University. He wanted to have a chat with that old friend of his.

PART 2
THE TRAGEDY OF THE LOGICIAN

Chapter 7

The first day of the fall term at Zhejiang University was unbearably hot. Yan Liang, a mathematics professor, waited for the next elevator.

Sun streamed into the hallway and cast his shadow on the wall. Professor Yan was so hot his scalp itched. He longed for his air-conditioned classroom.

Ding! The doors opened and Professor Yan quickly stepped inside.

"What the—?" Professor Yan nimbly moved to the back of the elevator, avoiding an unpleasant pile in the corner.

He squatted to look more closely at it and gasped. It was feces.

He started to sweat. His classroom was on the sixth floor and he didn't want to walk up six flights of stairs. If he could just hold out for a minute, he would be fine. He held his nose and pressed the button for the sixth floor.

The ride felt like the longest of his life. Then the elevator jerked and the doors remained shut. He pressed the "door open" button and the emergency button, but it took several minutes before he finally got out again. When the doors finally opened, Professor Yan stumbled out and sucked in the fresh air. Glancing up, he suddenly felt rooted to the spot.

A group of his students wrinkled their noses at the foul smell emanating from the elevator. He said in a loud voice, "Wait, wait, let me explain."

"Don't worry, Professor, we all have accidents," one of them said. "We promise we'll keep it a secret!" They all suppressed laughs, and one student even handed him a small pack of tissues. Turning red, he ushered them into the classroom.

He usually liked to start the year off with something lighthearted and had prepared a humorous lesson explaining why math was the "father of all academic disciplines."

But this year the students found him funny long before he had a chance to introduce himself. Instead, he taught two uninspiring lessons of mathematical logic. By the end, he just wanted to go home.

As he gathered his books, a male student read something on his phone to his neighbors. "A man has been lurking around west Hangzhou and repeatedly assaulting young women walking home alone late at night. According to a victim's description, the man is in his forties, has short hair, wears glasses, and looks respectable. The Xihu District Public Security Bureau reported that surveillance cameras have filmed him defecating in elevators. The police are making every effort to catch the criminal and are ramping up night patrols in the area."

As the student continued to read, more eyes focused on the professor. He matched the description perfectly.

Professor Yan was organizing his lecture notes when he noticed that the feel of the room had changed. Looking up, he saw suspicious expressions on his students' faces. He flushed.

At that moment, a girl came running back into the classroom. "Professor Yan!" she exclaimed. "The police are here. They say they want to speak to you."

The students saw two uniformed officers waiting at the door. Captain Zhao looked sternly at Yan. "Hurry up. We've been looking for you," he said impatiently.

The students all turned to look back at Professor Yan, surprised. They wondered if their teacher would leave the classroom handcuffed.

For a second, Yan couldn't move. He looked at Zhao, angrily stuffed his last few papers into his briefcase, and walked towards the door with his head hung low.

Chapter 8

Professor Yan clenched his teeth and glared at Zhao and Yang. "What are you doing coming into my classroom like that? In uniform, no less!" he hissed. He spied a Police Tactical Unit vehicle in the parking lot, the kind that typically transported criminals to police stations, and he was thoroughly irritated. "And you're driving a PTU. Thanks to you, I have now lost any shred of credibility I had with my students."

Zhao frowned. "What do you mean? I was on a case on Wenyi West Road and decided to swing by and see you. I'm sorry I didn't have time to change out of uniform."

"OK. OK. What's the matter? And don't ask me about one of your cases; you know I hate that. If you want to have dinner, I would be happy to go some other time. Just remember to come in civilian clothes." He quickened his pace. The last thing he wanted was to interact with the police today.

Zhao followed close behind and smiled. "Fine, let's grab something to eat. I'll change my clothes in the car."

Yan spun around. "Zhao, I know we're old friends, but what are you doing here?"

Zhao was a little embarrassed. "Actually I'm working on this case," he began in a low voice.

"That's enough! I left the force five years ago. I'm just a teacher now. I don't want to have anything to do with the police anymore; do I make myself clear?"

"I thought you might say that. But you know I wouldn't ask for help if it were just some ordinary case. You heard about last night's murder on Wenyi West Road, didn't you?"

"No, and I don't care."

Zhao coughed and pretended not to have heard Yan's answer. "It's been in the news. For three years there has been a serial killer at large in west Hangzhou. He leaves a note that says 'Come and get me' at each crime scene. Sound familiar?"

Yan couldn't help but feel a wave of schadenfreude wash over him as he heard about Zhao's tough case. "Yesterday was the fifth case, I take it?" He looked at Zhao. "But what does this have to do with me?"

"Come on, Yan, you were on the special task force for the Zhejiang PSB."

"I don't want to talk about the past. If you don't have anything else you want to talk about, then I'm going home. Good luck with your case, and please don't come back; it's a waste of time." Yan turned to leave.

Zhao caught his arm and said in a low voice, "If you don't want to talk about the case, that's fine. I just have one question. How did the killer pull his victim over seventy-five feet *of grass* without leaving a single footprint?"

"Crossing grass without leaving a footprint?" Yan's eyes flashed with curiosity, but he quickly resumed his disinterested expression. "Cops are the ones who are supposed to solve cases. Not professors."

"How about you just talk to me as a friend for a second? What do you say?" Zhao said.

"That's your only question?" Yan asked, hesitant.

Zhao nodded. "That's it."

"If I give you an answer, you won't bother me again?"

Zhao laughed. "If that's what you want, yes."

"I have one condition," Yan said.

"Go on," Zhao said, smiling, ready to hear his request.

"You're a high-ranking officer; you have some power in your bureau. I want you to put some pressure on the guys in the Xihu District PSB. Make sure they catch that pervert who's been hanging around in west Hangzhou lately.

Zhao's smile melted. "Do you mean the one on the news today?"

"Yes."

"Do you have any leads?" Zhao asked earnestly.

Yan pointed towards the elevator bay. "See that elevator on the left? I found human excrement in it this morning. I think it might have been left by the pervert."

Zhao ordered Yang to contact the university security team to review the footage from the elevator's surveillance camera. He then turned back to Yan. "Don't worry, it won't take long to get this guy. I'm going to handle it instead of the district PSB."

Yan looked surprised. "Why would you take on such an insignificant case?"

"Because we believe that this pervert also committed the murders."

"Really?" Yan was unconvinced.

"Last night, one of his victims told us that the assault occurred *right next to* the scene of the murder. The timing is close enough that one person could have committed both crimes. Right now our number-one priority is to catch that sick bastard. You're making me curious, Yan; why are you so interested in this case?"

"It's nothing. This morning I rode that elevator, and when I came out, a lot of people saw me and assumed—" He flushed. "It's just a misunderstanding; you don't have to worry. I mean, look, I don't look like the kind of person who would assault people; I teach, I couldn't possibly . . ."

Zhao had never seen Yan so inarticulate. He suppressed a laugh and patted him on the back. "OK, I won't worry. Let's go get something to eat."

Chapter 9

"Time flies, doesn't it? I can't believe you've been at Zhejiang University for five years now. First you left, and then the head of the Ningbo Criminal Science department Luo Wen left. I have to say, your replacements haven't been nearly as good," Zhao said before taking a sip of his drink.

Yan looked surprised. "Luo Wen is not in the force anymore?"

"You didn't know?" Zhao answered. "Oh of course, you left before he did, so you wouldn't have heard anything."

"Where did Luo go?"

"I'm not totally sure," Zhao said, shaking his head. "I heard a friend in Ningbo say that he's in business. That was over three years ago."

"Unbelievable. He resigned to go into business?"

"Everyone's trying to make more money, you know. Luo's superiors did everything they could think of to make him stay. They even signed the document he needed to get a special apartment reserved for public security authorities. But he wouldn't change his mind. I think someone said that he owned a couple of patents, so he could probably live off of that quite comfortably."

Yan exhaled slowly and nodded. "I remember. Most of his patents were filed in the name of his employer, but he did have a few in his name on micromeasurement. But I thought he wasn't interested in wealth or fame. He chose to be a forensic scientist because he loved the job. There must have been another reason for him to resign. What a shame."

"I know, it's a real shame when someone wastes their rare knowledge on teaching classes instead of solving real problems," Zhao agreed.

Yan smiled at Zhao. "Hey! You're having a dig at me, aren't you?"

"Yeah, and I learned it from you," Zhao said, then waved his hand. "OK, let's get back to business. I promised you I would catch the pervert. And you have to help me think about how the murderer didn't leave any footprints on the grass." Zhao lowered his voice and told Yan everything he knew about the crime scene.

When Zhao finished, Yan was silent for a long time. He finally raised his head and looked at Zhao. "Looks like you've met your match."

Zhao's eyebrows furrowed. "What do you mean?"

"The Zhejiang Bureau has invested a significant amount of manpower in these murders over the past three years. And yet nobody knows the first thing about the murderer. This guy must be brilliant at covering his tracks."

"That's right. Otherwise I wouldn't be asking you for help, remember?"

"But then he leaves a note to taunt the police."

"He is so arrogant!" Zhao said.

Yan Liang shook his head. "I think it would be hasty to say that. The killer took great care not to be discovered. He does not want to be caught by the police. In fact, if he hadn't left those notes, I think this case would be a plain old homicide, and it wouldn't have mobilized the Hangzhou and Zhejiang Bureaus. More importantly, it wouldn't be managed by someone like you, and there would be fewer officers working on the case."

Zhao nodded. If it weren't for the notes, nobody would have set up a joint special task force.

"He clearly left that piece of paper to capture the police's attention, which would make them more likely to go after him. Doesn't that sound contradictory to you?" Yan asked.

Zhao paused. "Well, what do you think?"

"I'm not sure. I am unable to deduce anything based on the current evidence, and guessing is not my strongest suit. To put it simply, if the police have not caught him for three years, the killer must be brilliant. And every action taken by a brilliant criminal is deliberate."

Zhao scratched his chin. "Never mind his intent; what I want to know is how he pulled someone that far across the grass without leaving any footprints."

"It's not impossible to pull someone without leaving footprints," Yan answered. "What I don't understand is why the killer would make his life so complicated."

"Tell me, how did he do it?"

"There are plenty of factors that narrow down the possibilities. First of all, the killer is human; he cannot fly. Second, the grass was muddy, and anyone who stepped on it would leave a footprint. There are only two ways that the killer dragged the body: either the killer actually walked on the grass or he never walked on it at all."

"What do you mean he never walked on it? How is that possible?" Zhao said.

"The killer could have strangled the victim, then tied the rope securely around the victim's neck and thrown the other end of the rope to the edge of the grassy area, then walked on the sidewalk to the other side. All he would have to do is pick up the rope and pull the victim across. It would work. There are only two problems with this theory. First, if the victim wasn't already dead, he would have run away when given the chance. Second, walking around to the other side of the grass would take a lot of time, and if a car or a pedestrian passed at the right moment, the killer would be seen."

Zhao was silent for a moment. "What if there were two people involved? One of them could hold down the victim and the other could pull the rope from the other side."

"I don't think so," Yan said. "You have already eliminated money and revenge as motives. Crime involving more than one person usually involves one of the two. Don't forget, in the five cases you've investigated, all the fingerprints belong to the same person. Besides, he probably wouldn't bother leaving all those strange clues if he were working with an accomplice."

Zhao nodded. "So you said it was possible that the killer actually walked on the grass but didn't leave footprints. How would he do that?"

"Simple. The killer would wear the victim's shoes. You found the footprints of the deceased, right? You might have guessed that the footprints were part of the victim's struggle to get away. But perhaps those footprints were left by the killer. That would mean that the killer not only wore the victim's shoes but also pretended to struggle while pulling the victim across the grass to make sure the footprints looked convincing."

"Hang on. If that's what happened, then we would still see the victim's bare footprints."

Yan looked keenly at Zhao. "But what if he was already dead?"

"He scratched the word 'local' on the concrete. He couldn't have been dead."

"Are you absolutely certain that the victim wrote it?"

Zhao considered this. "I'll have to go back and check. But why would the killer want to do that?"

Yan shook his head. "I don't know. That's something for the police to investigate. According to the clues, I don't think he was killed after he was dragged to the concrete. The writing on the concrete must have been left by the killer. I think you should speak with some handwriting analysts and try to confirm who scratched that word out. You should also contact the Zhejiang experts and try to find out who really left those footprints on the grass."

"OK." Zhao nodded.

"It's still a mystery why the killer would go to all this trouble, though," Yan added.

"What do you mean?"

"The most efficient way for him to achieve his goals is to kill the victim on the grass, toss the murder weapon in the bushes, and then leave as quickly as possible," Yan explained. "It's the safest way to execute the crime without getting caught. Why on earth would he want to drag the victim to the concrete and go through all that effort to hide his footprints? He definitely has his reasons, but I just don't know what they are. Captain Zhao," he said seriously, "over the past three years the special task force has been assembled multiple times because the killer is extremely good at not getting caught. I hope you're prepared for a long investigation."

Zhao sighed loudly.

Yan smiled, trying to lighten the mood. "You mentioned that you thought the pervert might be connected with the murder case?"

Zhao's grave expression faded. "Yes."

"What clues do you have for that case?"

"Exactly what you've been hearing in the news. The man is in his forties, he wears glasses, he's of average height and weight . . . that's about it." He laughed at Yan's pained expression and continued. "For the past few months, the killer has been targeting young women who walk home alone at night. He pulls them to the grass and sexually assaults them. He has evaded capture by wearing a cap and hiding his face. The victims only have hazy memories of the man, and it seems that he doesn't have any distinguishing features. The local police station has looked at the surveillance tapes after the reports and discovered that on multiple occasions he would go to any elevator in the nearby residential district and defecate. We're talking serious perversion here."

"So when you say 'assault' . . . what did he do exactly?"

Zhao frowned. "He unzipped his pants and jerked off in front of his victims."

"You mean he forced the victims to give him a hand job?"

"No, he did it all himself, but he made the victims watch, and when he ejaculated, some of the semen got on their clothes. None of the victims reported penetration, and no property has been taken in any of the cases."

"How strange," Yan said, clicking his tongue. "But why do you believe that it has something to do with the murder?"

"A woman reported an assault case at the west Hangzhou police station the night before last, just before midnight. She works the night shift at a bar, and she was assaulted on her way home, just after taking the last bus. She walked past a middle-aged man wearing glasses. At first she didn't notice anything unusual about the man, but just as they were passing each other he rushed at her with a knife and pulled her onto the grass. Then he assaulted her. The scene of our murder case is about fifty to a hundred feet away from that sexual assault. Dr. Chen thinks that the time of death would be very close to the time of the assault, so we have reason to believe that the pervert also committed the murder."

Yan smiled broadly. "I think the likelihood of that is practically zero."

Zhao's mouth dropped open. "Why?"

"In the last four cases you checked the surveillance camera and didn't see the killer in any of the tapes. That means that the killer successfully avoided all the cameras in the area, doesn't it?"

"Yes, there are a number of blind spots in the area; he must have done his homework."

"The killer is brilliant—he comes and goes without being seen, like a ghost. The only reason the pervert hasn't been caught is out of sheer luck. If someone happened to walk past while he was assaulting one of those women, he would probably be in the Hangzhou Bureau right now. He might wear a cap to hide his face, but you have still linked the defecating in the elevators to him. He leaves clues left and right. Basically these two are as different as night and day."

"That makes sense," Zhao said, thinking. "Well, if this were your investigation, what would you do next?"

"As an outsider, I don't want to know many details, but you mentioned that the murder victim's time of death was very close to the time of the sexual assault. You might be able to get more information if you catch that pervert. There aren't many other options."

"Thank you," Zhao said, his smile full of gratitude.

"Remember, I only talked about all this because you promised to help catch that pervert. I'm not a police officer anymore. Next time we eat together, I hope we can just enjoy the food," Yan said.

Zhao sighed and nodded. He would respect Yan's request. Still, he was pleased to have two new things to investigate. He wanted to show the word "local" to a handwriting analyst, and he wanted to check up on those footprints. If they matched a person of Sun's height and weight, then they could confirm they were actually Sun's footprints. If they didn't match, that would validate Yan's theory.

PART 3
NO EVIDENCE

Chapter 10

Guo Yu worked nonstop until 9:00 p.m. before finally going home.

He dragged himself to the bus stop. The bus trip lasted over half an hour. He got off at a stop next to a row of stands selling street food. Yellow Head and a few of his lowlife friends sat around a table, eating grilled meat and drinking beer.

The moment Guo Yu spotted them, he turned around. He hadn't forgotten the way Yellow Head smacked him in the back of the head. He was afraid of them—more than he cared to admit—and yesterday he thought that they might rough him up.

But today Yellow Head's attention was drawn to a pretty girl walking by his table. Her black miniskirt flattered her slim legs, and she wore a short-sleeved button-down shirt. Judging by her outfit, she was probably a sales assistant.

Yellow Head didn't care if the guy walking with her was her boyfriend; the beer in his belly made him reckless. He laughed. "Damn, she's hot. I would tap that." His friends all whistled at the girl.

The girl glared at them. "Assholes!" she shouted.

"Ooh, she's got a dirty mouth, too!" one of Yellow Head's friends called.

Her boyfriend said in a low voice, "Keep walking. Don't pay any attention to those fucking idiots."

Yellow Head stood up quickly and said, "Who are you calling a fucking idiot, you son of a bitch?"

The boyfriend saw the menacing look on his face. Feeling cowardly, he tried to save face. "I—I wasn't talking to you."

Yellow Head blocked their path and pushed the boyfriend in his chest. "What are you stuttering about, cocksucker?"

The girl pulled at her boyfriend's arm, urging him to walk more quickly.

"Don't try and swagger; you don't have the balls!" Yellow Head said, smacking the boyfriend on the head.

The boyfriend turned. "Hey! Don't mess with me!"

Yellow Head pushed him in the chest again. "Did you just talk back to me, motherfucker? Try that again." Yellow Head's friends stood up and encircled the two young men.

A bystander tried to break up the scene. "Hey. Don't make a big deal out this. Everybody cool it, OK?"

Surrounded by six aggressive young men, the boyfriend didn't know what to do. His girlfriend pulled his arm more insistently this time. "Forget it," she urged. "Let's go!"

Yellow Head kicked the boyfriend in his lower back. "I'm not going to let that slide, you son of a bitch!" The man collapsed to the ground.

Yellow Head's friends were already getting back to their beers. The Hangzhou police were known to patrol the area, so a few guys held him back before things escalated, urging Yellow Head to sit down.

Hearing his girlfriend cry out in fear, the young man picked himself up. He left with his head hanging down, not daring to make a sound. His girlfriend followed quickly behind him.

Guo Yu watched it all play out from a safe distance and let out a breath when it was over. They were real jerks, worthless guys, he thought. But there was nothing he could do. He reminded himself that he had to be careful and avoid them at all costs. Whenever they beat the shit out of somebody for no reason, the police were never there. Even if Yellow Head got arrested, they would only lock him up for a few days. Then he would be released and want revenge.

Suddenly he heard a voice next to him. "Are those boys always that bad?"

Guo Yu turned. It was that nice man who promised to take care of the mutt yesterday. Guo Yu nodded. "Everybody knows those guys. You see that one?" Guo Yu pointed discreetly at Yellow Head. "People call him the Little Gangster. He's the leader of the group. They do this stuff all the time."

"I see." Luo gave him an encouraging smile before starting to leave.

"Um, sir?" Guo Yu asked. "How's it going with the dog you adopted yesterday?"

Luo swiveled around. "I checked his injuries, and most of them are external. They will heal over the next couple of days. But he's still frightened of everything. He never leaves his cardboard box. I bought him some beef sticks, but he didn't seem to like them. He hasn't had much water either. It's a lot of work." Luo smiled weakly.

"Have you ever had a dog before?"

"A dog? Sure . . ." Luo thought of their family dog eight years ago. He was always busy, so he didn't spend much time with it. "I had a dog for a couple of months, but then one day I couldn't find him. I guess he ran away."

"If the dog is refusing to eat or drink, he's probably still getting accustomed to his new environment. All the dogs I ever had were like that when I first brought them home. After three or four days they get used to it and start eating again. That dog is probably a mixed breed. I bet he'll eat a lot when he gets used to your place."

"Is that right? I don't have as much experience as you seem to—if I ever have any problems, I'll come to you for advice."

"I like dogs a lot. It's a shame that I can't keep one in my apartment; there's not enough room for a pet. When your dog is feeling better you should take him outside to play. I can teach him some tricks like sit, sit pretty, and fetch."

Luo had lived in Hangzhou for three years but didn't have many friends outside of work colleagues. He was surprised at how pleased he was to hear Guo Yu's offer. He smiled. "I would be very grateful." He turned, took one last look at Yellow Head and his friends, and left.

Chapter 11

Guo Yu went to Chongqing Noodles for dinner, but he didn't arrive until 10:00 p.m. Zhu Huiru and her brother were already closing up for the day. So he was about to leave when Huiru noticed him and hurried over. "Do you want to order some noodles?"

"Never mind, you're closing." He looked down—he was still too shy to look Huiru directly in the eyes.

"It's fine. It's just before ten anyway," Huiru said, sounding enthusiastic.

"Um, OK. I'd like a bowl of wonton noodle soup, please."

Fulai went into the kitchen and Huiru sat down at a table across from him.

"You often get noodles later in the evening, but this is late even for you." She looked at him curiously.

Guo Yu could feel his face reddening and looked down shyly. "The company I work at makes me work overtime a lot."

"What do you do?"

"I'm a developer, I mean, a programmer. I write code for computer programs. You know?"

Huiru took out her phone and fiddled with it. "So you write the code for things like the games in my phone?"

"Yeah. But I don't work with mobile phones. I write programs for websites."

"Wow, you must be really smart. I can't read—it's really hard. You must have learned a lot at school to be able to do something like that."

At the word "smart," Guo Yu smiled and looked down bashfully. No one ever complimented him.

Before he knew it, the noodles were ready. Huiru stayed at his table and he tried not to freak out. He was afraid to take big bites like normal. What if she thought his table manners were disgusting? Still, there was a warm feeling in his chest. Maybe, just maybe, she was starting to like him. He didn't want to reveal his feelings about her, because he wasn't ready for a girlfriend. He was just barely managing to take care of himself and didn't yet have any big plans for the future.

Yellow Head entered the restaurant. "Hey, gorgeous, make me some fried rice. And I want you to deliver it to the park by the river."

Huiru's eyes narrowed at the sight of him. "Sorry, we're closed." Her voice was filled with contempt.

Yellow Head glared as he pointed at Guo Yu. "He's got food freshly made. What, are you playing favorites?"

"We're out of rice."

"Fine. Make me fried noodles with eggs. Hurry up."

"We don't have any noodles either." Huiru clearly didn't want his business, not after all the times he ate without paying.

"No noodles! What do you mean, no noodles?" Yellow Head made no effort to hide his anger.

At the sound of their raised voices, Fulai hurried over as quickly as his lame leg would let him to try to defuse the situation. "We have rice. We have everything. I'll make fried rice right now, OK?"

"Fulai!" Huiru complained.

Yellow Head leaned over her and said. "Well, gorgeous, I gotta go, but I'll see you real soon. You have to be the one to deliver the rice, got it? Relax, I'll pay for the rice and pay you back for those other meals too." He pulled a hundred-yuan note—enough for ten meals—out of his pocket and laid it on the table as he spoke. "Keep the rest for the next time I come around."

Huiru stood up grumpily, took the hundred yuan, and put it in a drawer with the rest of their cash. "Fulai, that guy is bad news!"

Fulai did his best to console her. "There's nothing we can do about it, you know that. We just run a little business; we have to take the good customers with the bad ones. If you don't want to deliver it, I'll do it."

"No, I'll do it. With your leg—" Huiru stopped. "It's probably better if you just stay here and clean up."

Guo Yu stared fixedly at her and asked quietly, "Why does he want you to deliver his food to the park by the river?"

"I don't know what he's up to," she said in a hushed voice. Every time she brought him a delivery, he groped her. Now he wanted her to deliver rice to a secluded spot in a park. *What if he was planning on . . . ?* She banished the thought, telling herself that even a thug like him wouldn't force himself on her. Or would he? As a precaution, she slipped a paring knife into her fanny pack when her brother wasn't looking.

The fried rice was ready in less than ten minutes. Huiru deftly placed it in a container and a plastic bag. She took the bag and started walking towards the park.

Guo Yu had a bad feeling about it all, but would he be able to protect her if something happened? He finally summoned his courage to follow her, but not before leaving correct change on the table.

Chapter 12

Due west from the noodle shop, a road led directly to the river, which was technically a canal with trees and landscaping on either side. The walk was not far, only about eight hundred yards. The park was not particularly beautiful; it was just a collection of fitness equipment that the city bought to form an outdoor gym. The outdoor gym was popular in winter. Fewer people came in summer because the mosquitoes drove everyone away. That night, the park was totally deserted.

Huiru carried the plastic bag into the park. She saw Yellow Head standing on a rotating metal disc, stretching his oblique muscles. Without a trace of friendliness, she placed the bag on the ground and turned to leave.

"Don't leave now, gorgeous!" He had a beer in one hand and stepped off the fitness equipment to pick up his meal. "It's a nice night; let's drink some beer and get to know each other better."

Huiru shook her head. "I'm busy. I'm going home and going straight to bed."

"Don't brush me off like that! Just sit with me for a while—maybe half an hour? I'm sure you can tell how much I like you." His sweet talk sounded unconvincing.

"I'm leaving now," Huiru announced.

"Oh come on, just stay a little while." He grabbed her arm. "Let's drink. Look, I bought two six-packs! I just want to talk. Really," he wheedled.

"Let go of me!" Huiru shouted and struggled against his grip. Yellow Head laughed and pulled her to the grass with one hand, carrying the six-packs in the other.

Against her will, Huiru was pulled closer to the river. With her free hand she slapped him as hard as she could. "Stop it! Let me go! I'm going to report you to the police!"

Yellow Head's hand stung from the slap, and the beer was having an effect on him. "I already told you, all I want to do is drink and talk; what's your problem? Stop squirming! Here! Now sit down!"

Huiru twisted her arm free and stepped back to run home. Yellow Head dropped the beers and grabbed her again, this time with both hands. "Give me a kiss! I won't take no for an answer!" He leaned towards her.

"Stop it! Let go!" She struggled with her whole body now. She pulled out the knife and pointed the tip at his chest. "One more move and I stab you!"

He stepped back in surprise and let out a cruel laugh. His breath reeked of beer. "You are just making this sexier." He swung at the knife in her hand.

She stepped back slowly, keeping a safe distance between them. She was terrified, but he didn't seem to notice or care. "If you come closer, I, I'll do it. I mean it."

Yellow Head's lips curled upward. "Don't get any ideas, missy. Now be a good girl and give me the knife. Let's sit down and have a drink. Daddy loves you."

"Don't come near me."

He suddenly lunged forward. Without thinking, Huiru closed her eyes and thrust the knife forward, stabbing wildly. When she opened her eyes, she saw that he had one wound in his chest and two in his stomach. Blood covered the front of her shirt.

Huiru screamed and pushed him away with her free hand. She stepped back a few steps, her arms and legs shaking uncontrollably. Yellow Head fell on his back and let out a low groan. Huiru suddenly noticed Guo Yu behind him, his eyes wide. He was gripping a rock in his hand. His face was ghostly white, and he couldn't take his eyes off Yellow Head.

"How . . . how could this happen?" Guo Yu shook as he watched Yellow Head, who stirred but couldn't get up.

As Guo Yu had watched Huiru being attacked, he had pushed any fear out of his mind and had sprung forward, bringing the rock down on the back of Yellow Head's head.

The blow had caused Yellow Head to stumble forward. Huiru had thought that Yellow Head was trying to take the knife from her. Panicking, she had stabbed blindly. Now all three wounds were gushing blood.

It was so quiet that they could hear the mosquitoes buzzing in the air. Huiru and Guo Yu stood motionless, not knowing what to do next.

Would Yellow Head die? If he didn't die, they would certainly have the threat of revenge hanging over their heads. How would he make them pay?

As the two young people stood silently, without a single useful thought forming in their heads, Huiru noticed a person standing on the edge of the grass. For a moment, she was struck dumb.

The man started walking straight towards them.

Chapter 13

Luo paused at the edge of the grass before walking towards them as quickly as possible. He saw Yellow Head on the ground, covered in blood, his hands and feet still twitching. For a moment he was too shocked to say anything. He looked at the boy and girl, who had lost the power to speak. "What did you do?" he demanded.

Huiru didn't say a word. Her face was white and her eyes were wide and fearful.

Guo Yu had trouble working his lips. "We should hurry and take him to the hospital," he said, his voice unsteady.

Luo squatted and looked carefully at Yellow Head and exhaled. "He was stabbed in the heart; there's nothing the hospital could do."

"There's nothing the hospital could do . . ." Guo Yu repeated, as he watched the body gradually stop twitching. Without warning, he burst into tears.

Luo watched them both hang their heads and weep. He considered the situation. "You should go to the police and turn yourselves in."

"Turn ourselves in—" Guo Yu reeled backward and stumbled. "But, but, he was going to have his way with her. Doesn't that mean it was self-defense? Do people go to jail for that? Do they pay money for damages?" His mind spun.

"Do you want to hear the truth?" Luo asked, looking directly at him.

He nodded dumbly.

"I see stab wounds in three places, including one that pierced the ribs and punctured the heart, an extremely difficult injury to inflict. The victim was bashed in the head and has three fatal stab wounds. Does that sound like self-defense? I think it would be hard to prove involuntary manslaughter."

"But that's exactly what happened!" Guo Yu said desperately. "He was pulling her and trying to have his way with her! How could that not be self-defense?"

Luo shook his head dispassionately. "The police look at evidence. Do you think they are going to take you for your word?"

"But!" Guo Yu felt nauseous and shut his mouth quickly. He thought about his pathetic savings. What about his parents living in the countryside? What about his disabled sister, who needed constant care? His world was coming to an end.

Luo looked at the two of them, sighed inwardly, and shook his head.

Suddenly Guo Yu looked up fiercely. He turned to Luo and said, "I did it. I saw him taking advantage of her, and I bashed his head, then I stabbed him three times. She didn't do anything!"

Luo was surprised to hear this. The knife was still in Huiru's hands, and her hands and clothes were covered in blood. Guo Yu did not have a single drop of blood on him. He was trying to take the blame, but why?

Huiru was just as surprised as Luo. "What? Why would you say that?" she asked Guo Yu.

"That's not important. I did it. You have a life to live." He looked down at his pockets and hastily pulled out his phone. "I'm gonna call the police right now. I'm going to tell them I did it."

"No. No! Stop! That's not what happened at all. I clearly killed him. It wasn't you." Huiru couldn't control her tears.

"Hang on, tiger," Luo said calmly. Guo Yu put his phone down. "You say that you killed this man. But why is the knife in her hands? Why is there blood all over her body and not yours?"

"Because . . ." Guo Yu couldn't finish his sentence. He realized that the police wouldn't believe him.

Suddenly Huiru stopped crying. She spoke calmly to Luo. "I did it. You saw me do it; you can be a witness. The knife is in my hands and I have blood all over my clothes."

Luo was surprised a second time. He had not witnessed the crime, but his keen instincts told him that both of them were involved.

"Are you trying to protect each other?" he asked them.

Neither of them spoke.

"Are you dating?"

Guo Yu blushed. "No, sir." Huiru shook her head.

Luo looked closely at Guo Yu. "Do you like her?"

Guo Yu looked up, startled. He nodded shyly.

Huiru's reaction indicated that this was completely new information. "You like me? But you never said anything."

"I . . ." He didn't know what to say.

"I see what's going on." Luo heaved a big sigh. "You both killed him, but it was an accident. Is that right? Based on the evidence here, I don't think the police would come to the conclusion that it was self-defense. Maybe if you turn yourselves in immediately, and you tell them what happened as clearly as possible, they'll decide that it was involuntary manslaughter. Hopefully that will reduce your sentence. Now I want to give you one piece of advice. Never ever take the blame for the other person. It doesn't help anyone. Even if you get the chance to set the story straight in the end, the police will doubt you." He turned and walked away. He was reluctant to leave them, but he did not want to get involved if he could help it.

Luo heard Guo Yu muttering, "How could this happen? How could this happen!" He turned back and saw the two of them still standing in the same place, looking utterly hopeless. Luo took a deep breath, determined to walk away. But his heart tightened.

The course of these two young people's lives would change completely from just one accident. Simply because a thug stirred up trouble. Should their lives be rewritten in this way?

Even if they got a light sentence and were only imprisoned for seven years, their precious youth would be wasted. And what would they do once they were released?

Luo fought it, but eventually, for the first time in his life, impulse triumphed over logic. He turned around and walked resolutely towards the girl and boy. "If there was a way to completely change this situation, would you want to try it?" His heart thumped wildly as he said it.

Luo was brilliant. He had worked on the Criminal Investigation Division of the Zhejiang Public Service Bureau and had been the head of the Criminal Science department of the Ningbo Bureau. He was a city captain by forty, and he had won awards for his forensic analysis. But this time would be different. This time, there would be no evidence. With his skills, he could save the lives of these two young people.

Chapter 14

"How could we do that?" Guo Yu asked earnestly.

"Well," Luo said hesitantly, "we could alter this crime scene until nothing here would be connected to you. You could keep living your lives as before."

"Would it work?" Guo Yu was overwhelmed. Fear, hesitation, confusion, and hope mixed together. He thought again of his parents and his sister. If he was imprisoned, they would lose their main source of income. When he left prison he wouldn't be able to get a job like the one he had now. How would he earn money? Would he go home and work the fields? Then there was the issue of compensation. Whenever a civil court case was broadcast in the news, the sums people were forced to pay were astronomical. It was the kind of money that he could never hope to pay off in a lifetime. He wished desperately that he could turn back time.

Huiru's eyes grew wide. "Do you mean we should run and hide?"

Luo shook his head. "No, but we should remove everything in this area that has anything to do with you. Right now only three people know that you have killed someone: the two of you and myself. As long as we don't say anything, the police will never figure it out."

Guo Yu weighed the advantages and disadvantages. "If the police discover that it was us, we would be charged with murder. There's no way they would charge us with manslaughter because we would have hidden evidence. Right? That would mean we couldn't explain what really happened."

"That's true," Luo said, nodding. "But the only way that the police would find out that you are the killers is if you confess." He saw that they were concentrating on his every word. "As long as you keep that secret, the police will never find you."

Guo Yu swallowed uncomfortably. "But . . . how can you be so sure?"

"I used to be a forensic scientist. I know exactly how the police handle cases. I can remove every single clue in this crime scene," Luo answered.

Guo Yu and Huiru looked at each other, neither willing to make a decision. But Guo Yu knew that if he turned himself in, he would waste away in prison for seven or eight years and have to make huge compensation payments until he died. His life would be completely ruined. If they pretended they were innocent, what's the worst that could happen? Still, there was something else bothering him. Why would this middle-aged man, practically a stranger, want to help them? He asked Luo outright, "Why do you want to help us?"

Luo smiled and answered calmly. "I don't think you two deserve to suffer." Then he looked at Huiru. "Thank you for giving me that dog."

Guo Yu was still hesitating when Huiru looked up and said, "Please, tell us what to do next."

Luo looked sternly at them. "Before you make your decision, I want to ask you a question. Think carefully! In the future, the police might come looking for you. If that happens, are you willing to lie to the police?"

"Lie to the police?" Guo Yu was so out of his depth that all he could do was repeat whatever Luo said. He had never had a single interaction with the police. In his mind, the police had godlike wisdom. They would see right through someone lying to them.

Huiru had already made up her mind. "How do you do it?"

"How to tell the lie is just a question of technique; I can take care of that. What is important is whether you would dare do it in the first place. If you don't want to, or if you are certain that you would panic when they spoke to you, then just forget this conversation and go and turn yourselves in. I don't want to go through all this effort without being successful, because that would mean that you will get a longer sentence and I'll be implicated. We would all go to jail.

Guo Yu and Huiru fell silent. Again, Huiru was the first to speak up. "I'll do it," she said. Her voice was firm. She looked to Guo Yu.

Guo Yu gritted his teeth. "I'll do it."

"Are you absolutely sure?"

"Yes," the two of them said in unison. If their plans went awry, they would just spend a few more years in jail than they would if they turned themselves in now.

"OK." Luo said, looking at his watch. "Four minutes have passed, and fortunately no one has walked by in that time. We need to hurry and alter the crime scene. Please follow every instruction I give you."

Chapter 15

Luo asked them both their names, and then took a pair of black latex gloves out of his bag. He carefully put them on, then said, "I'll drag the body over to the trees so that it is not discovered too quickly."

"Should I help you carry it?" Guo Yu asked.

"No, that will cause problems," Luo said. "There is already a lot of blood here, so it would be impossible to make the police believe that the crime occurred anywhere else. If two people carry the body, we won't leave any drag marks on the ground. Then the police will make note of that and have reason to believe that there were at least two people involved. If I drag it myself and deliberately leave drag marks, at least we will make them believe that one person committed the crime alone."

Guo Yu and Huiru nodded. Guo Yu was really starting to believe that this person was far more adept at this task than either himself or Huiru.

"Guo Yu, find a rock and turn the earth so that anyone walking by does not notice the blood on the ground," Luo said.

"Why do we need to do that? The police will find the blood, won't they?" Guo Yu said.

"If you know too many of the details, then it will be harder for you to face the police in the interrogation room. I'm sorry, but I can't tell you why."

"What should I do?" Huiru asked.

"You still have blood on your hands. Don't touch anything and go wash your hands in the canal water," Luo answered.

"What about my clothes?" The blood on Huiru's purple collared shirt wasn't too obvious at night, but anyone who came close would certainly see it.

"Don't worry about that now. I'll tell you what to do in a minute. We can't waste any more time."

As Luo bent down to pick up the body and pull it towards the tree, Guo Yu became worried.

"If you . . . if you take the body like that, won't there be footprints?"

"It's fine. I'll take care of it," Luo answered.

They made every second count. Huiru ran back to Luo, who was squatting between the trees, and said, "I washed my hands."

Luo carefully pulled out a phone from the victim's pocket. He kept looking at the phone as he spoke.

"I remember seeing a takeout box on the grass somewhere. Bring it here, please, as well as the bag used to carry the beer and one empty beer can. Be careful that nobody sees you on the grass—if you see someone, then just wait."

Huiru hurried to follow his instructions. She retrieved the fried rice, still untouched, and then picked up the bag of beer. She took the empty beer can, tossed it into the bag, and ran back to the trees. It was so dark that she tripped and fell in her haste. The beer cans rolled out of the bag, and Huiru started to pick them up.

"Don't pick them up!" Luo said sharply.

When she stopped it was already too late—she had touched several cans.

"It's fine," Luo said. "Your fingerprints will be on all the cans that you touched, but I'll wipe them clean. Don't worry."

"I don't remember which ones I touched," Huiru said.

"Then I'll wipe all of them."

One can of beer rolled out of sight behind the trees.

Guo Yu came over. "I'm done."

Luo stopped playing with the phone and stood up. He walked towards the ground where the stabbing took place and saw that the blood was more or less hidden. "Give me that paring knife."

Huiru handed it to him.

"Ten minutes have passed since the accident occurred. You don't have much time, so I'm going to wait to explain some things. Which way did you walk to get here? The road that passes by the noodle shop?

"Yes," they both said.

"There's a surveillance camera at the intersection of that street. I'm not sure if it would have picked you up when you came over, but we should prepare for the worst. We'll assume that the camera recorded you coming over. If you avoid the camera on the way back, it will look suspicious, so you need to take the same route that you took on the way here. Guo Yu, you're going to have to carry Huiru home on your back; that way nobody can see the blood on her front. If anyone asks, say that her leg is hurt. And we'll have to make it real because the police will probably ask questions. Huiru, are you ready? I'm going to hurt your leg."

"Do you have to hurt her?" Guo Yu sounded alarmed.

Huiru braced herself. "It's OK. I can take it."

"Excuse me for this." Luo picked up a rock and scratched it across her knee so that it left a mark. Her knee started bleeding immediately. Then he rapped her ankle with the same rock. Huiru stifled a cry of pain.

Luo handed the rock back to Guo Yu. "When you walk to the edge of the grass, make sure to put this rock in a place where it would be easy to trip. I don't care who asks you, you have to say that she fell down wherever you put that rock. OK, Guo Yu, carry Huiru on your back now. Make sure to walk back the way you came. Oh and Huiru, when you go home you should avoid your brother. You need to change your clothes without him noticing; we don't want him to become complicit. Naturally he would worry, but we also need to remember that every additional person who knows about the crime adds an element of risk. Can you do that?"

"Yeah. I'll call my brother and tell him that I fell so I need to go home and change," she said.

"Great. Guo Yu, after you take Huiru home, you need to go straight to the twenty-four-hour convenience store near your neighborhood. Buy some antibiotic ointment and some bandages, and remember to chat with the sales assistant so he or she remembers that you were there."

"That—that's it?" Guo Yu looked alarmed.

"No, of course not. I still have to take care of a few things, but you should go home for now. Do you both live close to the noodle shop?"

"Yes," they said in unison.

"I'll come get you at 2:00 a.m. and take you to my house so we can discuss how to deal with the investigation. Make sure not to wake anyone on your way out. Can you do that?"

They gave their addresses to Luo. They both still doubted that it would work, but when they saw the confidence in Luo's eyes, they relaxed. He seemed trustworthy, and that made them feel at ease.

After Guo Yu and Huiru left, Luo chewed his lip and surveyed the crime scene. He was confident that he could remove all the evidence, but those two were young and inexperienced. They could easily give something away in an interrogation. If that happened, his own plans that he had worked on for years would never come to fruition.

He was really going out of his way to help these two strangers. Was it worth it?

Luo felt like it was his fault that they landed in this mess, but he wasn't sure why. Maybe he had committed too many crimes and he wanted to do something good for once.

It wasn't worth debating now. He promised to help, so he would do his best. He just wanted to give them back their futures.

Chapter 16

At two in the morning, Luo picked up Guo Yu, then Huiru in his Audi SUV. He took a route back to his apartment that avoided any surveillance cameras.

"This is an Audi Q7, isn't it? You must have paid a fortune for it," Guo Yu said, admiring the interior. He was astonished that someone with so much money would agree to help them.

Luo just grunted.

"You're loaded." Talking about money made Guo Yu feel inadequate.

Luo smiled out of politeness. He never attached any importance to material things. He didn't care what car he drove or where he lived. When he was still a forensic scientist, he had a high-ranking title and was considered highly qualified. That entitled him to a salary that was much higher than the average police officer, among other perks. Still, he lived a very simple life and never spent lavishly. Three years ago, after he had resigned from the bureau, he finally learned how to drive and bought himself a car.

Before long, they drove through a neighborhood known for its luxury condominiums. Luo parked in the underground garage. "When we get out of the car, I want you to stay right behind me. There are a lot of cameras in this parking garage. I'm going to take the elevator and you will take the stairs. I'm afraid you'll have to climb seven flights. I know it's extremely unlikely that they will check the elevator camera, but if somehow that came to light, we would have no way of explaining why we met here in the middle of the night."

"How do you know where all the surveillance cameras in Hangzhou are?" Guo Yu asked.

"It's an occupational hazard," Luo said, laughing halfheartedly.

Guo Yu and Huiru were beginning to understand that Luo was much more enigmatic than they had realized. But they had no doubt that he could protect them from getting caught, and they did exactly as they were told.

When Guo Yu and Huiru arrived at the seventh floor, Luo had already opened his front door, and he motioned them inside.

The apartment was large and clearly expensive, but the decorations were minimal, even ugly. The floor was covered in cheap white tiles, and the walls were painted white. There was not a single work of art, and cables snaked across the floor, making the place look messy. His sofas had cheap upholstery. The dark window shades were pulled down, blocking out any view of the city. The door to his bedroom was open, revealing a single blanket and two pillows on the bed. The bedroom had no television or other furniture. The living room had a television and a computer.

Guo Yu looked around. "Did you just buy this place?" he asked curiously.

"No, I've had it for a few years now."

"Then, um, why don't you decorate it?"

"This is it," Luo said awkwardly.

Neither Guo Yu or Huiru knew what to say. His apartment was even more spartan than their tiny apartments.

Luo scratched his head and smiled. "I'm not much of an interior decorator, but I live by myself, so I don't mind."

Huiru quickly spotted the only decoration hanging on the walls. It was a small photograph in a simple frame. The man in the picture looked like Luo, only about ten years younger. It looked like a family photo, with a man, a woman, and a young child. Huiru looked at the photo. "This is your wife and daughter, isn't it? Why aren't they here?" she asked.

As soon as the question left her lips, she regretted it, because she could see the bed in the master bedroom was made for one, and all the other rooms were completely empty, making it highly unlikely that his wife and child lived here. Whether or not they were divorced, the way she asked the question made it sound like she was prying.

Luo's expression clouded for a moment. "My wife and child went missing several years ago. They still haven't been found." He turned his back, exhaled, and continued. "Let me get you something to drink. We have some very important things to discuss tonight."

He walked to the kitchen, and suddenly the two of them heard Luo cry out, "Oh no!" Guo Yu and Huiru ran over.

Luo was at his wits' end. "Why? Why does this dog poop all over the floor?"

The little mutt hunched in a corner, looking nervously at the three of them. Little brown packages were strewn about the kitchen.

Guo Yu and Huiru smiled at each other. Huiru found the paper towels and started to clean up the mess, while Guo Yu explained to Luo how puppies often didn't know better when they pooped all over the house. He then told Luo how they could be trained to only go in certain locations.

Luo thanked them again and again. Once the two of them had cleaned up the mess, Luo seemed to return to his normal self. He led them into the living room to discuss more serious issues.

Chapter 17

"Where did you get that knife?" Luo asked Huiru.

"From the shop," Huiru said haltingly. Thinking about the accident was still difficult.

"The knife looked relatively new," he said calmly. "When and where did you buy it?"

Huiru tried to remember. "My brother got it at the store across the street from the noodle shop. I think we got it a month ago."

"Do you have more knives like that one?"

"No, just the one. We bought it to peel fruit, but we haven't used it very much."

"Is the knife usually out on a counter or is it in a drawer?"

"In a drawer."

"Does your brother use this knife often?"

"He hasn't used it much at all, no."

"Does your brother know that you took a knife when you left to deliver the takeout?"

"I don't think so."

"Does he know that the knife is in that drawer?"

"He should know, but I don't think he pays much attention to that kind of thing."

"Right." Luo seemed satisfied. He asked both Guo Yu and Huiru to describe exactly what happened that night and then sat in silence, thinking. Finally he asked, "So that thug came to the noodle shop by himself and asked you to deliver takeout to him in the park by the river?"

Huiru nodded.

"Well, that means nobody else knew that you delivered the takeout to him, apart from the three of us and your brother." He thought it over for a moment. "But we can't depend on luck. Guo Yu, didn't you say that you saw him eating street food with his friends late at night?"

"Yeah."

"Then it's possible that he told friends he was going after Huiru. In that case, Huiru, if the police start asking whether you saw him yesterday and you say no, it will look suspicious. If the police ask you, you have to be honest and tell them that you saw him."

Huiru's mouth fell open. "I have to tell them the truth?"

"That's right. If the police come asking you questions, you have to tell them everything that happened exactly as it happened. The only thing that you leave out is the part where you killed him." He looked at Guo Yu. "Guo Yu, do you like Huiru?"

Guo Yu blushed and looked down. He didn't say anything. Before tonight, he had never expressed to anyone his feelings for Huiru. And now this man who was old enough to be his father was asking him so directly!

Luo chuckled. "That's the perfect reaction. If the police ask you about Huiru, give them that. You know that you like her, but you're bashful, so you can't say it out loud."

Huiru couldn't help but laugh.

Luo's tone grew more serious. "If you admit that you like her, that would be out of character. An experienced cop will speak to your friends and coworkers to learn about your personality. So remember, whatever you say, truth or lies, you need to keep the same expressions and behavior that you would normally have."

They both nodded.

"I'm going to go over how you will explain what happened last night, in detail," Luo said. "I'll tell you what questions the police would ask and teach you how to respond to them. I'll explain the words and tone of voice you should use. It may seem trivial, but things like your expression are extremely important. You have to get it right. I can tell that you're both clever, which is good. People who are slow can't be taught."

The boy and the girl smiled. Huiru thought that maybe her brother was the kind of person who might never learn.

"So, last night at around ten, that thug came to the noodle shop. He wanted some fried rice to be delivered to the park by the river. Huiru, you weren't thrilled by the idea, but you didn't want to cause any trouble, so you went. Guo Yu, you were eating your noodles. You secretly have a crush on Huiru, so when you heard the way that guy was speaking to her, you were worried for her safety. After she left, you decided to go to the park and make sure she was OK. Then, Huiru, once you delivered the rice, the thug grabbed you and you struggled to get away. You fell down while struggling, and at this point, Guo Yu comes by on the path. That thug sees that someone is watching and hides over by the river. You scraped your knee badly and you twisted your ankle. It hurt so much that you couldn't walk home. So, Guo Yu, you carried her home on your back and bought her some antibiotic ointment and some bandages at the convenience store."

"That's it?" Guo Yu asked incredulously.

"No, that's just an outline. I'll go through each step in a minute." Luo smacked his head. "Oh, I almost forgot!"

He put on a pair of latex gloves and opened a messenger bag. He took out two stacks of hundred-yuan notes and two pairs of unused latex gloves. He noticed the confusion on Guo Yu's and Huiru's faces. "Combined, these two stacks are worth twenty-five thousand yuan. Now I need your help. Put on those gloves and fold the money into heart shapes. I don't know how to do it, but I bet you learned in school. This is very important, but you can't ask me why. Just do it, please, and wear gloves so that you don't leave fingerprints on the bills."

Guo Yu and Huiru exchanged looks.

"This is something we have to do to alter the crime scene," Luo said. "Don't ask. All you need to know is how to describe the part of the night where you have to lie and how to answer the questions that the cops might ask. Don't ever ask cops about the details of the case. The body will probably be found in a few hours, and a lot of people are going to gossip about it. Be aware of what others are saying on the street, but don't get involved. You might unintentionally give something away."

Huiru and Guo Yu put on the gloves and started folding.

"Generally in a homicide case, the police need three things to get to the truth: witness statements, physical evidence, and a confession given by the suspect," Luo explained. "The so-called perfect crime is characterized by no witnesses, no physical evidence, and no confessions from any of the suspects. Now in terms of tonight's mishap, as long as I don't tell the police anything, there are no other witnesses. I have already destroyed almost all of the physical evidence—the last step is folding the money. Now we need to make sure the police don't extract a confession from you."

He paused to let that sink in. "The police might arrive at your door wanting to ask some questions. Experienced officers will use all kinds of techniques to glean information from you. Afterwards they will see if there are discrepancies in your respective statements. Any time there is collusion in a crime, the police can very quickly discover when people have fabricated a cover story, because the suspects' statements will differ."

Guo Yu and Huiru were once again filled with apprehension.

Luo smiled. "Let's work backward for a minute. Why can the police detect a cover story when there's collusion? Usually because of inconsistencies between one person's story and another's. You have to describe everything exactly as it happened before the accident, and then you have to tell the story I taught you."

Luo paused, then tried to sound more reassuring. "As long as you don't add any flourishes, you should be fine. Anything imaginative is extraneous and will lead to more problems down the line. If you don't know the answer to something, say so. Even if something the police say is different than what you know is true, don't help them in any way. When they ask you one question, you give them one answer. The more you speak, the bigger the risk."

Luo took a breath and continued. "Police will also tell you that your partner has already confessed to the crime. The weak willed often crack at this point. One of the main reasons why I decided to help you was because you both tried to take the blame for the other. That's very rare. Remember that. You both want to protect each other, which means that no matter what the police say, you can't confess. You need to believe that the other person won't break under pressure. As soon as one person talks, all three of us will be arrested."

Luo looked hard at each of them, and they nodded. Luo knew that the riskiest part of all this was the police interviews. Once they passed, they could all go back to their normal lives.

"When will the police come looking for us?" Guo Yu asked.

Luo smiled kindly. "They may or may not come to speak to you as part of a routine check of the neighborhood. In that case, they would not treat you as a suspect."

"If . . . if other people know that I delivered the fried rice, then the police would suspect me, wouldn't they?" Huiru asked, feeling uneasy again.

"Yes, at first, but they will give up that line of questioning if they are worth their salt."

"Why?" Huiru asked curiously.

"If they do it right, they will see that you both have an alibi, that you would not have had enough time to commit the crime. That should eliminate you as suspects." Luo broke into a small smile.

Guo Yu and Huiru looked at each other in confusion. They were clearly at the scene of the crime—the surveillance cameras would prove that. How could they possibly have an alibi?

PART 4

A GENIUS DESIGNS A PERFECT ALIBI

Chapter 18

At nine in the morning the next day, onlookers crowded the path in the park along the river.

As Lieutenant Lin Qi of the West Hangzhou District Bureau and his team crossed under the caution tape, he shouted at a subordinate, "You call this preserving a crime scene? What is going on here?"

There were footprints all over the grass and cigarette butts carelessly tossed on the ground. To make matters worse, the lower branches of the surrounding trees were broken.

Investigator Song was at his wits' end. "It looked like this when we arrived, I swear. Crowds of people swarmed the area. We haven't got a single useful footprint."

"Did these idiots move the body?" Lin asked.

"No. Two witnesses spotted the body and immediately ran to the station to report it. The crime scene has been clear ever since. It seems that people came to pick up the cash."

"What cash?" Lin furrowed his brow.

Song shrugged. "A street sweeper arrived at the park at 4:40 a.m. She found a hundred-yuan note folded into a heart. Eventually more and more little hearts, as well as some coins and other bills, were discovered. Soon it drew a crowd, which is why everything has been overturned. Much later, two people brushed away some leaves underneath the trees and discovered a dead body. That's when they called the police."

Lin shook his head in disbelief. He had been on his way to the station when he received the call. He could barely wrap his head around this case.

"It might be connected to the case, all this money strewn about. Then again, the money was folded into hearts. Maybe someone was trying to win the hand of a pretty girl. Or maybe the victim cheated on his partner, and she killed him and left all the money and letters." Song was thinking like a television script writer.

Luo would have never imagined someone would dream up a story like this—he had just wanted the money folded into hearts so that the bills would be smaller and harder to find, leading to more people destroying the evidence. If he had scattered unfolded cash, the street cleaner might have taken it all at once without touching the crime scene, thus wasting twenty-five thousand yuan. Instead, he had scattered money in the grass, in the tree branches, and under rocks. He even threw in loose coins so that people would continue to search for several hours. Nothing would excite the early risers and exercise fanatics more than discovering money lying on the ground. And they would attract enough attention to draw more and more people.

Lin stared at Song. He remembered that the young rookie had just joined the force and had only been involved in a handful of cases. It was understandable that he would have some absurd theories about the case. Lin sighed and led the forensic scientist, Gu, to the copse of trees where they started taking pictures. After double-checking that everything had been photographed, the two proceeded into the trees.

Two police officers were guarding the body, which was already starting to decompose in the summer heat. Lin was used to the smell, but shuddered at what he saw. "How much would you have to hate some-one to do that?"

The victim's shirt was cut apart and cast aside. There was a large gash near the victim's heart, and blood had coagulated around the area. There were two other stab wounds in the abdomen, deep enough that Lin could just make out the victim's intestines. But the killer had gone further: the victim's abdomen, chest, and arms were covered in long cuts, meticulously inflicted with the tip of a knife blade. The distance between each cut was almost equal. It looked like the victim was wear-ing a striped shirt.

Gu looked up in awe. "Looks like you got yourself a big case today, Lieutenant Lin."

Lin frowned. If he had just found a dead body in a park, he would call it a run-of-the-mill homicide. But these long incisions clearly took a long time to make, which meant this was the kind of murder that put people into a panic. His team would soon be under a huge amount of pressure to solve this case.

Gu reached for his forensic kit. "The victim died yesterday, although we won't know the exact time until we do a complete autopsy. The tem-perature is too high for us to make a guess by sight alone. The victim's phone and wallet were not stolen, so you will be able to identify him. Looks like a revenge killing."

He clicked his tongue as he examined the victim's arm. "Why does he have so much dirt under his fingernails? Odd. Based on everything I've seen so far, I think the thin cuts were made soon after the victim died. Otherwise the blood would have coagulated and they wouldn't look like stripes."

Lin nodded.

"The cause of death is this stab wound, close to the victim's heart," Gu continued. "It looks like the weapon was a dagger. When we get back in the lab, I can analyze a cross section of how the weapon entered the body. These two stab wounds on the abdomen were not fatal. I found a mark on the back of the head that suggests the victim was hit by a blunt object. I'm not sure how much I'll be able to recreate of the crime scene—we will have to wait and see. But I'm not holding my breath."

Lin frowned impatiently. "Well, do the best that you can." He noticed the beer cans on the ground. "Old Gu, could you please take a look at those for me?"

Gu took off his used gloves and exchanged them for a fresh pair. He picked up a can and moved to a shady area to check the surface with a magnifying glass. He raised his eyebrows slightly.

"What is it?" Lin asked.

"This case is much more complicated than I expected," Gu said, looking up. "I thought the killer just wanted revenge and took the time to cut those long, thin lines because he was extremely angry. If that were the case, I'm sure you could interview the victim's friends and enemies to narrow down a suspect. But this can has been wiped clean. There isn't a single fingerprint on it."

Lin shook his head. "Criminals watch detective dramas all the time these days. Most of them have learned not to leave fingerprints, just like thieves know to put a towel on a door handle before they force a door—" He stopped midsentence. "This isn't just a homicide; this is premeditated murder. Why else would the killer wipe off fingerprints? And then there's the money! If the killer left it there deliberately to make sure that people would gather and destroy evidence . . ." Lin drew a sharp breath.

"Have you ever seen a move like that?" Gu asked seriously.

Lin shook his head slowly. "No, never. I have never come across a killer that thinks like this."

Gu nodded. "Let's just hope that we are overestimating our killer, then. It's highly unlikely that he's some kind of genius."

Lin tried to console himself as he nodded at Gu. In the decade that he had worked for the police, he had learned that most killers were not well educated. Some of them learned a thing or two while watching television, but they never managed to fool the police.

Gu and his team started to pick up all the beer cans and put them in evidence bags. He was about to finish, when one of his men called out, "Dr. Gu? I found another one over here."

Gu walked over and saw a can laying in the shrubs. He could tell just by looking that it was different. "This one has prints!" he shouted.

Chapter 19

It was dusk. Lin was sitting in his office when two investigators came in, each carrying toolkits.

"Lieutenant Lin, we spoke to nearly everyone in the area about the victim. His name is Xu Tianding and he was born in a rural area. The government selected his family's house, among many others, to be demolished for development. We have learned from his friends and local residents that he was a well-known small-time gangster. He went by the nickname Little Gangster and has been in and out of the police station ever since junior high. He used to extort money from students at school and spent most of his time causing trouble—it seems that he got into fights almost every day. He started to make friends with other gangsters, most notably Zhang Bin. Zhang Bin and Xu Tianding have been friends since childhood. According to Zhang, he, Xu, and four other friends were out eating street food at around ten o'clock last night. Xu finished and went off for a walk. We spoke to someone at a small supermarket close to the crime scene and found out that the victim purchased two six-packs of beer, which we found at the crime scene. He nearly finished one can, but the other eleven were unopened."

Lin thought for a moment. "What was he doing buying all that beer for himself? Did he plan on sharing it with someone?"

The investigator shook his head. "It's not clear. When we asked his friends, they said he didn't mention it. The cashier at the supermarket didn't know anything either."

"Based on what we know," Lin said, "our motive here is almost certainly revenge. So who would have wanted him dead?"

"Oh, lots of people," the investigator said, scoffing. "All of his neighbors hated his guts, said he was a complete jerk. Apparently he went to the restaurants and shops owned by migrant workers and bought things on credit but never paid. They didn't want any trouble, so they kept quiet. He behaved inappropriately on multiple occasions. Some female workers complained that he would harass them when they walked by. In fact, he was very close to getting in a fight about a girl sometime last night."

"Just last night?"

"That's right." The investigator explained how Xu and his friends catcalled at the girl and attacked her boyfriend.

Lin pursed his lips. "It sounds like we might have several pages of possible suspects just from our initial investigation."

"I'm not sure you could list them all—maybe just the people he and his gang friends offended recently. But who knows how many people he hurt when nobody else was looking?"

"That's true." Lin thought hard. "Tomorrow, keep talking to local residents to see if we can identify any primary suspects. Make sure to find that girl and her boyfriend—I want you to interrogate them as thoroughly as you can. Are there any surveillance cameras around the crime scene?"

"There aren't any on the road next to the river, but there is one on the intersection nearby."

"OK, make sure you check that. I'm going to speak to Dr. Gu."

Lin went to the forensics lab, where Gu was having noodles. A pair of bloody latex gloves lay in the trash can next to him. Lin swallowed back disgust. "So, what do we have so far, Old Gu?"

Dr. Gu stood. "Xu Tianding had a lot in his stomach at the time of his death. Do you want to take a look?" he teased.

Lin emitted a dry cough. He had known Gu for years but still could barely tolerate his humor. "No thanks, Dr. Gu, I just had lunch. You clearly have a stronger stomach than I. Just tell me the results, please." He looked from the noodles to the gloves and turned his back. He had seen many dead bodies in his tenure, but had yet to eat food next to one. He didn't plan on trying it any time soon.

Gu laughed at Lin's squeamishness. "This young man really could eat," he said, turning to Xu. "He might look skinny, but he apparently had a big appetite. I found remnants of grilled meat in his stomach, plenty of beer, and some fried rice still in his esophagus. There are a number of possibilities here. Either he drank too much beer and he needed to vomit, or he was struck with a rock and it caused autonomic neuropathy. Alternatively the food might be in his esophagus because he was attacked right as he was eating and didn't have time to swallow completely. Either way, the food in his stomach was almost completely undigested, which tells us that the time of attack was very close to the time that he ate that fried rice."

"But where would he get fried rice?" Lin asked.

"As soon as I discovered the rice, I asked someone to check back at the crime scene. Sure enough, they found a takeout box in the grass, half-filled with fried rice. As far as we know, the attack was far from the trees, in the open area of grass, close to where the takeout was found. We found a lot of blood in that area, but it was almost entirely mixed into the earth thanks to all the people stomping around. Still, it was clear that the murderer killed his victim in the grass and then dragged him eighty feet into the copse of trees. The killer also loosened the dirt near the trees."

"Why would he do that?" Lin asked.

"I think the killer purposefully scattered money to attract lots of foot traffic. That way they would remove all traces of his footprints. But he knew that fewer people would walk into the copse of trees, so he destroyed that part himself."

"Have you pinpointed the time of death?"

"We can tell from the time that he was last seen and from the autopsy that the time of death was between ten and eleven o'clock last night. But when we looked at Xu's phone and his call records, it shows that Xu called his friend Zhang Bing at 10:50 p.m. I asked Song to speak to Zhang Bing about it. Zhang claims that Xu asked if he wanted to have lunch the next day, but then Zhang heard sounds of a struggle and then the call ended. When Zhang tried to call back, nobody picked up. Eventually the phone was turned off. Zhang had no reason to suspect that Xu was being attacked. He didn't think anything of it. So based on the phone call, the time of death was at 10:50 p.m."

Lin nodded. It was extremely helpful information. "Do you think that the killer knew Xu?"

"Knew him? Why do you think that?"

"Xu bought those two six-packs of beer at a supermarket close to the crime scene. He had already been drinking and couldn't have finished that off himself. If he took two six-packs of beer to the park, he was probably planning on drinking it with someone else. But his friends claim not to know anything about it."

"That's a good point," Gu said. "There's another thing that's been bothering me. Why would he go right by the river, where he would surely get bitten by mosquitoes?"

"That's true," Lin said. "It doesn't make sense. And I don't understand why he only ordered fried rice if he wanted to share with someone. Tomorrow I'll send someone to find out where and when he ordered that rice. Something might turn up."

"While you're at it, ask if anyone saw a person with a lot of blood on their clothes that night."

"You think the killer had blood all over their body?"

"Absolutely," Gu said. "The stab wound closest to the heart especially would have produced a gush of blood. The killer would definitely have blood all over their hands and their clothes."

Lin nodded slowly.

Chapter 20

Zhao kept hearing bad news. Four different teams had come into his office already and the day was not even over.

First, the officers who checked the surveillance cameras said that they didn't find any suspects. The killer was able to hide in the blind spots, and the park off of Wenyi West Road was not covered by the cameras. It wasn't surprising, since he had also avoided being caught on camera for the other four murders. Still, it gave Zhao a sinking feeling.

Then the officers who spoke to the victim's friends and family said they didn't turn up anything useful. Nobody knew why Sun would be walking by the park on the night of the murder. Nobody knew that he would stop on the side of the road to relieve himself, which meant the killer must have followed the victim instead of waiting for him to appear. Yet nobody noticed anyone, meaning that the killer must have been incredibly careful. There were a handful of people who hated Sun enough to kill him, but they were struck off the suspect list after producing alibis. The police came to the conclusion that the victim did not know the killer.

The third piece of bad news was about the note. Apparently the paper, the ink, and the printer were all common brands. It was impossible to trace its original source.

And finally, the group interviewing local residents wasn't making any progress. They spoke to people who had passed by the park that night and nobody saw anyone suspicious. Zhao told the investigators to keep looking. Someone might have seen something; it was just a question of connecting that person with the police.

The investigation had only begun a day ago, and yet they already seemed to be facing dead ends. Zhao was frustrated.

At least the investigation into the jump rope left him something to mull over.

An officer had taken the jump rope into all the toy and fitness stores in west Hangzhou and discovered that the particular brand of jump rope was discontinued two or three years before.

Zhao felt a chill go up his spine. Was it possible that the killer had planned on committing a series of murders *three years ago*?

He had examined the jump rope multiple times. It was clearly new, not taken out of the trash or stolen from a playground. He flipped through the photos on the previous four cases and looked carefully at each jump rope. They all looked very new but had slight differences, so the killer probably bought each one at a different store, ensuring that he didn't become a memorable customer. It was a very cautious move.

If the jump rope was bought several years ago, it would be impossible to find out where the murder weapon was bought.

Zhao leaned all the way back in his office chair and stared at the ceiling. Every possibility led to a dead end. Would it be impossible to catch this killer, even after five homicides?

Zhao didn't want it to be true. It looked like all they could do was register more local fingerprints in the hopes they would get a match. It was like looking for a needle in a haystack.

Dr. Chen walked into his office carrying a file. "The Zhejiang handwriting expert examined the word that was scratched on the concrete. I have the results here."

Zhao immediately sat up. "Well, what does it say?"

"It is impossible to determine if the word was written by Sun Hongyun."

"Why?"

"There weren't many examples to compare it to—Sun didn't write much. We turned his house upside down and only found a handful of receiving notes from his freight business. We sent them to the expert, who said that even though the handwriting on the ground was very different from the handwriting on the receiving notes, he could not confirm that the word 'local' was not written by Sun. Not to mention that he was struggling with the attacker as he wrote. Anyone in that situation would have drastically different handwriting."

Zhao frowned. "Well, what about the footprints in the grass?" he asked. "Can we confirm that they were made by Sun? Is it possible they were made by someone wearing Sun's shoes?"

"The footprints are more complicated, so we've contacted some mechanics researchers at Zhejiang University and asked them to help us do some tests."

"Alright, then we'll just have to wait until we hear from the university," Zhao said.

Chen hesitated before asking as delicately as possible, "I heard Yang mention that the teams have encountered some difficulties in this case."

Difficulties? They didn't have a single clue. Zhao sighed. "We could still get a breakthrough if we catch that pervert. I'll assign some more officers to the case tomorrow and we'll see what happens."

Chapter 21

The sun had started to sink when Luo walked to the noodle restaurant. His steps were calm, as always.

He stopped at the door and looked inside.

Guo Yu was sitting at a table eating noodles and Huiru was cleaning off the countertop. They both noticed Luo at the door and stopped what they were doing, looking anxious.

Luo avoided their gaze and quickly surveyed the sidewalk. He finally entered, as if he chose this restaurant by chance. He didn't sit at Guo Yu's table, but took a seat at another free table and carefully studied the menu on the wall.

Huiru came to his side. "What can I get for you, sir?" Then in a quieter voice, "Why aren't you sitting with him? He wants to talk to you."

Luo was not at all worried by whatever Guo Yu had to say. He was confident that he had changed the crime scene enough to fool the police. If something really bad had happened, Guo Yu would already be in the police station and not sitting in a noodle restaurant.

"Let me see . . . how about noodles with tomato and egg? No, I've had that a lot lately. Just a minute, let me think . . ." Luo said, and dropped his voice to a whisper. "It would be odd for me to sit at his table. I need a reason." Then he raised his voice again. "I'll take that noodle dish with beef and green peppers, please."

"OK," Huiru said.

She passed Luo's order to her brother, and then took a woven tray to Luo's table. "I'm sorry, we're going to put some rice cakes on this table so they can cool. Could you please move to that table there?"

Luo was happily moved to sit across from Guo Yu, who began to speak. Luo discreetly put his finger to his lips and whispered, "Talk while you eat."

Guo Yu did as he was told and picked up his chopsticks, pretending to eat. "Huiru said she saw the police stopping into a lot of stores. They didn't stop here." He smiled, relieved.

Luo was not surprised. "It's only the first day. They're doing a preliminary investigation. I think they'll make it over to Huiru and her brother in the next day or two."

"In the next day or two? Really?"

"Don't get worked up," Luo said quietly. "It will be routine. The police will want to know when the man ordered takeout and when she delivered it. She won't have any problems as long as she follows the plan."

"Oh," Guo Yu said, nodding nervously.

"When did she tell you this?"

"Just now, when I entered the shop."

"You two need to be more careful," Luo chided. "Whatever you do, don't talk about it on the phone. That includes texts."

"Got it."

Huiru brought Luo's noodles to the table.

Thinking quickly, Luo picked up the small bottle of vinegar and dumped it into his noodles. He looked up. "Excuse me, could you bring some more vinegar?"

Huiru took the hint and ran into the kitchen to get some vinegar. She refilled the bottle at his table as slowly as she could.

Luo spoke to both of them quietly. "You don't look like you have everything under control. Remember, you and I are strangers. If you see me in future, act like it. And Huiru, you injured your leg recently; you need to act like it's difficult to walk. Which reminds me, how many times did you wash your clothes?"

"A dozen, like you told me. They look good as new," she said without moving her lips.

"They might look new, but the chemicals they use in bloodstain analysis are very sensitive. I would soak it in a mixture of detergent and water a few more times."

Huiru finished pouring the vinegar. "Can I have a little more, please?" Luo said. He then quickly took a paring knife out of his bag and handed it to Huiru under the table. "This is new and it's identical to the old one," Luo said. "Take it. Remember, if the police come by in the next few days, just answer their questions the way I taught you."

Huiru nodded. Both she and Guo Yu had come to trust this man entirely.

Luo stood up as soon as he finished eating. Huiru didn't want to take his money, but Luo smiled kindly. "Remember, we are strangers," he said. Then he said in a loud voice, "Can I get change for a twenty?"

Chapter 22

The next day at 9:00 a.m., Fulai went to the market to buy fresh vegetables. Huiru was cleaning the shop and preparing for the lunchtime crowd when Song and Li, two young police officers, entered the shop.

"Hello, madam," Song greeted her. "We'd like to ask you if you've seen this man before." He showed her a picture.

Huiru was a little startled, but soon recovered. She moved closer and saw that it was Yellow Head. "Yes . . ." Huiru's throat had gone dry and she coughed. "Yes, I have. He lives in the neighborhood. Why, what happened?"

"You didn't hear?" Song found this odd. The noodle restaurant was less than a mile away from the park, and the other shop owners on the street all knew about the murder.

"What is it?" Huiru felt herself getting nervous. Luo had covered a lot of territory, but he wasn't perfect. He didn't expect that the police would ask such a simple question. Huiru tried to act natural and speak slowly, like Luo had said. Still, this was the first time Huiru had spoken to the police in her life.

Song tried to jog her memory. "You heard about the murder in the park by the river? This is the man who died. His alias is Little Gangster."

"It was him? Oh!" Huiru shook her head, trying to sound surprised.

"Do you know him?" Song asked, looking meaningfully at Li.

"Not well; I just know that he orders food at our restaurant and doesn't pay. He's always causing problems for us," Huiru said angrily.

The police officers were well aware of Xu Tianding's penchant for ducking out on his bill. Her disdain seemed very normal. After interviewing so many of the local residents, the police had concluded that everyone was glad to see him gone. Everyone except for the Xu family, of course. All of Xu's neighbors thought he was wicked, and the local business owners wished he would get in a car accident. But at home, Xu was just a boy. His grandmother had cried her heart out. Unfortunately very few people had tried to comfort her.

"When was the last time you saw him?" Li asked.

"The last time?" Huiru wrinkled her eyebrows in thought. "The night before last."

"What time was that?"

"We were closing up shop, and he came over and ordered fried rice. I didn't want to make it, and I told him we were out of rice. But he started acting mean, and my brother is afraid of him, so—"

Song interrupted her before she could finish. "You made the fried rice?"

"Uh huh." Huiru nodded.

"Then what happened?" Song asked.

"He said he had to leave, but he asked me to deliver the rice to him at the park by the river."

"He told you to meet him in the park?" The police looked at each other and perked up.

"Uh huh." Huiru's face was calm.

"How many orders of rice did he ask for?" Song asked.

"Just one."

"And you delivered it to him?"

"I didn't want to, but my brother has a lame leg and he can't walk very fast. I always do the deliveries. I didn't have a choice."

"So what happened next?"

"He . . . he . . ." Huiru hesitated.

The two officers braced themselves; they could tell that something important was coming. "What happened?" Song asked.

Huiru spoke reluctantly. "He was drinking all by himself in a park, and he had a plastic bag with beer in one hand. After he saw me, he came . . . came towards me and told me to have a drink with him. He even . . ." She trailed off.

"What did he do?" Li asked, his tone urgent.

"Nothing." Huiru lowered her head.

Song looked sternly at her. "Madam, we need to investigate every detail of this case. Please tell us exactly what happened."

Huiru hesitated before stammering, "He pulled my arm and wanted me to drink, and—and he groped me."

"How could he!" Song shook his head angrily. "And then what happened?"

"I wanted to get away from him, but he wouldn't let me go. He kept pulling me and saying I had to drink with him. I don't know how drunk he was. I shouted for help and he tried to cover my mouth. I finally managed to escape and run away. He stopped chasing me, but right before I reached the road, I fell and my leg started bleeding. I twisted my ankle and couldn't walk. My friend happened to pass by, and he picked me up and carried me home on his back. It scared . . . scared me to death." She looked truly frightened. Luo had told her to think of how she felt when she realized Yellow Head was dead when she needed to act frightened. Sure enough, it worked.

The two officers took a careful look. She was wearing jeans, so they couldn't see her injury, but they weren't willing to ask her to undress.

They asked a few more questions, but there weren't any more useful clues to glean from her story. Eventually they agreed to speak to a few more business owners on this street and then report their findings to their superiors.

Chapter 23

"Do you really think she injured her leg?" Lieutenant Lin asked, scratching his chin. Investigators Song and Li had arrived to report what they learned from the girl in the noodle restaurant.

"She seemed to be favoring one leg, but she could still walk. If she is injured, it's not bad." Song said.

"That's not what I'm asking," Lin said, shaking his head. He paced back and forth. "If she fell, it's likely that she hurt her ankle. But did she bleed a lot?"

"That's what she said, yes."

"Did you see the injury?"

"No, we couldn't. She was wearing jeans."

"Long jeans?"

"Yes. What's wrong, Lieutenant?"

Lin nodded, turned, and paced some more. "That's reasonable, actually," he said, his eyebrows furrowed.

"What's the matter?" Song and Li were at a loss.

"It's summer. When you get a scrape in summer, the best thing to do is to leave it uncovered so it doesn't get infected or start itching. It heals faster when it's uncovered."

"Are you saying that she didn't hurt her leg, and she was just pulling the wool over our eyes? She wore long pants so that we couldn't see her injury!" Li was an excitable young officer.

Lin thought carefully. "When you asked her what happened at the park, was she quick to tell you that Xu Tianding groped her? Or did it take her a long time to finally explain what happened?"

"At first, she just said that she delivered the rice and nothing else happened," Song remembered. "But we pressed her, and she eventually told us what happened."

"That's right," Li said. "Song over here told her that we were investigating a case and she had to tell us everything exactly as it happened. Then she finally told us."

"That's reasonable too," Lin said. "She was sexually harassed, and she didn't want anyone to know. If she was too forthcoming, I would say she was acting."

"So does that mean that she's not a suspect?" Song asked.

"Not necessarily," Lin said, looking out the window. He turned back to look at the young officers. "Everything checks out, but what if she is much smarter than we think?"

Song laughed. "I don't think that's possible, sir. If she's acting, then criminals are getting too talented. We'll never solve another case!"

"I agree with Song," Li said. "Migrant workers aren't that clever. If she killed him, she would want to make up a cover story and show us her injury. I can't imagine that she would deliberately do the opposite."

"And what about the crime scene?" Song added. "Gu told us about the folded hundred-yuan notes in the grass. He estimated that there was anywhere between ten and thirty thousand yuan on the grass. Where would a migrant worker get all that money? How could she come up with such a neat solution to destroy the crime scene? Think of the stripes cut into the victim's skin, those thin long cuts. I don't think a young lady would do something like that, do you?"

Lin pursed his lips and grudgingly agreed. "That's true. But we can't ignore her. As far as we know, she is the last person to see Xu Tianding alive. We now know that he bought all that beer with the intention of drinking it with Huiru—he wanted her to let her guard down. We now know that Xu deliberately chose the park by the river because it was secluded. Now, most of the beer cans were wiped clean, which means those fingerprints have something to do with the killer. So after she left, who did come to kill Xu Tianding, and why did they touch the beer cans?"

"But there was one can that had Xu's fingerprints and someone else's, right?" Song said. "If we compare those fingerprints to Zhu Huiru's, then we can determine whether she has something more to do with the case."

"Yes, yes, we'll compare the fingerprints," Lin said calmly. "But right now we can't be sure that the fingerprints on that can belong to the killer. They could be the prints from the person who sold the beer to Xu or the prints of some delivery person. If we compare the prints now and discover that they are not a match, then we might recklessly come to the wrong conclusion. I would like to have a chat with Ms. Zhu myself. Please find that clip in the surveillance tapes so I can see what she looked like on the night of the murder."

Chapter 24

One hour later, Lieutenant Lin stood by a computer. Investigator Song pointed at the screen. "This is where it gets interesting. At 10:19 p.m., Zhu Huiru walks past carrying the fried rice toward the river. At 10:20 p.m., a male walks quickly past, also in the direction of the river. At 10:42 p.m., the same male walks back towards the residential district, carrying Ms. Zhu on his back."

Lin squinted at the screen and did some calculations in his head. "It's just over a quarter of a mile from this intersection to the crime scene. I think it would take her about three minutes to walk there, judging by her pace. So subtracting three minutes each way, she would have stayed there seventeen minutes. That's a long time. If they had an argument and then Xu assaulted her and groped her, it would take less than seventeen minutes."

"She said she stayed by the side of the road for a while when she hurt her leg. Maybe she spent a lot of time checking her injury," Li suggested.

"If that were the case, someone walking by would have noticed her sooner. But nobody mentioned it, did they?"

"No, but that doesn't mean that she wasn't telling the truth. It was late; there wouldn't have been a lot of people on that road."

"Have you spoken to the friend who was with her that night?" Lin asked.

"She told us it was a friend," Song said. "We didn't ask more about him."

"That young man was hurrying somewhere. We need to talk to him as soon as possible. The killer stabbed the victim three times, pulled the body into the copse of trees, and destroyed nearly all of the evidence. I didn't think a young woman could do it by herself, but a young man could have."

"But there is no blood on him," Li said. "Dr. Gu said that if the victim was stabbed three times, including once to the heart, a lot of blood would have gushed out."

"The light isn't good in this video," Lin said, leaning forward. "Are you sure he doesn't have blood on his clothes?"

"It doesn't matter. If he was covered in blood and walking on a busy road like this, somebody would have seen him," Li said.

Lin nodded. Even late at night that much blood would be noticeable. He squinted at the image of Huiru. He couldn't tell if there was blood on her clothes because she was being carried by Guo Yu.

What if that was why the young man was carrying her? So that nobody would see it?

But it seemed highly unlikely that a young woman like that would stab her victim three times. Suddenly someone behind him said, "They can't be the killers."

Lin spun around and looked at Dr. Gu, who had just entered the room. "Why not?" Lin asked.

"Xu Tianding was killed at 10:50 p.m., remember? That's when he called his friend Zhang Bing. Zhang Bing swears that he heard Xu's voice on the phone, so we have no reason to believe the phone call was faked. But you can see those two on the surveillance at 10:42 p.m., and they didn't come back this way afterwards. It's possible that they used a different route, but I looked at a map. They couldn't have made it back to the park by 10:50 p.m. This surveillance video gives them an alibi."

Lin was stumped. Mr. Xu was attacked while he was on the phone, and the call was made at 10:50 p.m. But Ms. Zhu and that young man left before 10:42 p.m. It was a cast-iron alibi.

"We still don't know who that man is," Gu said. "But based on what we know of Zhu Huiru, I don't think she is capable of committing the murder. The killer destroyed all the possible evidence, including the victim's fingernails. Do you remember how his nails all had mud in them? The killer cut the victims nails, removed any dirt from the nail bed, and put the victim's fingers into mud. If Xu scratched the killer, there would have been DNA evidence under Xu's fingernails. But we couldn't get any evidence from them because the killer cleaned it all up. The thing that really confuses me is the stripes of blood. They were made so meticulously, they were so evenly spaced—that must have taken a lot of time. I don't know if it's significant or not."

"What do you think?" Lin said, his eyebrows furrowed.

"I don't know," Gu said. "In some cases the killer leaves something behind as a sort of message. In the case handled by the Hangzhou Bureau, that serial murder, the victim always has a Liqun cigarette in his mouth. I looked at plenty of case records to see if any of them had cuts like the one we found on the victim, but nothing turned up."

Lin nodded, still dissatisfied with the lack of evidence. "I think we'll have to pay a visit to Zhu Huiru again. She stayed at the scene of the crime for seventeen minutes. I want to ask her how long she was on the side of the road. One more thing. Do you know what the dimensions of the murder weapon would be?"

Gu pulled out a document for Lin to examine. "Based on the size of the wound, it looks like an ordinary paring knife. Nothing professional."

"A paring knife?" Lin looked at the document thoughtfully.

Chapter 25

The investigation of the serial murder was in full swing at the Hangzhou Bureau.

Dr. Chen took a stack of files to Zhao's office. "We have the results from the mechanics researchers at Zhejiang University," he said. "The person who left the footprints in the grass weighed between 130 and 170 pounds. The victim weighed over 190 pounds. Thus, we can conclude that the footprints were made by the killer. The researchers also said that the marks indicate that the victim was dragged without a struggle. Afterwards, the killer put the shoes back on the victim. I'm impressed by how realistic it looked."

Zhao took the report and scanned it briefly. The results were exactly as Professor Yan had predicted. Despite having a limited number of clues, Yan was able to determine what had happened just from the lack of the killer's footprints. He hadn't changed a bit.

Another of Yan's predictions had been confirmed: the victim was killed before being dragged to the concrete. There were no footprints of Sun's bare feet. It all checked out.

"Did we learn anything else about the killer's body type?" Zhao asked.

"No," Chen sighed. "The footprints were too messy—plus they were made while the killer was dragging a heavyset man. On top of that, the consistency of the dirt changes daily depending on the water content, and the drag marks change accordingly. Since the researchers did their experiments days later, they couldn't get precise answers. All we have is a height between five foot six inches and five foot nine inches and a weight between 130 and 170 pounds. I'm sorry, the results are just too imprecise to work with."

Zhao pressed his forehead in dismay. The results only confirmed that the killer was not extremely short, tall, or overweight. That meant that almost anyone in the city could be the killer.

"Oh, there is one other piece of information," Chen said.

"What's that?" Zhao asked.

"Based on previous evidence, we believed that the killer was left-handed. But the footprint evidence tells us that the killer's right leg has more power than his left."

"So? What does that mean?" Zhao said, intent on Chen's next words.

"The killer might not be left-handed after all. He might have deliberately used more force with his left arm to fool us."

"I can't imagine someone going through all that effort," Zhao said, somewhat unconvinced.

"It's certainly unusual. If anything, left-handed people often leave evidence to make it look as if they were right-handed, leaving with police with a larger search pool. I've never heard of the opposite being the case."

"Would you call your theory reliable?"

Chen shook his head. "No, it's just a guess. It is possible that the person has a stronger right leg but is still left-handed."

Zhao exhaled loudly. After all that research, everything was possible. But they couldn't make any progress if they couldn't exclude some possibilities.

"When the victim went to relieve himself at the edge of the grass, he was killed where he stood. And while the body was dragged, only one person made footprints. We now know that those footprints belonged to the killer. That's all still true, right?"

"Yes."

"Then the word on the concrete couldn't have been scratched by Sun Hongyun. The killer must have done it and then put the rock in Sun's hand."

"Yes, that's right," Chen said, nodding.

"So that brings us to a new question: Why would the killer write the word 'local' using Sun's hand?"

"I have no idea," Chen said. "It's just like the Liqun cigarettes. It doesn't make sense."

Zhao closed his eyes and let out a long breath while he tried to gather his thoughts. "I can think of two possibilities. Either the killer isn't local, so he left those words to put us on the wrong track, or the killer is actually a local and he's an egomaniac. He's confident that the police will never catch him, so he's starting to leave us clues. But I'm just grasping at straws here."

"So what should we do next?" Chen asked.

Zhao rubbed his eyes. "What else can we do? We've got to catch that pervert and see if he has any connection to the murderer."

After dismissing Chen, Zhao sat and thought. The killer was leaving false clues left and right, tampering with evidence in a way they had never seen before.

What if everything they had found thus far had been deliberately left by the killer to put them on the wrong track?

He pursed his lips and took another look at all the files related to the pervert, then the notes from his visit to Ms. Liu, the latest woman to be assaulted. He knew there was something off, but he couldn't put his finger on it.

He put her report aside and looked at the sketches of the other women who reported assaults, letting them all float through his head. He compared all the notes side by side. Suddenly he sat upright.

There *was* something wrong!

In all the past cases, after the pervert finished his assault, he would brandish the knife, threaten them, and then swagger off. But in the most recent case, which occurred on the same night as the murder, Ms. Liu said that the pervert looked nervous and ran away.

What had made him so nervous?

Chapter 26

In the evening, Luo Wen took his cross-body bag and walked to the noodle shop. When Huiru saw him through the window, she pretended not to know him and focused on her work. Then she flashed him a look.

Luo walked in and pretended to look at the menu. Huiru moved closer. "The police came and asked questions today." Her voice was low.

Luo smiled and nodded. "I'll have the noodles with beef, please. Do you deliver? I have some things to do, and it would be great if you could bring the food to my apartment."

Huiru nodded. "Sure. Just tell me your address and I'll bring it over."

Ten minutes after he arrived at his house, the doorbell rang. Luo opened the door where Huiru stood with his noodles.

"Please, come in," Luo said.

The small dog with the golden fur ran over and barked twice. Then he ran back to the sofa to hide. Huiru smiled. "Wow, he's all better! Look at him running around!"

Luo couldn't help but laugh as he watched the dog. "Yes, he healed very quickly. He started running and jumping just a few days after I brought him home." But his smile soon faded. The other dog had had a lot of injuries too. He remembered how happy his daughter had been when her dog had healed. She gave the dog a bath with the help of her mother and then let the dog sit in her lap. When Luo saw this he took the dog away, worried that his daughter would get sick. But she knew how to get her way. She started crying immediately, and Luo gave up and let her play.

It was bittersweet to think about the past. His eyes moistened. He wished he could go back in time and relive those happy moments.

Luo exhaled and forced himself to come back to the present. He poured a glass of water for Huiru. "What happened today? Don't rush, just take your time."

Huiru told Luo about her conversation with the police, trying her best to remember every detail.

Luo listened attentively and smiled broadly when she finished. "Well done! That's what you should have said. And were you wearing these jeans this morning?"

"Yes, I was. Just like you asked."

"That's good. How is your knee doing?" Luo said.

"I already have a scab."

"OK. Could you let me take a look, if it's not too much trouble?"

"Of course." She started to roll them up but the jeans were too tight to roll all the way to the knee. "Um, should I go to the bathroom and change into something?" Huiru asked.

"Oh no, no, you don't have to do that," Luo said quickly. "You're a young lady, and I don't want you to change clothes in my house. Just push up the jeans a little higher."

She smiled warmly. She really felt like she trusted this man like a nice uncle. He sincerely wanted to help.

She kept rolling her jeans, and Luo looked at her knee as best as he could. "It's been really warm for the past few days. The wound is healing faster than I expected. Does it itch?" Luo asked.

"It itches a lot, but I know I shouldn't scratch it. It's pretty awful."

"OK, tomorrow you can wear a short skirt to air it out. But wear a sheer overlay skirt to hide your scab a bit. That way they will just barely be able to see the injury and know you were not making up a story. When your scab starts to fall off, you can just wear a normal skirt. And continue to put antibiotic ointment on it."

"I can do that."

"That reminds me, how is your ankle?"

"It was sore yesterday, but it doesn't hurt anymore."

"That's bad," Luo sighed. "I didn't hurt you enough to make it realistic. Ideally your ankle would have swollen. But it's hard for me to hurt your ankle properly because I can't register your pain. It reminds me of a story by Zhuangzi: I am not a fish, so I do not know the happiness a fish feels. In the next few days, try your best to walk as if you were still hurt. Take it really slow. Do you understand?"

Huiru nodded quickly.

"Have you seen Guo Yu today?" Luo asked.

"He came in not long after you left the restaurant. I told him that I was coming to see you to talk about the police interview. He said he would come back with some snacks so we could chat."

"OK. Tell him that in the next few days the police will probably speak to both of you and ask you to explain what happened. Just follow the plan. And remember, no matter how urgent, do not call or text each other," Luo said.

Chapter 27

The next morning, Lieutenant Lin and Investigator Song walked into the noodle restaurant.

Fulai greeted them. "I'm very sorry, but we don't serve breakfast. Could you come back at lunch?"

Lin smiled. "We're actually here to speak to Zhu Huiru."

Fulai looked anxious for a moment. "Is this . . . is this about Little Gangster again? His death has nothing to do with us. When she delivered his order, he was so out of line that she hurt herself trying to get away from him. She hurt her ankle quite badly."

"Is that so?" Lin asked gently. He looked Fulai up and down. One of his legs was shorter than the other because he had had polio as a child. That certainly explained why Huiru delivered the rice instead of Fulai.

Huiru came out from the kitchen. When she saw the police she stopped in her tracks. "Do you still have questions for me, officers?"

Lin smiled. "I'm sorry to bother you again, but since you are the last person to have seen the victim, we wanted you to confirm some details." He could tell that she was tense and added, "We apologize for the inconvenience, but cooperating with the police is the duty of every citizen. I hope you understand."

"Of course," Huiru said. There was nothing else to say.

"Would it be possible to talk somewhere private?" Lin asked, his tone serious.

"Where would we go?" Huiru asked carefully.

"Perhaps you could take us to the river and tell us exactly what happened again? It would be extremely helpful for our investigation."

"OK." Huiru lowered her head and started towards the door.

"Look at that!" Lin said, watching her gait closely. "Your leg is better now?"

Huiru hadn't realized how quickly she was walking and blushed.

As soon as this police officer stepped into their restaurant, she had a feeling that he was different from the two who came yesterday. He seemed all knowing and completely in control, and his uniform indicated a higher rank. It looked like today would be a lot more challenging.

The more she thought about it, the more nervous she got. But Luo taught her to act naturally no matter what situation she found herself in, and she managed to keep that in the forefront of her mind.

"My ankle doesn't hurt much anymore. I can pretty much walk now."

"Then it healed quickly," Lin said. "Just three days ago you sprained it so badly that you couldn't walk. Wow."

Huiru smiled weakly.

"How about your knee?" Lin asked. He saw that she was wearing a skirt with a sheer overlay that showed a small scab on her knee.

Huiru followed Luo's instructions and answered truthfully. "It formed a scar already. I think it will be better in the next few days. It doesn't hurt; it just itches."

She thought that Lin would keep asking questions but he didn't. "Fine, let's go to the river. I'll do my best to keep this short—I don't want to keep you from your work too long."

As they walked, Lin asked Huiru where she was from and when she had arrived in Hangzhou, chatting with her about the noodle restaurant and how their business was doing. He didn't ask anything related to the case.

When they arrived at the river, Lin stopped in his tracks and looked Huiru up and down. Huiru felt scared and looked down, but then thought that would be unnatural, so she looked at Investigator Song instead.

"Ms. Zhu, could you please tell us what happened that night?" Lin said.

"I was holding the fried rice, and I walked to this spot here. I saw him on the fitness equipment over there." She pointed at the disc where Xu Tianding had stretched his oblique muscles. "I put the takeout box on the grass and was about to leave—"

"Just a minute." Lin smiled knowingly. "Did you forget to collect his payment?" He watched her face carefully.

Huiru answered without missing a beat. "When he came into the restaurant, he said he wanted fried rice. I told him we wouldn't make it because he had ordered food without paying so many times. He tossed a hundred-yuan note at me and said that it was payment for the past orders and that night's order. He would do whatever it took to make me deliver that rice."

Lin nodded. Judging by her expression, she was telling the truth.

"Continue," Lin said.

"Then he approached me. He wanted me to sit and chat and have a drink with him. He said that he bought a six-pack just for me. I refused, but he grabbed me so I couldn't leave. He dragged me very forcefully. I resisted, but I'm not that strong, so I couldn't get away. He dragged me all the way to the grass behind the fitness equipment."

"Where exactly?"

She walked to a place on the grass and pointed. "About here."

"Alright. Please continue."

"Then he groped me. I fought against him but it was really tiring. Finally I pushed him away and ran straight for the road, screaming for help. He was still coming after me, but fortunately my friend walked past, so he gave up. But right before I reached the road, I tripped and fell, and that's how I got hurt. I don't know where he went after that."

"So when you were struggling to get away, where was the take-out box?"

"I set it on the ground and didn't pick it up again," she said confidently.

"Do you remember where you fell down?" Lin asked.

"I tripped on a sharp rock over there." Huiru took them to the rock. A sharp edge was pointing out of the dirt, which was exactly how they left it.

Lin squatted down to look at it. He took a pair of gloves out of his pocket and extracted the rock from the mud. Upon close inspection he did see a trace of blood. He put the rock in an evidence bag and handed the bag to Song. "What's your friend's name?" he asked. "Could you give us his contact information?"

Huiru gave Guo Yu's name and number, and Song wrote it down.

"Do you still remember approximately how long your fight with Xu Tianding lasted?"

"Umm . . ." Huiru tapped her foot in thought. "Just a few minutes."

"Can you be more specific?"

"About four or five minutes, I think."

"After you were hurt, did you and your friend go directly home?"

"No, I couldn't walk. I was afraid that . . . that . . . you know, that guy would come back and get me, so I massaged my ankle for a bit and then my friend took me home."

"How long did you and Guo Yu stay here?"

"Hmm, a long time I think. About ten minutes."

Lin gritted his teeth. He couldn't poke any holes in her story. Could it really be possible that she had nothing to do with Xu Tianding's murder?

"Well, he tried to assault you, but he didn't get very far. Why didn't you report it to the police?

"Report it?" Huiru did not attempt to hide her disdain. "Even if the police locked him up, they would release him again in a few days. And as soon as he was released, he would come to the restaurant for revenge. My brother and I run a small business; we can't afford to get into trouble like that. We have no choice but to take whatever comes our way." She looked up.

Lin shifted on his feet, feeling awkward. When a civilian didn't want to report an incident to the police, it meant the police were doing something wrong. "Oh, one more thing. You and Guo Yu were by this road for quite some time. Did anybody walk by?"

"Yes."

"Do you remember who?" This could officially take her off the list of suspects.

"No, I didn't see anyone that I knew," Huiru said, shaking her head.

It was a normal answer, Lin admitted to himself. When you pass a stranger on the street, you're not going to remember what they look like a few hours later, let alone a few days.

"Do you know if one of them was walking two dogs on that night? One man said he was walking his dogs and saw a young man and a young lady on the side of the road. Perhaps he saw you two."

Lin had invented the man with the two dogs, but he wanted to see how Huiru would react.

But Luo had taught Huiru how to handle these tricks. She knew not to help the police answer more specific questions. If you knew the answer you could say it; if you didn't you should say that you didn't know.

"I don't think I saw them."

Lin nodded and remembered the beer can with the fingerprints on it. "Did you touch any of Xu Tianding's beer?"

"No. He wanted me to, but I didn't drink a single drop."

"Did your hand ever touch one of those beer cans?"

"No."

"What were you wearing that night?"

"Um, a purple collared shirt." Huiru knew that the surveillance tapes would prove that she wasn't lying.

"Could you bring that shirt to me so we can take a look at it?" Lin asked.

"The shirt?" She hesitated, like she didn't understand why it was necessary.

"Don't worry, this is part of our routine investigation. We will return the shirt to you as soon as we've finished."

"OK."

Lin and Song followed her to her apartment block. She handed the shirt to them, and Song and Lin made their way back to the police station.

Song waited until they were out of earshot before saying, "Lieutenant Lin, surely Zhu Huiru can be taken off the suspects list now."

Lin had a frown on his face. "Her answers were airtight."

"You mean you still think she has something to do with the case?"

"She was a little bit unnatural. I just have this strange feeling that she's lying to us," Lin said. He wasn't willing to say outright that he thought she did it.

Investigator Song, on the other hand, was ready to strike her off. "But most people are nervous when they are interrogated by the police, especially in a murder case. We now know what happened that night. We know that Xu deliberately asked for his fried rice to be delivered to the park, and deliberately bought all that beer, so he would have a chance to assault Zhu Huiru. Her description of Xu matches what everyone else has said about him. The autopsy shows that Xu had fried rice in his stomach. He didn't eat it when Huiru first arrived, because he was thinking about something other than food. But after she left, he probably started to eat. Plus Huiru and her friend Guo Yu left the scene at 10:42 p.m., but Xu died at 10:50 p.m. That's a very strong alibi."

Lin didn't agree or disagree with Song. "OK, let's find out a little bit more about this Guo Yu," he said. "If we don't find any discrepancies between their statements, then we can confirm that they have nothing to do with this murder."

Huiru walked all by herself back to the noodle restaurant, her heart beating wildly. It seemed like she had passed this test. She hoped that the police would stop bothering her, at least.

Chapter 28

In one of the offices of the West Hangzhou Bureau, Investigator Li reported his latest findings to Lin. "Dr. Gu ran the tests on Zhu Huiru's shirt and didn't find any traces of blood on it."

"I see," Lin said.

"We just typed up Guo Yu's statement," Li said, handing his boss the document. "His answers are consistent with Zhu Huiru's story. We didn't find a single discrepancy. He came home late after working overtime. His employer confirmed that. He was eating at the noodle restaurant when Xu Tianding entered, threw a hundred-yuan note on the table, and ordered fried rice. Xu said that Zhu Huiru should deliver it to the park. After she left, Guo felt very worried for Ms. Zhu's safety. He was afraid something bad would happen. So he followed her. When he first got to the river, he didn't see anyone. About five minutes later he saw her running across the grass away from the river, Xu chasing behind. Just before she reached the road, she tripped and fell. He hurried to help. That was when Xu noticed Guo and retreated, presumably to the park. Ms. Zhu massaged her ankle for a long time, but it hurt too much to walk. Finally they decided that Guo should carry her home. He guessed that someone walked past during those ten minutes, but he doesn't remember who they were or what they looked like. Neither of them grew up in Hangzhou, so they don't know very many people in the area."

"Huh." Lin said thoughtfully. "So he's Ms. Zhu's boyfriend?"

"No."

"No?" Lin asked.

"Guo's coworkers described him as very timid," Li explained. "At first he told us that he and Ms. Zhu were just friends. Only after we pressed him did he admit that he liked her. He was very shy about it and asked us to not tell her."

"Is that a believable answer, in your opinion?"

"Yes, he is widely known as an introvert. Next, he said that at 11:00 p.m. he went to a twenty-four-hour convenience store near his apartment to buy dressings and antibiotic ointment for Ms. Zhu. Dr. Gu estimates that the killer spent at least half an hour making those thin cuts on the victim's body. There's no way a young lady like Ms. Zhu could have done something so grotesque. And Guo was in the convenience store at eleven; there is surveillance footage to prove that. He wouldn't have had the time to do it."

Lin nodded but did not speak. It all checked out, but he couldn't stop thinking about the way Ms. Zhu looked uneasy when he saw her that morning. Was she simply nervous about speaking to the police? Or was she feeling guilty?

"Lieutenant Lin?" Li said. "Their statements are consistent and match the facts. Neither of them had enough time to commit the crime. We can rule them off as suspects, right?"

"Yes, let's go in another direction," Lin said. He didn't have any choice.

At that moment, a group of officers from the task force knocked and entered. One of them said, "Lieutenant Lin, we looked for a murder weapon that matched the cross section of the wound that Gu gave us, and we found this paring knife."

He handed the knife to Lin and continued. "This knife is sold in many of the supermarkets and stores in the area. We tried to find a record of a recent purchase but couldn't."

Lin looked at the knife and put it on his desk. "How are the interviews coming with those who had a dispute with the victim?" he asked the group.

"We spent a lot of time speaking to Xu's friends, including Zhang Bing, and came up with a list of about seventeen people who might have held a grudge against Xu. Some were attacked by him; some say he owed them money. One man told us that Xu was seen torturing a dog. The dog was rescued by a Good Samaritan, but Xu wanted him back, so the man finally bought the dog for three hundred yuan. And those are only the people Xu has wronged recently. We were unable to get the names of all the students who were bullied into giving him money, restaurants where he ate without paying, or people that he harassed on the street."

"What a mess," Lin said, knitting his eyebrows. "But we don't have any other choice. We have to investigate them one by one."

"I would start with the man who was beat up by Xu at the outdoor market on the evening of the murder," the officer suggested. "We spoke to him already, and he claimed he was at home that evening. The only person that can vouch for his whereabouts is his girlfriend. He was adamant that he would never kill someone for something so insignificant. Should we bring him to the station?"

"No," Lin said tersely. "If we bring him in without cause or any evidence, then we should be bringing in everyone on that list. We have to be more careful—otherwise he might file a complaint."

"So what do we do?" the officer asked, at his wits' end.

"Try speaking to the girlfriend; it might be easier to tell if she's lying." Lin said.

"I guess we don't have any choice," the officer agreed.

Lin clapped his hands to get everyone's attention. "OK. You've all worked hard today. It's about time we went home. We'll continue this tomorrow."

He picked up the knife and followed them out of the office.

Chapter 29

It was dinner time, and the restaurants near Luo's apartment were all bustling.

Luo approached the noodle restaurant, but all of the tables were taken. He was about to leave when he saw Guo Yu sitting at a table and giving him a look. As always, he stayed where he was and casually checked his surroundings before walking into the restaurant and sitting next to Guo Yu.

The minute Luo sat down, Guo Yu whispered, "The police came to see me today."

Luo smiled almost imperceptibly. He knew that Guo must have answered the questions well, otherwise he wouldn't be here. "The police asked me some questions too," he said.

"Why . . . why would they speak to you?" Guo Yu said, raising his eyebrows.

Luo gave him a discerning look, and Guo Yu quickly went back to eating. "The police are investigating anyone who has a connection with the thug and might hold a grudge against him."

Guo Yu put down his chopsticks. "Why would you hold a grudge against him?"

Zijin Chen

"I bought his dog for three hundred yuan, remember?" Luo said.

"That . . . that counts?"

"The police might think that I resented him for making me pay so much. So they came and asked me some questions."

"How did they find you?"

Luo leaned in a little closer. "They said they asked Zhu Fulai, Huiru's brother. Fulai was there when I bought the dog and knows my face. I have ordered delivery several times, so he has my number."

"So what did you say?" Guo Yu asked, growing anxious.

Luo spoke calmly. "I happened to be at home, so I said I would meet them at the entrance to my apartment building. They asked me what I was doing that day and I said I was out on a walk. When I showed them my work credentials, they were convinced." Guo Yu didn't know exactly what Luo did for a living, but he knew that he had money, so he guessed it was for some important company. It made sense that as soon as the police saw his work certificate, they believed that he wouldn't kill someone just for three hundred yuan.

"How about you? How did your little chat go?" Luo asked.

"I did everything the way you taught me, and they believed me," Guo Yu answered.

"Did they ask you to describe your relationship with Huiru?"

"Yeah. I said we were just friends and then when they asked me repeatedly, I said that I liked her but wanted to keep it a secret. I heard that they spoke to my colleagues too." Guo Yu smiled with a touch of pride. "I think I did pretty well."

"Very good," Luo said, nodding. "You probably won't have any more trouble then."

"So it's over?" Guo Yu said, in disbelief.

"I think so. Even if they do come again, just stick to the story. By the way, where is Huiru? Is she making a delivery?"

126

"Yeah. She was here when I first arrived and then she left to deliver some noodles. I spoke to her for a little bit, and she said everything went OK." Guo Yu looked relieved as he picked up his chopsticks.

"Stop smiling; it's too obvious." Luo said.

"Oh." Guo Yu wiped the smile off his face.

At that moment a plainclothes officer walked into the noodle restaurant. Neither Luo nor Guo Yu could tell that he was with the police.

Chapter 30

Lin changed into casual clothes when he was finished with work and walked to the scene of the crime. His heart was filled with conflicting emotions as he stood by the canal.

What should have been a straightforward homicide case had suddenly turned into a complete quagmire. He felt like his head was bursting with information.

In the past, whenever he handled a case involving gangsters, he usually apprehended the suspect within a few days. Typically the killer was not very good at covering his tracks. Whenever there was not enough evidence, they would just speak to the friends of the victim and identify a suspect in a short amount of time. They were weak people—as soon as they saw the police at their door, they were quick to show guilt.

He had never seen a case where the killer was willing to spend tens of thousands of yuan to destroy the crime scene.

Then there was the fact that the killer dragged the body into the trees and spent at least half an hour making shallow cuts into the corpse. He still didn't understand the underlying reason for this, but it showed that the killer was of a different caliber.

The killer knew to remove all footprints and wipe the cans clean of fingerprints. This was important. The cans were bought in order to get Ms. Zhu to drink and stay with Xu Tianding. They weren't meant for anyone else. So after Ms. Zhu left, who saw Xu? Why would they touch the cans but not drink them?

It would be easy to explain if Zhu Huiru were the killer. She might have touched the cans inadvertently and wanted to wipe the cans clean to make herself look innocent. But Xu was killed after she left the park. Surveillance cameras didn't lie. Guo was in a convenience store at 11:00 p.m., so he wouldn't have the time to make all those shallow cuts on the body. And no matter how he tried, he couldn't find any problems with their statements.

What could have possibly happened that night?

Lin realized he was hungry. He turned back to the residential area to find a restaurant.

He entered Chongqing Noodles and recognized Huiru's brother. Guo Yu was seated at one of the tables, but since Lin wasn't the one to take his statement, he didn't recognize him.

Zhu Fulai immediately recognized Lin. He shuffled over and said, "Hello, Officer. Would you like to order? Or did you have . . . have more questions for us?" There was a trace of panic in his voice.

Guo Yu and Luo couldn't help but sneak a look at the man as soon as they heard Fulai say "officer."

"I'll have some noodles with shredded pork," Lin said. He started looking for a table before suddenly remembering something. He wanted to try his luck, and he pulled out the paring knife that his team had given him earlier. "Excuse me, have you seen this knife before?"

Fulai looked down at the paring knife, suddenly alert. "It's just an ordinary kitchen knife. Does . . . does . . . the knife have something to do with the case?"

"Yes. Have you seen it anywhere?" Lin asked, looking closely at Fulai.

Luo held back a smile. If Fulai got the replaced paring knife from the kitchen, then Huiru would be in the clear.

Luo specifically bought a new knife for Huiru after the accident, whereas the murder weapon showed signs of use. An expert like Lin would see the difference immediately. It would be perfect for Fulai to hand over the knife, because he was not connected to the case.

Fulai's answer was so unexpected that Luo was stunned. "No, I've never seen it before."

Lin stared hard at the cook. Finally he smiled politely and sat down at the table next to Luo and Guo Yu.

Just as Luo was puzzling over Fulai's answer, Huiru returned. Lin immediately pulled her aside and said, "Ms. Zhu, have you ever seen a knife like this?"

Huiru deliberately acted as if she didn't understand the point of the question. "Does this have something to do with the case? It's just a paring knife."

"Yes, it does. The killer used a paring knife to stab the victim. We need to know where it came from," Lin said, not taking his eyes off Huiru.

"OK . . . looks like a very normal knife to me," she said, peering at it. "I think my brother bought one that looks similar. It's usually in the cutlery drawer; let me check."

Luo pressed his lips together tightly.

Huiru turned and opened the drawer. She moved a few things around and quickly found the replacement knife.

Luo sighed inwardly. Huiru and her brother had conflicting answers. That spelled trouble.

Lin examined Huiru's knife briefly. The edge looked brand new. It could not be the murder weapon. Still, it was strange that Ms. Zhu and her brother had inconsistent answers. He looked a little more closely at the knife and said, "It looks like this knife has never been used before."

"We bought it to peel fruit, but we just put it away and forgot about it," Huiru answered.

"When did you buy this?"

"Um . . . a month or two ago, I think. My brother bought it; I'll ask him. Fulai, come here a minute! When did we get this knife?"

Luo cringed. Huiru just said that her brother bought the knife, but then why would he say that he had never seen it before?

Fulai came over, coughing awkwardly. "Where is this knife from?" he asked.

"It's our knife, from that drawer over there," Huiru said.

"Oh, right," Fulai said quickly. "I bought it in the supermarket across the street, about two months ago. But I haven't touched it since, so I totally forgot."

"Ah." Lin's smile seemed to have some underlying meaning. He returned the knife to Huiru and sat back down.

Chapter 31

Luo heard a knock and opened the door to a jittery Huiru. "Come in," he said.

Huiru stared at her feet. She didn't even sit down.

Luo poured her a glass of water. "What happened today? What was your brother thinking?"

"I, um . . . I asked him myself, after the police officer left. My brother thought—thinks—I killed that thug," Huiru stuttered.

"Why would he think that?" Luo asked, frowning.

"He said that he put the pieces together when I came home really late after taking the paring knife from the drawer. I didn't know that he saw me take it. Then the police came looking for me . . . so he thought it was me. He lied to help me cover it up, which is how . . . how everything went wrong. I'm really sorry, this is all my fault. This is all my fault!" She sobbed.

Luo pressed his lips together and paced back and forth. "That officer was very experienced; I could tell by the way he interrogated you."

Huiru choked as she said, "That same officer came by earlier today. I think he . . . he thinks I did it."

"Oh?" Luo stopped pacing and looked at her. "What did he say earlier?"

She described everything that happened.

"I'm positive you answered all those questions correctly," Luo said. "Maybe . . . do you think you might have looked nervous?"

"A little, yeah."

"If he were more professional, he would stop bothering you. They must have checked the surveillance cameras by now and know that you have a solid alibi. The autopsy would show that you wouldn't have enough time to have committed the crime," Luo said, thinking it through. "Hmm. He must have a gut feeling about you. It was probably something about your expression. If he actually had something to incriminate you, he would already have an arrest warrant. Don't worry, it will be fine."

"Do you really think so?" Huiru asked, wiping her eyes.

"If he examines the evidence, he has no reason to suspect you. It's a shame that you and your brother gave different responses, though. I'm afraid the police will come back now."

"It's all my fault, how I dragged you into this. I'm so sorry."

"Sorry you didn't tell your brother that you killed someone? The more people who know the truth, the riskier everything becomes." He smiled to try to make her feel better. "If anyone is at fault, it's me. I didn't anticipate what your brother would do."

"Don't talk like that," she said.

"What's done is done. What we need to focus on now is how to handle the situation. Soon, when the police discover that the case—" He stopped and changed his wording. "In the end, I'm sure that the police will take you off of the list of suspects. You didn't say anything wrong, but in the future, make sure that you pay attention to your tone of voice and facial expressions. You could try practicing saying the answers somewhere where you brother won't overhear. As long as your statement is bulletproof, they won't be able to do anything. But I think

I'll need to play a few more cards in my hand so I can get you out of this situation."

"What are you going to do?" Huiru asked. Her eyes widened.

"The less you know, the better," Luo said. He stroked his chin, muttering under his breath, "I could go to his apartment tomorrow and have a good look around. Guo Yu would be at work, so it's just Huiru that I have to worry about." He looked up and said, "What do you normally do in the daytime? I mean outside of restaurant hours."

"I usually get up late. Then I help my brother buy fresh vegetables or clean up the restaurant and get ready for the lunchtime customers. In the afternoon I usually take a nap, or sometimes I go window shopping and walk around. That's all."

"Do you go to the movies?"

"Not anymore," she said, shaking her head. "I used to go when I was little; we had a theater in my hometown. But then it went out of business."

"I don't go anymore either," he said, turning to look at the dog and smiling bitterly. "I think it's been eight or nine years now."

"Why not?" Considering his income and all the free time he seemed to have, she assumed he went all the time.

Luo coughed. "I was thinking about telling you to go to the movies on your own or with your brother on Friday. But if you suddenly go now it will seem out of the ordinary. Hmm. Can I see your phone, please?"

She handed him her phone.

"This is the phone you use when people call to order deliveries, right? Do you have another one?"

She pulled out another, this one decorated with sparkling stars.

"How much did this cost you?" Luo said, turning it over.

"About twelve hundred. Why do you ask?" She looked confused.

Luo took some cash out of his bag with one hand and threw the phone forcefully with the other.

"Ah!" Huiru was shocked. She quickly picked up her phone.

Luo handed her the money, "This is two thousand; go and get a new phone on Friday. Remember to tell your brother that you dropped your phone and broke it. Around 1:00 p.m. go to one of the stores in downtown Hangzhou and get a new phone. Don't tell your brother about the money; he'll just worry. Go to a place that sells a lot of phones—the bigger the better. If you can, ask one of your friends to come with you. Spend plenty of time shopping and don't come back until you have to start work again."

"But . . . why?"

"It's better if you don't know," he said, his eyes twinkling.

Huiru didn't want to take his money. "I can't take this; you have helped Guo Yu and me so much already. If you want me to get a new phone, I'll buy one with my own money."

He pushed the money back in her hands—his decision was final. "Take it. I have no use for it."

"Why . . . why . . . are you helping us like this?" she asked with trepidation.

Luo smiled broadly. "I just want you to have a bright future. For my part, well . . . it might be atonement for things that I have done. I'm very sorry that I can't tell you more about myself, but I promise that I am just trying to help. When this is all over, I hope that you forget me completely." He was sincere.

She didn't know what he meant by that, but she knew that he wasn't a bad person. If he had wanted to take advantage of her, he would have done so already.

Chapter 32

Captain Zhao rushed down the hall of criminal investigator offices. Investigator Yang looked up when he entered. "Wow, you came back fast."

"Of course I did! As soon as you told me you caught the pervert, I came as quickly as I could." He headed towards the interview rooms. "What room is he in?"

"Number 2."

"Has he confessed yet?"

"His lips are sealed. He keeps saying that he doesn't know why we arrested him."

Zhao stopped in his tracks. "We got him in here and he won't admit to a thing? Are you sure we got the right man?"

"Absolutely." Yang had a smile on his face. "We found a knife and a hat in the trunk of his car. We're contacting some of the victims to ID him."

"How did you get him so quickly?"

"We found a stretch of road with two surveillance cameras. He walked by but never came back. A while later, a BMW drove off in the other direction, so we thought it could be his car. We searched his license plate number and got his address." Yang leaned back, looking pleased.

"Well done, Yang," Zhao said, nodding in approval.

"But there's one other thing that I should tell you."

"What's that?"

"The guy's wife is here. She claims that we got the wrong man and brought two television reporters with her. She says we have no right to arrest him without giving a reason. She wants answers."

"Oh . . ." Zhao frowned. He hated when the media got mixed up in their work. Then a smile spread across his face. "You said he won't talk, huh?"

"That's right. He claims he doesn't know why we arrested him. He looks guilty, though."

Zhao chuckled. "You tell his wife that we'll bring her husband out in just a moment."

Yang handed the pervert's file to Zhao before leaving. The man's name was Jiang Dehui. He was forty-one and from Hangzhou. His expensive car and his address indicated that he was rich.

Zhao walked briskly into the interview room. The guards greeted him. Zhao nodded and pulled up a stool. "You're Jiang Dehui? The one who has been sexually assaulting women for the past few months, is that right?"

Jiang shook his head vigorously. "No! Absolutely not! I don't know what you're talking about."

"So you didn't do it?" Zhao said, a smile creeping up.

"I didn't do it. I wouldn't possibly do a thing like that!"

"OK, OK," Zhao said breezily. "Your wife is outside. She says that you've been wrongfully accused. Looks like she brought a few reporters with her. How about I take you out there and we wait for the victims to come to the station? We'll let them confirm whether or not you were the one to assault them. If they say it wasn't you, I'll apologize to the television reporters and let you go."

When Jiang heard the word "reporters," his face went white as a sheet. He started to tremble.

Zhao smiled. "How about it?"

Jiang slumped in his chair. "Could you, uh . . . could you tell my wife to go home?"

Zhao shrugged. "Your wife came here of her own volition; we don't have the right to tell her to go anywhere. I'm afraid there's nothing I can do."

"I—I—"

"Are you ready to come clean?" Zhao leaned against the wall and crossed his arms. "If you cooperate, we can protect your privacy. I'm guessing that your wife has no idea what you've done, otherwise she wouldn't be making such a fuss. Is that right?"

Jiang turned bright red. ". . . Please don't tell them what I've done. I'll tell you everything."

"Very good," Zhao said. He turned to the guard next to him. "Give him his phone and let him call his wife.

Jiang held the phone, and took a deep breath. He called his wife and told her that he was involved in a tax-fraud case and would have to stay at the police station for the next few days and that she should go home.

When Jiang finished his call, Zhao turned to the guards. "Bring me his statement as soon as you finish."

Chapter 33

Soon after Zhao arrived in his office, Yang entered. "The reporters are gone. They left with the wife."

Zhao smiled. He actually wished the reporters could have stayed. The string of sexual assaults had made headlines for several months, taking the city by storm. It would have been nice to announce that they caught the guy. Then again, the case was still extremely sensitive. It was better this way.

"Two of the victims have already confirmed that he was their assailant," Yang said. "I don't know why he suddenly was willing to confess."

Zhao knew, but he didn't explain this to Yang. It was partly thanks to Jiang's wife. She brought all those reporters, causing her husband to worry that if he was on television for even a minute he wouldn't be able to show his face in public ever again. The only thing bothering him now was that he didn't know who the serial killer was.

Yan Liang, the professor, had very quickly come to the conclusion that Jiang was not the killer, given how careless he was. Zhao was uneasy. He had wanted Jiang to be the killer, because that would mean he was nearing the end of the murder investigation.

Before long, an officer returned from the interview room. "He admitted to all of the assaults, but . . . he says he didn't kill Sun Hongyun."

Zhao pursed his lips. "Did you get his fingerprints?"

"Of course. They don't match the ones on the murder weapon."

Zhao took the interview report and pored over the text.

On the night of the murder, Jiang Dehui entertained some clients until eleven o'clock. Then he drove to Wenyi West Road. He got out of his car and waited for an unaccompanied woman to come along. Sometime later the victim walked towards him. He grabbed her and dragged her onto the grass to assault her, threatening her with a knife. He zipped up his slacks after he came and was about to threaten her again when he saw a man standing behind a copse of trees, facing him. He was only twenty or thirty yards away, but it was dark, so he couldn't see the man's face clearly. Even so, Jiang was quite certain that he saw him wearing a cross-body bag. He also thought he saw something in his hands. When Jiang realized that the man was approaching, he knew that the man had witnessed the assault. He panicked and fled.

Something clicked. Zhao went back to the victim's statement, confirming that she said Jiang had run off, looking nervous. Whereas in all the other assaults, Jiang threatened the women one last time before leaving. Jiang had run away because he saw the killer walking towards him.

Jiang saw the man, but he did not witness the actual murder. The woman didn't see the murderer, suggesting that the killer hid or he went in a different direction. Either way, the killer didn't follow Jiang.

Zhao whistled. Jiang had been extremely lucky that night—if the killer had gotten any closer, he might have offed him.

According to the statement, the killer was wearing a cross-body bag. It wasn't much to go on.

There wasn't anyone on the surveillance cameras wearing one. They had already interviewed and eliminated everyone who walked by with any kind of bag. And Zhao couldn't be sure that the killer always walked around wearing one.

Ultimately it seemed that Jiang's case did not have a very strong connection to the murder. Jiang admitted to threatening the woman and defecating in the elevator. He claimed that he was dealing with a lot of stress at work and needed a thrill. He knew that it was risky, which was why he never committed rape or forced the women to give him the hand job. He simply masturbated in their presence, never thinking it would be considered sexual assault. It was clear that Jiang was mentally disturbed, but Zhao couldn't think about scheduling the team psychiatrist just then. He had a splitting headache.

Chapter 34

A police car slowly pulled up to the corner across from Chongqing Noodles. It was dusk.

Lin was about to get out when young Li pointed at a young man entering the restaurant. "Hey, isn't that Guo Yu going in?"

"That's Guo Yu, huh?" Lin watched the skinny man with glasses, recognizing him as one of the customers from the day before when he asked about the paring knife. "Does Guo Yu come here every day?" he asked thoughtfully.

"I'm not sure, but if he has a crush on Huiru, he probably comes often."

"Perfect. While we're here we can get his fingerprints too." The two of them stepped out of the car and headed across the street.

Business was always good in the evenings. The tables were full, and everyone looked up when the officers approached the counter. Guo Yu was the only one who looked down, hunching his shoulders over the table closest to the counter and farthest from the door. His reaction didn't escape Lin's notice. He stopped at the counter as Huiru did her best to act welcoming. "Would you like something to eat, officers?"

"Not today, thanks," Lin smiled. "We just need to take your fingerprints. It shouldn't take long; don't worry."

"Fingerprints?" Huiru looked confused.

Lin coughed and lowered his voice, but Guo Yu could still hear everything. "Yes, we found some prints at the scene of the crime and think they might match the killer. We need to collect prints from everyone involved in the case. It's a funny story, actually. Guess where we found them?"

"I don't know," Huiru answered quietly. She had a feeling he was testing her.

"There were eleven cans at the scene of the crime, and each was wiped clean with a cloth. Then we found a twelfth can behind a tree. It was empty, but the prints were intact. I assume that it was dark and the killer missed it when cleaning up the scene."

Her heart skipped a beat. She remembered touching some of the cans before Luo told her to stop. He had promised to wipe off all the fingerprints.

Did one of the cans go unnoticed? Or were the officers just testing her again?

She forced herself to stay calm. "Oh . . . well, that means you'll probably find the killer pretty soon. Do you want to take my fingerprints right now?"

"Yes." Lin looked at Li, who took out a piece of special paper and asked Huiru to press her fingers on it.

Huiru had no choice but to obey.

"Can you get your brother here? I'd like to take his fingerprints too." Lin said.

Huiru went to the kitchen to get her brother. He nervously put his hands on the paper and gave his sister a look of concern before wordlessly returning to the kitchen.

Lin curled his lips in a smile as Li turned to Guo Yu's table without missing a beat. "Oh, hello, Guo Yu. We need your fingerprints for the case too. Sorry for the inconvenience."

Guo Yu's smile was somewhat forced, but he did as he was asked.

As they left the restaurant, Lin reflected on their guilty faces. But he would have to wait until tonight before knowing if he got a match.

Luo came into the restaurant one hour later. He looked intently at the menu. Before he could order, Huiru whispered, "The police were here today. They took my fingerprints and I—"

"Noodles with beef, please!" Luo said, interrupting her. "I need to take care of some things. Could you deliver them to my apartment as soon as they're ready?"

Ten minutes later, Luo let Huiru into his apartment. "Make it quick; it's possible that a plainclothes officer is following you."

That only made her more nervous.

"Sorry, I didn't mean to scare you," Luo said awkwardly.

"It's fine. About an hour ago the officers came to see me again. They wanted fingerprints, not just mine but Guo Yu's and Fulai's too."

Luo frowned. "Of course, your brother lied yesterday, so now they suspect him too. But it won't affect you; he doesn't have anything to do with the case."

She nodded. "The police said that they found a can behind a tree, and that they think the fingerprints on that can belong to the killer."

"That's it?" Luo smiled gently.

"Uh huh." Huiru looked uncertain.

"So you're worried that I missed a can?"

"Um, I . . ." She didn't know how to answer. He had done so much to help them. She couldn't blame him if he overlooked something.

"Were you worried when they spoke to you?"

"I . . . I felt pretty nervous, and it probably showed."

"I told you before, no matter what they say, you can't look like you're afraid of them." Luo knitted his eyebrows.

Huiru's eyes welled with tears. "It's all my fault, all my fault . . ."

"Don't blame yourself. I expected too much of you two. Anyone who is interrogated by the police is going to feel nervous. But remember, if someone acts unnatural during an interview, the cops may get suspicious, but if they can't find any evidence, they'll assume you're just not used to speaking to the police."

"Do you mean that?" Her expression brightened.

"Those aren't your fingerprints on the can."

"Then whose are they?" She looked up quickly. "Are they yours?"

"Don't think about it," Luo said, avoiding the question with a wry smile. "Now you just have to face a few more questions. Did you tell your brother that you're going to buy a new phone tomorrow?"

"Uh huh. He didn't say anything about it."

"Good. Then everything is going to plan. OK, you should go before it gets suspicious." Luo gave her an encouraging smile.

Huiru felt her heart pounding as she left Luo's apartment. Did he really leave his fingerprints on the can? Wasn't that an enormous risk? Why was he so intent on helping them anyway?

Chapter 35

"None of the fingerprints are a match," Gu reported in Lin's office.

"None of them?" Lin's mouth fell open.

"Of course. Why are you so surprised? I told you that neither Zhu Huiru or Guo Yu could be the killer. Their alibis are rock solid."

"But Zhu Fulai doesn't have an alibi, does he?"

"I don't see why you have any reason to suspect him," Gu replied, his disdain showing. "He has a lame leg and trouble walking. And I hear that somewhere between ten and thirty thousand yuan were scattered in that park. Where would a migrant worker get that kind of money?"

"I . . ." Lin was stumped.

"What do you have against them anyway? You should follow the clues and stop wasting valuable time," Gu said aggressively.

"I'm not wasting time. I think there's something fishy here. We need to keep investigating until we get to the bottom of it." He explained how Zhu Huiru and her brother gave different accounts about the knife yesterday.

"That's it?" He snorted in disgust. "You're letting an initial hunch get the best of you. The knife was bought months ago; it's reasonable that Fulai would forget about it."

"No, listen," Lin said, shaking his head. "You didn't see the looks on their faces!"

"You mean they looked nervous and stammered? Did they seem to want to avoid being investigated by the police?" Gu said.

"How did you know?" Lin said, surprised.

"That's a very normal reaction!" Gu looked disgusted. "You and your colleagues have visited that restaurant four times in three days about a murder investigation. Any normal person would be nervous—don't you agree?"

"Uh . . ." Lin considered it for a moment. "I guess so."

"Were they that nervous the first time you asked them about the case?"

"I didn't go on the first day; it was Song and Li. They, uh, said that the suspects acted normally."

"There you go. I've known you for many years. When an aggressive cop like yourself comes along, anyone would get a little scared, don't you think?"

Lin nodded, feeling embarrassed. But something was off. "You've been pretty aggressive yourself today. What's wrong?"

"I'm not happy with the way you're handling this investigation. You're wasting time, and that means I have to keep working overtime. Comparing fingerprints is not rocket science; anyone can do it. I don't think it's necessary for me sign my name on every report."

"OK, I get it; I've been asking too much of you. I'll lay off," Lin said sincerely.

"I've known you for years, and you've never changed." Gu softened. "Besides, you shouldn't worry so much about this case; you're not going to crack it just by sheer skill."

"Old Gu, could you have a little bit more confidence in me?" Lin said. "We're only a few days into the case."

"Stop dreaming. I don't even think you could solve it if we gave you a few years."

Lin's face flushed with displeasure. "You make it sound like this is my first day on the job! I've solved more crimes than anyone else in the bureau."

"I know," Gu chuckled. "Everyone in the West Hangzhou Bureau wishes they could crack as many cases as you, but that isn't going to make a difference here."

"Do you know who did it?"

"No, but I do know that the Zhejiang Bureau and the Hangzhou Bureau dedicated an awful lot of manpower to solve an important serial murder, and they still weren't able to catch him."

"What are you talking about?" Lin looked seriously at Gu.

"Do you know anything about the case that Zhao is working on?"

"Captain Zhao, yes." Lin's eyes grew wide. "You mean . . . ?"

"I was flipping through the papers sent down from the Hangzhou Bureau today, and the fingerprints looked very familiar. I just confirmed it—they're a match."

Lin sat up and swallowed.

Even with the combined experience of criminal investigators and police officers, they had never come close to finding the serial killer.

His throat suddenly felt very dry.

PART 5

AN EQUATION WITHOUT A SOLUTION

Chapter 36

The West Hangzhou Bureau director and vice director walked briskly towards Lin's office. Captain Zhao followed close behind.

"Lieutenant Lin, you remember Captain Zhao," the director said. "Your murder case is going to be handed over to the special task force of the Hangzhou Bureau. We need your full cooperation on this."

Lin nodded. He had worked with Zhao a handful of times. He was known for cracking cases. Plus, as a captain, Zhao's rank was higher than Lin's.

Lin handed over a bundle of case files. Zhao accepted them graciously. "If I have any questions, I'll let you know."

"Certainly."

Zhao went to the small meeting room next door and pored over the records. Other members of the special task force met with the West Hangzhou officers assigned to the murder case.

He read and reread the section on the crime scene investigation, but just skimmed the part about Xu Tianding's friends and enemies. They were looking for a serial killer, which eliminated a lot of potential suspects.

But as he quickly went down the list, one name leapt off the page.

Luo Wen? He checked the man's occupation. Chairman and technical senior consultant of Pro Micromeasurement Instruments Company, Ltd.

His eyes narrowed. *Luo Wen is a pretty rare name. Could this be the same Luo Wen from Ningbo?* he thought.

He was forty-eight years old and had a Ningbo identity card. *Is it really him?*

Zhao stood and went into Lin's office. He pointed at Luo's name. "Have you spoken to this man?"

"No," Lin said, shaking his head. "Someone else on the team interviewed him."

They summoned Investigator Li immediately to look at a picture of Luo from an old news article. "You've seen him; is this the same guy?" Lin asked.

Li looked carefully and quickly confirmed Zhao's guess. "Yes, that's him, although he looks much older now."

"Of course he does," Zhao said. "The picture here is several years old." He frowned slightly. "I can't believe he's in Hangzhou."

"Do you think he should be added to the list of suspects?" Lin asked, confused.

"What? No!" Zhao smiled. "I'm just surprised."

"Well, what's his story?" Lin asked.

"Do you know the former director of the Ningbo Public Security Bureau Criminal Science department, the one directing Forensics and Material Evidence?"

"I think so. You mean that's him?"

"That's right," Zhao said, nodding. "He was one of the best forensic scientists in the country, an absolute genius. He is the editor of many forensic science books and worked for the Criminal Investigation Division of the Zhejiang Public Security Bureau. He became the director of the Ningbo PSB before he even turned forty."

"Why did he resign?" Lin asked, looking over the interview record.

"He wanted more money, surely. He's the chairman and a senior consultant at this huge company. He must be rolling in it!"

"Definitely. He drove off in an Audi Q7," Li answered.

"See? If he continued working for the bureau, he wouldn't be able to buy himself a fancy car because others might criticize him. Now that he's at a private company, he's making more money and he can spend it however he wants. Did he give you any advice on the case when you saw him?"

"Not a word. We had no idea he used to be a forensic scientist. He seemed like he wasn't the slightest bit interested in the case," Li said.

"He used to be a cop; how could he not be a little curious?" Zhao murmured, thinking of Yan Liang.

Chapter 37

"Come on, old Zhao, the people who typically sit in this chair are doctoral students. What do you think you're doing, charging in here with your puny bachelor's degree?" Yan said angrily as Zhao pulled up a chair.

"You don't have to be so grouchy. I have some good news for you."

"Good news?" Yan smiled. "Did you catch the pervert?"

"Yep."

"When will it be on the news?" Yan asked, leaning forward. After that embarrassing first day of class, he couldn't shake the feeling that his students looked at him differently. He desperately wanted to clear his name.

"In the next few days," Zhao answered.

"You don't look very pleased about this."

"The pervert's not the killer. And we learned that the killer has struck again, in Hangzhou. It's driving me crazy!"

"That's odd. Why would there be another murder just a few days after the fourth? Doesn't he usually wait about sixth months?" Yan asked.

"Yes, but this murder is totally different from the others. There was no Liqun cigarette, jump rope, or note. And the killer must have spent a lot of time cutting thin lines on the victim's body. Still, the prints match. No one can figure out what it all means. Which is why I came to you."

"I'm sorry, but if you can't figure it out, there's no way I can." Yan knew exactly what Zhao was getting at and wanted to make it clear he was not going to get dragged into Zhao's case.

"You're sure you don't want to help out?"

"I think I made myself clear already, Zhao."

"Forget it," Zhao sighed. "I knew you were going to be like this. I guess you also don't want to hear about our new development."

"What do you mean?"

"We stumbled upon Luo Wen."

"So he's working for the police again?" Yan asked, his eyes brightening.

"No, he's doing well for himself at a big consulting firm. He got into an altercation with the latest victim over an abused dog. So our investigators ended up speaking to him."

"Talk about a thorough investigation!" Yan chuckled.

"We didn't know where to start," Zhao protested. "We had no idea that the thug was killed by the serial murderer, so we had to start with the victim's enemies. And if we hadn't, we definitely would not have found Luo."

"You should really speak to him instead. Luo's got a real sense of justice. He always said that committing a crime was shameful, no matter the reason. That's why he became a forensic scientist in the first place." Yan paused to think. "He used every forensic technique at his disposal to bring criminals to justice. I know he's not a cop anymore, but I'm sure he would give you some advice if you ask. He's not like me; you know that." Yan laughed somewhat uncomfortably.

Zhao smiled but his mind was thinking about the past. Yan was the best criminologist Zhao had ever met, an expert at getting to the bottom of difficult cases by analyzing the behavior of the accused. But he didn't play by the rules and was forced to resign after a disastrous mistake.

Zhao looked at Yan and shook his head. "My men said he didn't seem interested in the case. He probably has his reasons, just like you."

Zhao's phone rang. He took the call, hung up, and immediately stood to leave. "Sorry, I have to take care of something. If you want to contact Luo, you can call this number." He threw a piece of paper at Yan and strode out, a serious look on his face.

Chapter 38

It had been Lin on the phone. Apparently Zhang Bing, Xu's best friend, was at the bureau reporting a threat. His family found a piece of paper at their doorstep that said "I'm coming for you next." It was now at the Hangzhou Evidence Lab.

Zhejiang University was very close to the West Hangzhou Bureau. Zhao made it to his office in ten minutes. Lin immediately took him into a meeting room, where a young man with longish hair and a white undershirt sat cowering in his chair. He played with the cup of water in his hands.

Zhao coughed gently. "You're Zhang Bing, is that right? Don't be afraid; my colleagues and I take your safety very seriously. We won't let anything happen to you. Now, could you tell me when you picked up that piece of paper?"

Zhang Bing looked up at Zhao's calm and reassuring face. He swallowed. "It . . . my dad saw it when he was leaving the apartment. It was rolled up and wedged behind the door handle."

"And the paper wasn't there in the morning?"

"I didn't leave the house this morning; I was on the computer all day. My dad left at about midday and he didn't see anything then."

"What time did your dad notice the paper, then?"

"Three o'clock. He told you, didn't he?"

"Yes," Zhao said. "Have you noticed anyone suspicious lately?"

Zhang Bing thought carefully. "No, I don't think so."

"Let me put it this way. Who do you think would want to kill both you and Xu Tianding?"

"Shit . . ." Zhang Bing walked Zhao through a few recent arguments. Zhao knew that there was almost no chance that one of the thug's rivals would be a serial murderer, but he didn't want to say that. An office assistant patiently wrote down all the details just in case.

Soon, Zhao and Lin had finished with their questions and sent Zhang Bing on his way.

"Lin, that piece of paper will probably turn out to be a cruel practical joke. But if the results suggest that the murderer placed it there, then I'm making you responsible for Zhang Bing and his family."

"No problem," Lin said. "I think the paper was meant for Zhang Bing. His parents were relocated to Hangzhou after their building was demolished. Their main income comes from renting out their properties. According to reports, the father likes to gamble but otherwise he doesn't get into trouble. The killer targeted Xu Tianding, who was a childhood friend of Zhang Bing, so it makes sense that Zhang Bing is the next target. But it's better to play it safe. We'll give them twenty-four-hour police protection; I'll organize the shifts."

"Good," Zhao said, satisfied. "We can't afford to make any mistakes, especially when the killer has openly made a threat. We need to be on alert. And that piece of paper was discovered at three o'clock; do you think we can find anything on the neighborhood surveillance cameras?"

"I'm not sure. There are two or three in the area, but they're all in the parking lot. I'm not sure if that will be of any help."

"Then we'll have to ask the neighbors. Try and see if anyone saw something."

Lin's phone rang. When he hung up he sighed loudly and turned to Zhao. "I had strong suspicions that the last person to see Xu Tianding, a young woman named Zhu Huiru, was somehow connected to his death. I had someone following Zhu Huiru and her brother. The brother was in the restaurant, she was buying a cell phone, and her friend Guo Yu was at work. None of them could have put the paper in that door handle. Looks like I was barking up the wrong tree."

Zhao had never paid much attention to the Zhu siblings or Guo Yu. All three of them had alibis, and their fingerprints did not match the ones found on the scene. Considering their backgrounds and their means, especially the fact that there were tens of thousands of yuan at the crime scene, Zhao thought it was impossible that any of them were the killer.

"That's alright," Zhao said, patting Lin's shoulder. "I'll let you handle things here. I'm going to the Hangzhou Evidence Lab to see what they can tell us."

Chapter 39

After work, Professor Yan parked his car in Luo's neighborhood. He pulled out a bag and stood by his car, watching his surroundings. Before long he spotted a man with a cross-body bag.

They both smiled as Yan approached. He gave Luo Wen a strong handshake. "Luo! It's been ages!"

"Too long. How have you been?" Luo asked.

"Can't complain! I'm teaching at Zhejiang University. It's a lot less stressful. How about yourself? I heard you're in business. I bet you've got a nice, healthy bank account now?"

"Not bad." Luo smiled. "I just wanted a calmer life."

"Well, you still look like the same old Luo."

"Really? Why do you say that?"

Yan pointed at his bag. "The first time we met you were wearing a bag just like that one. When I asked you about it, you said it was a habit from working in the bureau. It was handy for carrying tools. So you haven't changed one iota."

"Huh, I never noticed." Luo laughed. "I guess I must really be set in my ways."

"It's a good thing you took to that mutt; otherwise I wouldn't know you were here. When I resigned five years ago, I wanted to call, but you were still a forensic scientist. I didn't want to have any connections with the police after the incident, you know. I didn't know that you resigned too."

"But how did you find out that the police interviewed me?"

"You know Zhao Tiemin? He invited me out and happened to mention you."

"I've heard of him. When I was still a forensic scientist in Ningbo, I think he was . . . the captain of the Hangzhou Criminal Investigation Division?"

"That's right. He's still there now. He was directing the investigation of a murder in west Hangzhou and noticed someone named Luo Wen. When he checked the details, he realized it was you. That's how I found you." Yan smiled.

Luo inwardly felt the need to be more alert, but it didn't seem like Yan was testing him. He relaxed.

"So you're helping them investigate the case?" Luo asked.

"Who, me? Goodness no! I don't want any part of it. Besides, even if I wanted to help, do you think the police would even allow it after what happened?"

"About that . . . ." Luo lowered his voice. "I still don't think you handled it the right way."

"I know," Yan said, nodding. "I always knew you would disapprove. But I don't regret what I did. Anyway, we shouldn't dwell on the past. Let's go up to your place so you can drop off your things."

"What things?"

Yan opened a plastic bag so Luo could see inside. "I wanted to bring you something. But you don't smoke and you don't drink—even I enjoy a glass or two at home in the evening. Then I remembered that you just got a dog. I brought him some treats."

"Oh . . ." Luo blushed and looked down. "But I don't have anything for you."

"Don't be silly. I happened to drive past a pet shop and I thought of you, that's all."

"Alright. We can go to my place, but I don't normally entertain, so I'll have to take you out to eat."

"Wow, you have an apartment in this neighborhood? That can't be cheap."

"I got it for a pretty good price. Now the prices are thirty to forty percent higher; I don't know exactly. A lot of agencies call me asking if I want to sell. It's a pain."

"Did you pay for it all at once?" Yan smiled.

He nodded humbly. He didn't like showing off his wealth.

When they entered Luo's apartment, Yan stopped in his tracks, his mouth hanging open. "This is your apartment?" The property was worth at least two hundred thousand yuan. Yan estimated it was at least one thousand square feet. Yet it was poorly furnished. Internet cables were crossing the floor, and the little mutt was filthy. The dog followed them as they walked. Luo looked embarrassed. "I know it's not very fancy."

"Not fancy?" Yan laughed. "I call this not even trying."

Luo scratched his head. "I'm not very good at things like decorating, but I live by myself, so I can keep it simple."

Yan sighed. Luo was a brilliant forensic scientist, but he was the kind of person who put all his energy into his work and didn't really pay attention to the quality of his life.

Yan noticed the family photo on his wall. He frowned. "Still haven't found them yet?"

Luo answered in a low voice, turning his back. "It's been eight years. I'm starting to think . . . I might never find them."

The silence in the room was oppressive. Yan coughed and took out a dog bone. He threw it to the dog, who picked it up and trotted to a corner so he could chew on it in peace.

"Look at him go! He must have strong teeth," Yan said.

"You really think of everything," Luo said, a smile returning to his face. "I never thought to buy him some treats."

"How should I put this?" Yan paused, looking at the family photo again. "It's been a long time now. Have you, uh, thought about remarrying?"

"I like my life just the way it is," Luo said, laughing.

"Well, there are certainly a few catches at the university."

Luo cut him off. "You don't need to be my matchmaker, Yan. I appreciate the offer, I really do, but I don't need your help."

"You're not going to live the rest of your life all alone, are you?" Yan said, frowning.

"Why not? I enjoy the freedom."

"Stop fooling yourself." Yan shook his head. "You were always more passionate about forensics than me. I think you resigned so you could start over in a new place."

Luo smiled but said nothing.

"You've got yourself a dog to fill that hole in your heart. But you need to find another person to share your life with."

"No," Luo sighed. "That's not why I got the dog. My daughter had a dog just like this one here. When I saw this poor little puppy, I let my emotions get the better of me and decided to take him home."

They were silent again.

Luo cleared his throat. "It's almost dinner; how about we get something to eat? My treat."

They left Luo's neighborhood and talked for over three hours at a nice local restaurant about anything but work. Luo realized that he hadn't been this happy in a very long time.

They walked back to Luo's place after dinner. Just as they were about to part, Yan said, "Zhejiang University is just around the corner. We should meet up more often. Are you very busy these days?"

Zijin Chen

"No, I'm almost never in the office," Luo said. "We should definitely do this again."

"That's surprising. What is this new job anyway?"

"You know that I have a bunch of patents, including some on micromeasurement. I lend them to the company, but they don't require much work on my part. As for the titles, the company thought it would be convenient to give them to me so I could sign off on any new projects they might have."

"That sounds really nice," Yan said, nodding. "Teaching at the school is not quite so liberating—they control what course materials I use and so on."

They finally reached the entrance to Luo's neighborhood. "Thank you again for the dog treats."

"Don't be so polite, Luo!" Yan said, chuckling. "You paid for dinner, remember?"

"I know you enjoy a glass of wine in the evenings, but I don't have a taste for it. I just remembered that a client gave me a bottle of Château Lafite. I'm not sure if it's real, but perhaps you can test its authenticity." Luo laughed. "It's in my car; I'll get it for you."

"Oh, a Lafite! That's very generous of you," Yan said.

Yan followed Luo to the parking lot, and they stopped in front of an Audi Q7. The car automatically unlocked upon recognizing Luo's key in his pocket. As Luo carefully took the wine out of the trunk, he turned to see Yan speechless.

"So is it a real Lafite?" Luo asked.

"I think so, but I can't really tell myself." Yan turned the bottle in his hands as if it were his baby. When he was finished admiring the bottle, he looked up. "I thought you couldn't drive. Did you finally take lessons?"

"Yep. When I was still in Ningbo, I didn't have the time. But when I resigned I didn't have that excuse anymore," Luo explained.

"I see. Is it a company car?"

164

"No, it's mine."

"That probably cost you over a million. When did you get it?"

"Um . . . almost three years ago now. Just after I moved to Hangzhou."

"Look at you, buying such an expensive car. I'll trade you my car for your car any day," Yan said teasingly.

"Don't say that," Luo said, laughing. "You're a teacher. If your students saw this car, they would be less interested in cultivating their minds. I can have a nice car because I'm not working as a professor or a police officer."

"Looks like you've changed, Luo. You never showed off your wealth in the past. But now you've got a flashy car . . . Was it hard to get used to it?"

Luo's smile was strained. "Actually I still don't like driving. I often take public transportation to work because it's more convenient."

Yan's expression changed ever so slightly as he considered Luo's comment. "If you don't drive this car to work, then what did you buy it for?"

"You know, when I go out, or go window shopping. It's, uh . . . kind of nice," Luo answered calmly, not noticing the wrinkle between Yan's eyebrows.

"It's for the status, isn't it?"

"Yeah, I guess you could say that." Luo flashed a genuine smile.

"So do you go shopping alone or—"

Luo gave him a look that shut him up. "I don't have friends in Hangzhou. I go out by myself."

Yan laughed it off and nodded, but he felt very sad for his friend. He said a quick good-bye and walked to his car with slow, thoughtful steps.

Chapter 40

It was nine o'clock, but Zhao was still in his office working.

"We got the results from the threatening note," Chen said, handing Zhao the report as he spoke. "The paper, ink, and printer are all consistent with the ones the killer used in the previous murders. The paper was well preserved because it was found indoors soon after it was placed there. We used an identification device imported from the United States to detect faint fingerprints on the paper." He looked at Zhao for his reaction.

"Based on the fingerprints, we can eliminate Zhang Bing and his father as suspects," he continued. "These match the fingerprints in the previous murder cases. We were hoping to test some sweat from the paper, but the sample was insufficient."

Zhao propped his head on his hand. "Our killer is getting bolder. He has killed two people in just a few days. Now he's left a note announcing who he plans to kill next. Or is this some kind of stunt to mislead us?"

"Why would he try to mislead us when we know so little about him in the first place?" Chen said, pursing his lips.

"Good point," Zhao said. "That would be taking an unnecessary risk. I guess he does intend to kill Zhang Bing."

"It's very likely," Chen said.

"We have men from the West Hangzhou Bureau watching Zhang Bing and his family around the clock. The family understands the gravity of the situation, and they are willing to cooperate. In theory, we will catch the killer if he tries to attack. But I have no idea what he will do next."

"What about poison?"

"Poison?"

"What if the killer managed to put something toxic in their food?"

"We have had cases like that before," Zhao said, nodding. "I'm glad you thought of it. I'll remind the guards to keep a lookout tomorrow morning."

"The report on the murder of Xu Tianding is very thorough, but I didn't find any more leads that I would want to investigate."

"All we have are those fingerprints," Zhao said after a long pause. "We can keep screening locals to see if we can find a match. Two people have died, and Zhang has received a credible threat. We have to do something! We'll gather some officers and make sure to record every single fingerprint in the neighborhoods closest to the crime."

Zhao's phone rang. It was Professor Yan. "I need to talk to you about the case."

Zhao was surprised, but he wasn't about to miss the opportunity to speak to Yan. "Come on over. I'm in my office right now."

Yan arrived shortly after Chen had left. As soon as the door was closed, he sat down and leaned forward. "I want to help you with the case."

"But . . . last time . . ." Zhao said hesitantly.

"We've been friends for many years," Yan explained. "I just had dinner with Luo Wen and he inspired me to offer you some useful advice. If you want to hear it, of course."

"Alright," Zhao said, smiling. "There's just one thing." He paused. "We need to keep this hush-hush. You're not a police officer anymore, and I'm afraid if you were openly involved in the case . . ."

"I know; I have a criminal record," Yan said frankly.

Zhao coughed in case anyone was listening at the door. "That's not what I meant. Please don't get me wrong."

"Fine. Whatever you want to call it."

Zhao looked Yan up and down. "What happened? You met up with Luo Wen, and now you're a completely different person?"

Yan shrugged. "We, uh, just talked about a lot of previous cases and it rekindled my interest."

"Right." Zhao nodded. "So what do you need?

"I want a copy of the entire investigation, please," Yan answered.

"That will take you days to read."

"It doesn't matter. I have time."

"I'll have someone make copies tomorrow morning and deliver it to you myself." Zhao smiled.

Yan nodded. "Oh, by the way, did you say that all the victims were ex-convicts?"

"Except for the last," Zhao said. "He was just a thug. He was held at the police station a number of times, but he never actually went to prison. It's odd; the last case was totally different from the previous five."

Yan frowned slightly before saying thank you and leaving.

Meeting Luo Wen again after so many years had made Yan very happy. But now he was filled with a sense of foreboding.

Chapter 41

"Good morning, Lieutenant Lin."

Upon hearing the knock on the door, Lin raised his head. The man was in his fifties and wearing a delicate pair of glasses. Lin looked puzzled until realization dawned on him, and he smiled in surprise.

He remembered their first meeting like it was yesterday. *"I know that none of you are thrilled to be taking this class. Most police officers think that criminology is no better than criminal psychology or behavioral sciences and that it can provide answers only after a case is solved. It's true that everyone in this room is good at collecting evidence at the scene, walking their beat, and checking surveillance videos. You have solved hundreds of cases by using these fundamental tactics. But criminology is about sitting at a desk and thinking. Some may even call it 'armchair strategizing.' I agree that you don't need to use something as sophisticated as criminology to catch your usual criminal. Today I'm going to use real cases to prove to you that math is the father of all academic disciplines and that logical reasoning is the best weapon against the more talented criminals."*

He had listened to that lecture six or seven years ago when he and twenty other officers were invited to go to the police academy at the Zhejiang Bureau to attend training courses organized by the provincial government. Like the other officers, Lin looked down on teachers at the police academy who were full of hot air. The officers were excited to take advanced courses in crime-scene investigation but had no interest in psychology. Professor Yan's course was an exception.

Most of the examples Yan used were actual cases that he had worked on. He was a full-time cop, not an academic. He only designed this course after the Zhejiang Bureau begged him to teach the next generation of promising officers. He was high ranking too: assistant director of the Zhejiang Criminal Investigation Division. By the age of forty, Yan had already become a criminal investigation expert. His example cases opened the young officers' eyes. They learned that meticulous logical reasoning would not only greatly decrease the amount of work they would have to do, but could also help them decide which direction an investigation would take.

Yan himself had admitted that logical reasoning still needed to be supported by concrete evidence. Still, the officers thought he was a genius. Lieutenant Lin immediately recognized him, even after all those years.

"Professor Yan! What are you doing here?" Lin's quickly stood to shake Yan's hand.

Yan smiled. "I'm here to help with Zhao's case. But you should know that I'm not in the force anymore."

Lin had heard about Yan quitting the force five years ago to teach at Zhejiang University. He had been surprised, but he didn't know what had happened and wasn't in a position to ask about it.

"Zhao and I are old friends, and it seems like this case is unusually challenging, so I—"

"So you're helping to crack it!" Lin said.

Yan hesitated. "No, I'm not an officer anymore, so technically I shouldn't be helping with cases as all, especially classified ones. I'm just really curious . . ."

"I understand," Lin said quickly. "You want me to keep it between us. Is that right?"

"Well . . . yes." Yan paused and smiled. "You could put it that way."

"The only thing is . . ." Lin hesitated. "I'm not sure if Captain Zhao authorized . . ."

"I've already read the files for all six murders," Yan said.

Lin relaxed when he heard this, relieved he would not have to worry about breaching confidentiality. Still, it was going against bureau policy to let a nonofficer get involved. Everything would need to be kept very quiet.

"How can I help?" Lin asked.

"I want to reinvestigate the murder of Xu Tianding."

"Well," Lin said, "we only found out that our serial killer was connected when the prints found on a beer can matched the prints in Zhao's other cases. I don't think it will give us a breakthrough."

"On the contrary," Yan said. "If there's any case that will give us a breakthrough, it's this one."

"But that crime scene was totally wrecked! At least the previous crime scenes were well preserved."

"Well preserved, yes, but did the police find anything of value, anything to get us closer to the killer? No," Yan replied. "The killer cleaned up the past five crime scenes himself. In the sixth case, he scattered money on the ground to get a group of strangers to destroy evidence for him. Why?"

Yan pressed on before Lin could guess. "He wouldn't have gone through all that trouble if he could have cleaned it up himself. That means that something did not go according to plan."

"So what?" Lin seemed unconvinced.

"If he was rushed, he probably didn't cover his tracks perfectly. We have to find where he made his mistake."

"That makes sense." Lin nodded.

"I wanted to ask you about the victim, Xu Tianding."

"Everything I know is already written in the case file," Lin said.

"Yes, and a lot of it mentions your interviews with Zhu Fulai, Zhu Huiru, and Guo Yu. You even had people following them. I wanted to ask why. Is it because Ms. Zhu was the last person to see Xu Tianding?"

Before Lin could explain, Yan started pacing the room. "Because you found alibis for Ms. Zhu and Mr. Guo very early on. They should have been eliminated as suspects. I know that anything subjective can't go in the report. Still, sometimes a hunch can lead us to more clues."

Lin was shocked by Yan's keen perception. Even Captain Zhao didn't give a second thought to Ms. Zhu simply because he believed she wasn't tough enough to kill a man.

Lin explained that he spent more time on Ms. Zhu, her brother, and her friend because when he first interviewed her, she briefly had a strange expression on her face. And later when asking about the knife, Ms. Zhu and her brother had different answers. It seemed like they hadn't gotten their stories straight before Lin turned up.

He sighed. "But those were all guesses on my part. The evidence is solid—it shows that my suspicions were misplaced. First of all, the three of them have alibis."

Yan nodded.

"Then we examined the knife in their restaurant. It was new, so it couldn't have been the murder weapon," Lin continued. "I had one of my men bring their photos to all the nearby shops to check if any of them had bought a chef's knife recently, but got nothing. And the set of prints match our serial killer, but Zhu Huiru and her brother weren't even living in Hangzhou three years ago."

"Right. Go on," Yan said.

"They're not what you'd call rich. They couldn't possibly have thrown away ten to thirty thousand yuan to ruin a crime scene. And their statements line up so well—even if they were pros, we would have found some inconsistencies by now. To top it all off, yesterday afternoon a friend of Xu's named Zhang Bing got a threatening letter, and we know it was written by the killer. Ms. Zhu, her brother, and her friend all have alibis."

"Really?" Yan said. He had not heard about that.

"I thought about it for a long time," Lin said. "But it was a waste of the team's time and resources—if I hadn't spent so much time investigating them, we might have found some valuable clues by now. Five days have passed since the murder; we may have already missed our opportunity. I have to admit I feel responsible in a way."

Yan listened sympathetically as he took notes.

After he left, he thought harder about what Lin had said. Lin had kept investigating those three young people even when the evidence showed they should be eliminated as suspects. They must have been acting very unnaturally. But Yan wasn't there to see Ms. Zhu's expression, so he had no way of telling if Lin was unduly affected by a preconceived idea.

He knew that some officers were enamored with the pseudoscience of criminal psychology. They would scrutinize every action and word and even check if the person was looking to the left or the right whenever they answered questions. According to some officers, subconscious actions and microexpressions would show if the person was telling the truth.

Yan didn't believe any of it. He would much rather focus on the content of a person's answer to see if there were any holes in their logic. The pros operated on a completely different level—once they had their story straight, they convinced themselves that it was the truth.

On the other side of the spectrum were people who were naturally timid in front of the police. Even if the case had nothing to do with them, their nervousness could be interpreted as guilt. Yan couldn't determine anything for sure until he met them himself.

Chapter 42

It was Saturday and Luo needed dinner. As per usual, he stood on the side of the road until he confirmed that he wasn't being followed, then walked nonchalantly into Chongqing Noodles.

"Hi, I'd like a bowl of *pian'er chuan* today." Luo looked at the menu and then over at Huiru. She seemed calm.

Huiru waited until the noodles were ready and then whispered, "I don't think any cops have come by since two days ago," as she placed the bowl on his table.

Luo smiled. "That's because you've been eliminated as suspects. Completely eliminated."

"So now, we really—we really don't have to worry?" She tried to suppress her delight.

"You can relax. It's finally over."

Huiru nodded happily and went back to work.

Luo was certain that the police would stop investigating Huiru and Guo Yu.

First, the timing of the threatening letter would leave them with solid alibis. More importantly, Yan had told Luo that Zhao was taking over the murder of Xu Tianding, and recently the special task force discovered that the prints from the serial murder case matched the latest killing. It was impossible for Huiru and Guo Yu to be responsible for all six murders.

He was finished helping those two young people. Now it was time to see how the Hangzhou Bureau would handle the case.

He smiled and picked up some noodles with his chopsticks. A real burden had been lifted off his shoulders. Helping them cover up the case had been extremely difficult—it was easier when he worked alone.

Luo heard a familiar voice behind him. "I'd like a bowl of *pian'er chuan*, please." Luo turned and his eyes met with Yan's.

Yan's eyes narrowed slightly before he smiled broadly. "Luo Wen! What a coincidence, running into you again in a little place like this!"

"I live just down the road and come here all the time. What are you doing here?"

Yan took a seat facing him. "I was visiting another professor in my department this afternoon who lives near here. I was feeling hungry, so I stepped in. You said you come here often?"

"Yeah." Luo smiled shyly. "You know that I'm too lazy to cook for myself. I almost always eat out."

"And you typically come to this restaurant?"

Luo hesitated for a fraction of a second but didn't hide anything. "Yeah."

Yan leaned forward. "Do you know the owner well?"

Luo hesitated again. "He makes delicious noodles, so I see him a lot."

"That's not what I mean. I heard that the young woman, Zhu Huiru, was the last person to see the victim, that thug. She was on the suspects list, wasn't she?"

Luo felt deeply surprised. Yan knew Huiru's name. He must have spoken to the police about her. Perhaps his visit to the restaurant wasn't a coincidence.

Zijin Chen

Luo knew exactly how police officers worked. But Yan was different. He was unpredictable.

His mind was racing but he didn't pause. "Is that so? I heard that the killing was pretty brutal. You'd never think a lady could pull off something like that."

"Oh really? I don't know all the details." Yan let out a weak laugh. "But I'm really glad I ran into you. There's something I want to ask you."

"Oh?"

"Zhao Tiemin wants me to help him with his case. He nagged me until I had no choice but to say yes. But I only understand logic, not methodology. You might know, though!"

"Well? Go on."

"All the victims in the serial murder were strangled from behind, using rope."

"So? Maybe the killer is so good at attacking from behind that the victims aren't able to fight back."

"Yes," Yan said, shaking his head. "Though it's odd that there is no trauma to the body besides the ligature marks. We didn't find any evidence of skin or clothing under the fingernails, but the victims were all ex-convicts, so they knew how to fight. It just doesn't add up."

"You're right that it wouldn't be easy to strangle someone to death from behind," Luo said. "Usually victims struggle violently."

"So my question is," Yan continued, "how does he do it?"

Luo pretended to think for a moment. "He might knock them unconscious and then strangle them."

"Maybe, but autopsies show that there was no trauma to any of the victim's skulls."

Luo was on edge. He didn't understand why Yan wouldn't stop asking questions. Was he working for the investigation?

As an experienced forensic scientist, Luo could think of a number of answers to Yan's question. If he didn't offer them up, would Yan become suspicious?

176

He thought harder. The method of killing was not the crux of the case, so it wouldn't hurt to tell Yan. And it would surely backfire if Luo tried to hide anything; Yan was just too smart.

"I remember a few similar cases," Luo said. "One of the county-level cities near Ningbo had a string of serial murders, and there was never any evidence of struggle." Luo paused. "In this case, though, the murder weapon was a knife. The killer used an electric baton to incapacitate his victim before stabbing them to death. And in the case of strangulation, if the victim woke up, he still wouldn't have the energy to resist his attacker."

"Wow," Yan said. "Would we be able to see any evidence of that on the body?"

"The electric current will excite the central nervous system and cause a person to faint. The current leaves the body, so you cannot detect it in an autopsy. However, you could look at the skin of the victim for shock marks. They look very similar to bruises, so they are easy to miss."

Yan nodded. "But I still don't understand why the killer would use strangulation. If he shocked the victim like you said, why wouldn't he just stab them afterwards?"

Luo didn't know what to do. He couldn't give Yan a straight answer; he might uncover too many details. Luo smiled. "I don't know about that. Every killer has their favorite weapon. Some use knives, others rope, and others poison. Some even use a gun if they can find one. Maybe the killer was squeamish and wanted to avoid blood by using a rope."

Yan laughed. "How could a criminal be afraid of blood but have the gall to kill six people?"

Luo didn't answer.

When they finished eating, Yan and Luo walked outside together before parting ways, both deep in concentration.

Chapter 43

After saying good-bye to Yan, Luo started home. Just as he was passing the park, he saw Guo Yu walking impossibly slowly towards him.

Luo turned and acted as if he didn't know him, but Guo Yu shouted, "Sir!"

Luo hushed him quickly, looking in both directions. "Come this way but keep a distance." Luo approached the outdoor gym and started rotating his oblique muscles, indicating that Guo Yu should use the pull-up bar next to him.

Guo Yu did a few pathetic pull-ups, his least favorite exercise.

"Is something wrong?" Luo asked.

"Nothing. It's just . . ." he paused and bit his lip. "I was just at the noodle shop, and Huiru said that the police haven't been to see her and everything is fine. I . . . don't know how to thank you."

"It's nothing," Luo said, smiling. "You don't need to thank me. I hope you can forget about all this and forget about me. I just want you to lead your lives as if this never happened."

"I know." Guo Yu concentrated and managed another pull-up with difficulty. "You've saved our lives, but we still don't even know your name. That's just not right."

"But I told you before," Luo said, laughing. "You and I don't know each other. We're strangers. That's better for you and it's better for me. If you want to do something for me, just remember that rule."

Guo Yu's vision blurred. He stopped doing pull-ups and bowed his head. "I will," he said. "What about in a few years when this has blown over? Could we be friends then?"

"Why do you want to be my friend?" Luo looked at him closely.

"Because . . . because you did so much for me," Guo Yu stammered.

"It was nothing." Luo turned to the river. Then, in a voice so quiet that only he could hear, he whispered, "This helped me too."

"But . . . could we be friends if we wanted?" Guo Yu said.

Luo waited before answering. "I have a lot of things I need to take care of," he finally said. His voice was dispassionate.

"Oh," Guo Yu said, looking deeply disappointed.

Luo smiled again. "So how are things with you and Huiru?"

"What do you mean?"

"Oh come on, you don't have to be so shy," Luo teased.

"We're, uh, the same as before," Guo Yu said, blushing.

"What?" Luo was surprised. "After everything, you two aren't boyfriend and girlfriend yet?"

"It's . . ." Guo Yu's face was now bright red. "It's just that I can't make her happy."

"Why do you say that?" Luo asked gently.

"I don't have a great job, and . . . my family is poor." Guo Yu found it difficult to talk about such matters, but he wanted to tell the truth.

"You don't have to be so fixated on money. I can tell that Huiru really likes you."

Guo Yu let out a sigh. "Maybe I can save up more in the next few years."

"And then you'll ask her out?"

"Maybe." Guo Yu looked down.

Luo shook his head sadly. "You don't have to be rich before you allow yourself to be happy. You haven't even tried to make her happy yet; how are you sure that you can't? Do you think that all she wants is money? Men think it's more important to focus on their careers. They often don't make time for their family. But ignoring your loved ones is the most selfish thing you can do."

By the time Guo Yu lifted his head, Luo was already walking away with his head bowed.

Chapter 44

Captain Zhao wore a determined expression as he walked into Professor Yan's office, though he had at least been considerate enough to change out of his uniform before barging in on his friend. His eyes flicked across the students sitting there and then focused on Yan. "I want a word with you."

Yan stood and took Zhao to an empty meeting room next door. "What is it?" he asked after closing the door.

"You talked to Lieutenant Lin about the case behind my back." Zhao glared at him.

Yan smiled and sat down. "Are you regretting involving me now?"

"This puts me in a really awkward position, you know that." Zhao sighed.

"Relax," Yan said. "I made it perfectly clear to him: I'm not a cop anymore. He knows that nobody is allowed to know that I'm involved in the case."

"Oh." Zhao's face softened. "Sorry, I got a little worked up there."

"Never mind," Yan said. "You're a captain; you have to think about your division and your job."

Zhao cleared his throat. "So, what have you got?"

"I've made some progress, but I need more evidence."

"What did you find?" Zhao said excitedly.

Yan shook his head. "I haven't found anything, and before I have evidence, I can't tell you my theories."

"Yan!" Zhao's face turned red. "You're afraid that your theory might be wrong and you'll lose face, is that it?"

"Basically, yes," Yan said.

"You've got to be kidding me!" Zhao banged the table with his fist. But Yan was not easily persuaded.

"Just give me some time," Yan said, sighing. "This is a real pro. The answers to this case might surprise you."

Zhao knitted his brows. Finally he said, "What do you need to find that evidence? I can send someone to help."

"I might need some help in the future; I'll tell you when I do," Yan answered.

Zhao watched Yan for a long time. He knew he wasn't going to get any information out of him. "So what are you going to do next?"

Yan picked up a piece of chalk from the blackboard. "So far we have six homicides. I think you can simplify it into two categories: five nearly identical homicides with a shocking lack of evidence and the homicide against Xu Tianding. Everything in Xu's case is different from the previous cases, which is why I think it should be in a different category. Do you agree?"

"OK, sure."

"Now I have to explain a few mathematical concepts. Have you heard of quintic equations?"

"I know quadratic equations, cubic equations . . ." Zhao was not expecting Yan's question and didn't see why it was relevant.

"Those are all polynomial equations," Yan said, nodding. "A quintic is a fifth-degree polynomial."

"Right. Get to the point."

"I'm sure you would have learned about quintic equations in high school or at least in college."

"Umm . . . I don't think so."

"Even humanities students learn about quartic equations in high school or college," Yan said. "Fine, you might not have been introduced to quintic equations before. Quadratic, cubic, and quartic equations all have formulas, so you can always get an answer. Whereas polynomials with a degree higher than four cannot be solved. There aren't any ready-made formulas for solving them. So what do we do with quintic equations? Use substitution. Make an educated guess about what the answer might be, plug it into your equation, and see if the number was too big or too small. Then adjust your guess accordingly and repeat until you zero in on the true answer."

"What the hell does this have to do with the case?" Zhao said, baffled.

"It's the same logic for cracking a case," Yan said with a trace of excitement. "Most cases are simple, like cubic or quadratic equations. All we have to do is investigate, collect evidence, and put all the clues together. But this case is different. There aren't many clues and we don't have a suspect, so it's like a quintic equation. In other words, we can't use our normal procedure to get to the answer."

Zhao squinted at Yan. "If we can't use our normal procedures to find a suspect . . . what do we do?"

With a flourish, Yan wrote "substitution" on the board.

"So you want to find a suspect, assume they are the criminal, and then see if it all fits with the other aspects of the case?" Zhao said.

"Exactly," Yan said. "We have to do it backward. Find a killer and then determine whether or not he committed the crime. But all the details will have to line up perfectly."

"So do you have a potential suspect?" Zhao asked immediately.

Yan nodded.

"Who is it?" Zhao asked urgently.

Yan pursed his lips. "I can't tell you until I'm completely sure. I never expected everything to be so complicated. The two categories are totally different, like two quintic equations. And there might be multiple unknowns." Yan looked out the window. "The first step to solving an equation is determining how many unknowns you have," he continued. "Then you plug in some numbers and see if they give you the answer you're looking for. Once I determine the unknowns, I can find some suspects and put them in the equation. If we get the answer we're looking for, I'll need your help to collect more evidence."

"Alright," Zhao said, suppressing his impatience. If any of Zhao's subordinates had wasted his time with a lesson on solving equations, Zhao would have throttled them. But Yan wasn't a cop anymore. He couldn't be pushed to work faster.

"Do you have any theories about the cigarettes left at the scene of the first five murders or those long cuts across Xu Tianding's chest?" Zhao said.

"I already told you—we are dealing with far too many variables," Yan cautioned. "The person who committed the crime is too clever, so we have to go backward. Your questions will be answered only after we check whether our suspect fits the details of the case."

Zhao had a sudden desire to burn down the entire mathematics building, but he quickly calmed down. "It's very unconventional," he mumbled. "Might as well try it . . ."

"I have two questions for you," Yan said.

"Go ahead."

"Are Sun Hongyun's remains still at the Hangzhou Coroner's office?"

"Yes, in the forensic facilities. They haven't been cremated yet."

"Can you get someone to check his neck? I want to see if there are any electric shock marks."

"What? Why?" Zhao perked up.

"I spoke to Luo. The victims were strangled but there wasn't a struggle. He thought the killer might have shocked the victim with an electric baton. Apparently there was a similar case in Ningbo. That would leave distinct marks on the neck, which is why we need to examine Sun Hongyun again."

"Excellent. That Luo is a pro, I tell you," Zhao said.

"Of course he is," Yan said quietly. He turned again to the window.

"What was your other question?" Zhao asked.

"Prisoners are required to register their home addresses when they are released, is that right?"

"Yes, that's a policy."

"Where can I look up the address of an ex-convict?"

"On the internal website for the Hangzhou Bureau," Zhao said hesitantly.

"Can every police officer access that database?"

Zhao nodded. "The guys working in the prison, members of the Politics and Law Committee, officers at local police stations, and criminal investigators are all able to search it."

"So a lot of officers can access the database?"

"Yes, because every jurisdiction needs to know about ex-convicts in their area. We deal with a lot of cases of recidivism, so we need to know who has a criminal record. Yan, why do you care so much about our database?" Zhao asked.

Yan changed the subject. "What do you think the killer's motive is?"

"He's taking the law into his own hands," Zhao said with certainty. "Sun Hongyun and the other victims of the first five homicides were all ex-convicts. Xu Tianding had never been to prison, but he was in the system."

"But how do you think the killer found these ex-convicts? How did he know their criminal records?"

"All the victims lived in west Hangzhou. The killer has probably lived in this area for years. He must have known their histories," Zhao guessed.

"But *how?*"

"It can't be that hard to figure out. When there's a criminal on your block, everyone is going to hear about it."

"You're not thinking critically, Zhao," Yan said, shaking his head.

Zhao was offended. After all, as the captain of the Hangzhou Criminal Investigation Division, he commanded several hundred officers. He frowned. "What do you think?"

"I can't imagine the killer going around and asking all of his neighbors who committed crimes. If I gave you a day to try to figure out who had a criminal record just by asking people on the street, you wouldn't get a single name. Not only that, people would think you were crazy, and it would leave a deep impression. The killer wouldn't want people to remember him like that."

Zhao grunted, but Yan had a point.

"If someone wanted to identify ex-convicts, the only way is by looking at the database on the bureau's internal website." Yan gave him a serious look.

Zhao couldn't speak for a few seconds. "Do you think someone in the bureau did this?" he asked in a low voice.

"Not necessarily," Yan said hurriedly. "Someone might have hacked the system."

Zhao turned away and closed his eyes. Yan's hypothesis terrified him. What if it was an insider? What if a police officer killed all those people? Even if they solved the case, it would have major repercussions in Hangzhou, not to mention law enforcement. It would be huge.

Yan saw the worried look on Zhao's face and said, "Don't worry; I don't think a cop did it."

"But . . ."

"I already told you, everything I know is based on assumption. I don't have any evidence now, but I'm confident that I'll find the answer soon," Yan said, determined.

Chapter 45

That evening, Investigator Yang told Zhao the results of Dr. Chen's second autopsy. There was indeed a mark on Sun Hongyun's neck that could have been caused by an electric baton.

Dr. Chen also reviewed the photographs of the other four victims. All of them had similar marks on their necks. He concluded that the first five victims were also attacked by electric batons and then strangled to death. But the sixth victim—Xu Tianding—didn't have the mark.

Zhao nodded. As Yang was about to leave, Zhao stopped him. "Go and tell Professor Yan everything that Dr. Chen told you," he said.

"Yes, sir," Yang said.

"One other thing," Zhao said, hesitating again. He stood up and approached Yang. "I want you to arrange for someone to follow Professor Yan for the next few days. Be discreet; I don't want him or anyone else to know."

"Sir?" Yang looked confused before his eyes widened. "You think Yan is the killer?"

"Nonsense!" Zhao huffed. "Where did you get that idea? He's not brave enough to kill someone."

Yang lowered his head awkwardly. "Then . . . why do you want to follow him?"

Zhao frowned. "He says he's already found some clues, but he won't tell me anything! I want to know where he's going and who he's seeing. Ideally the officer tailing him could take pictures. Yan never reveals exactly what he's thinking, but this time I think he's hiding something important. You have to keep this strictly confidential. Understood?"

"Of course," Yang said, nodding. "But what is Professor Yan doing in the bureau in the first place? He's not a cop. That's . . . not really appropriate, is it?"

"He used to be a criminal investigator—one of the best. Then something horrible happened." Zhao paused. Yang was young, but Zhao didn't see any reason to hide the story. "He used to be part of a team of criminal experts for the Zhejiang Public Security Bureau."

"Really?" Yang's mouth fell open. He knew that it was very difficult to be selected for the criminal expert team. It was one rank below the head of the Zhejiang Bureau. Yan must have been a phenomenal investigator and very well known.

"Yan Liang was also a guest professor at the Zhejiang Police Academy," Zhao continued. "He helped the higher-ups in government solve cases when they were still working at the local level; they held him in the highest respect."

"Then what is he doing teaching math at Zhejiang University?" Yang asked incredulously.

"He got emotionally involved in one of his cases," Zhao said, looking out the window. "About five years ago, sometime in October, construction on some new high-rise apartments in east Hangzhou was stalled," Zhao said. "It was supposed to be finished at the beginning of the year, but the real estate company had cash-flow issues. The boss took the money and ran off. The whole project turned into a bunch of unfinished buildings. The district government looked into it and decided to let a state-owned enterprise acquire the real estate company. They would only have to add plumbing and electricity. Still, it took the better part of a year before the apartments were made available to the flat buyers."

Yang nodded, listening closely.

"Then on the day that the proprietor came to inspect the buildings, they found a body on one of the rooftops. It had decayed so much that only a skeleton remained—the coroner could only determine that the victim was male and killed approximately three months before by a strike to the back of the head, where a hole was found in the victim's skull. He guessed that the victim had been killed in June and rotted away over the course of a summer. The police did not find an ID card or any articles of clothing to help identify him."

Yang's eyes widened.

Zhao nodded grimly. "Roof access was protected by a locked iron gate. We're talking a very secure door; only a hand could fit between those iron bars. There's no way an entire person could squeeze through. According to the real estate company, the door was never broken into during the six or so months that the project was suspended. There were no marks to suggest that the gate was forced open. The key was kept in a drawer in the real estate company's office, where a director was responsible for keeping it safe. She was pregnant and had a strong alibi, so she was eliminated as a suspect."

"How is that possible?" Yang asked, squinting in confusion. "The gate was not damaged and never opened. The key was in good condition and safely kept in an office. There's no way the victim could have gotten up there, let alone his attacker. Maybe the killer used a machine to get the body onto the roof?"

"It's a high rise," Zhao said, shaking his head. "Twenty floors."

Yang pursed his lips.

"The district bureau discovered the victim's identity a few days into their investigation. A middle-aged woman had reported her husband missing in June. She lived in an older neighborhood close to the high rise in question. The police compared the DNA and it was a match. The police learned more about the situation after interviewing the woman, her teenage son, and a few of the neighbors. The family was very poor, but the man still wasted money on drinking, gambling, and entertainment. Sometimes he would not come home for several days. He had many affairs," Zhao explained.

"But all the evidence was three months old, and nobody could figure out how the body got on the roof. How was the case solved?" Yang asked.

"From the face of it, the rooftop seemed completely closed off. It garnered a lot of attention because a lot of people were at the scene when the body was discovered. Still, the district bureau was unable to find any leads. The Zhejiang government put Yan on the case. His specialty is the type of case that seems to defy logic. He quickly deduced that the killer used a drill to remove all the bolts from the door, removed the entire door, laid the body on the rooftop, and finally put all the screws back in place."

"Oh!" Yang said.

"After interviewing the victim's wife, Yan quickly discovered inconsistencies in her testimony. Then he found a power drill at her house. Yan accused her of the crime, and she admitted to it."

"Wow." Yang couldn't think of anything else to say.

"She said that her husband was always gambling and carousing," Zhao explained. "He frequently came home drunk, and if she or her son said the wrong word, he would beat them. Their son was a sophomore in high school. He wanted to take summer school classes to have a better chance to pass the college entrance exams, but he needed five hundred yuan for the fees. The father had lost a lot of money gambling that night, and he lost his temper. The woman couldn't bear to watch her son mistreated anymore—it was the final straw. The next day while her son was at school, she struck her husband in the head with a hammer."

"And then what happened?" Yang asked.

"She needed to hide the body, of course," Zhao said. "She remembered the new flats being built nearby and was certain that there weren't any security guards there. In the middle of the night, she dragged the body all the way to the roof and then reported her husband missing a week later. She even fooled her own son."

"That's incredible," Yang said, shaking his head.

"She went to the station a few more times to follow up so the police swallowed the bait," Zhao said. "They even felt bad when she was caught because her husband was a real bastard. Still, homicide is inexcusable. The best they could do was collect some money for the son's college tuition."

"Where did Yan go wrong?" Yang asked, clearly confused.

"You didn't notice anything wrong with that story?" Zhao said.

"What do you mean?" Yang asked awkwardly.

"How could a middle-aged woman carry her husband up to the roof of a different building? Even if she had the strength, how did she remove all the screws on the iron gate?"

He knitted his brows and tried to work it out. "Did her son help her move the body?"

"She wasn't the killer at all: it was her son," Zhao said. "Two weeks after the mother was taken into custody, the son turned himself in. He claimed his mother took the blame to try and protect him. On the day he asked for money, the drunk father started beating him, and the mother stepped in between, trying to protect him. Watching his father lay a belt on her put the son over the edge. He grabbed a hammer and used all his might to strike his father on the head. The mother went into shock. The son wanted to turn himself in."

"But that didn't happen, obviously," Yang said.

"Before he could leave, his mother threw herself at his feet. If he went to prison, she would lose the will to live. She just wanted him to have a future. The son had earned top grades throughout high school and was on track to get into a top university, like Peking University or

Tsinghua. He didn't want to rob his mother of her last hope. So they came up with a plan together," Zhao said.

Yang didn't speak.

"They picked somewhere close by to dump the body," Zhao continued. "The abandoned residential buildings seemed like the perfect choice. The mother wanted to leave the body on the top floor, but the son thought it would be safer if they got the body on the roof. He looked at the lock and saw that it was covered in dust. It had not been opened in a long time. But if they broke the lock, a guard walking by would notice and would certainly take a closer look. Pretty smart, huh?"

Yang nodded but didn't speak.

"With the help of a power drill, he removed all the screws on the gate and hid the body behind a ventilation pipe so that it wasn't visible to anyone standing at the roof access. A few months passed. They thought they were in the clear. But soon after the body was discovered, Yan was hot on their trail. The mother wanted to protect her son by taking the blame for the murder. She threatened to kill herself if he and her son did not cooperate. Yan allowed the mother to take the blame. But two weeks later, the son couldn't cope with the guilt. He went to the police station and told them what actually happened."

Yang shook his head. He had come across too many tragic cases where a scoundrel of a husband destroyed his entire family. But no matter how much the police empathized with their situation, they couldn't let them go.

He looked up. "But how did Yan get in trouble? Did the son give him up?"

"He helped them falsify evidence."

"What!?" Yang was shocked.

"When the son turned himself in, one of the officers checked the original case and discovered that Yan went to the son's school to check his attendance record. The murder happened on a Sunday, when he should have been at an evening study session. The actual school records showed that the son asked to be excused from that session. He was late for classes on Monday too. But in the case files, the school record showed that he attended the session. The police officer reported his findings, and they came to the conclusion that Yan forged the attendance records and tampered with the statement issued by the school. He even changed the woman's testimony at the PSB to make everything consistent with the other documents in the case file. Everything fit like a glove."

Yang raised his eyebrows.

"A police officer falsifying evidence is a serious transgression," Zhao continued. "The Zhejiang PSB was deeply shocked. They could have taken strict disciplinary action, maybe even fired him on the spot. But the heads of the Zhejiang PSB mulled it over and amended their decision, since the end result of the case was the same and Yan made his decision out of empathy and not to further his own interests. Most importantly, he had an excellent record and had made important contributions to the force, including training the next generation of police. Still, Yan eventually decided to resign, saying he no longer felt suited for police work. That's why he went to teach at Zhejiang University."

Yang didn't know what to say.

"When Yan spoke to me about it privately, he said that he knew that it violated his professional code of ethics to help them. It was all for nothing in the end, but he told me he didn't regret his decision."

"No wonder you said he's not fit to be a police officer," Yang said.

Zhao nodded. "He is extremely effective at using criminology, but his ideals get in the way of him doing his duty. I'm glad that he is helping us with the case, but I think it's very strange how he suddenly asked to be involved. That's why you need to find someone to follow him. I don't want to be responsible for another fiasco like that in the Zhejiang PSB. Know what I mean?"

Yang nodded slowly, biting his lip. "Of course. I'll keep a close watch on him."

PART 6
COVERING ONE'S TRACKS

Chapter 46

There were only a handful of customers eating at Chongqing Noodles, typical for lunchtime. The restaurant was slow in the early afternoon.

Yan parked his car across the street from the restaurant. He sat and observed the surroundings before leaving his car and heading in.

"What would you like, sir?" Huiru recognized Yan's face but she couldn't remember why.

Yan studied the menu, taking the opportunity to watch Huiru. Finally he asked for a bowl of braised noodles and a bottle of soda.

He sat in the same seat that Luo had taken yesterday, conveniently located next to the cash register. When Huiru returned from the kitchen, he took a sip of soda and asked with a friendly smile, "Do you know Luo Wen very well?"

"Who is Luo Wen?" Huiru asked, a blank look on her face.

Yan studied her expression to see if she was faking. But she didn't flinch. Was it possible that Luo Wen never told her his name? How did they know each other?

"The man who was sitting here yesterday," he added. "I sat across from him."

Huiru's face flickered, and she looked away for a minute, straightening things on the counter. "Yesterday? We have a lot of customers every day. I'm not sure I know who you're talking about."

"But didn't you let him take that puppy home?" Yan asked, paying close attention to her face.

Huiru's heart skipped a beat. She didn't want to look at Yan for too long. "Oh . . . yes, that man. I guess he was sitting here yesterday. Is there something wrong?"

"Do you know him well?" Yan asked, his kind smile unwavering.

"No." She shook her head. "When I saved that puppy, he just happened to be there and offered to take him home. Are you sure there isn't something wrong?"

"No, no, I'm just a friend. I heard that he has noodles here fairly often; is that true?"

"Um . . . yeah."

"What does he like to order?"

Huiru remembered that they were laughing together the day before. They must be friends. But she kept Luo's advice in mind and answered as naturally as possible. "Oh, noodles with egg, noodles with beef, noodles with pork and bean sauce. He likes all kinds of dishes. I don't know what his favorite is."

"Oh? I thought you knew him better," Yan said.

"Why would you think that?"

"He doesn't help you out with things? Besides the dog?" Yan said, his stare now bordering on rude.

At first Huiru didn't respond. She was on high alert, and she focused her gaze on a speck of dirt on the counter, trying to be calm. "What things?"

"He said that he did you a big favor. Did you already forget?"

"I don't know what you mean." She spoke loudly to try to cover up the tremor in her voice.

"He said it was something big."

"Oh . . . it must be the puppy, then," Huiru said quickly. "I didn't know what to do with the dog after I brought him into the restaurant. My brother said I had to get rid of him, and I didn't want to abandon the poor thing. Just when I needed him, a nice man said he would take the dog home. He solved that problem for us."

"I also heard that afterwards some thug came over, claiming the dog was his. He wanted to take the dog back, and my friend had to pay three hundred yuan to keep him. Is that true?"

"Yes."

"And then the very next day, that thug was killed, right?"

Huiru tried her hardest to think of a way to end the conversation, but nothing came to her. "Yeah, something happened to him over by the river."

"I heard that you were the last person to see him before he died. Is that true?"

"Yes. The police investigated his death a while ago."

"The stab wounds in the thug's chest match a knife that you guys have here in your restaurant. Is that right?" Yan asked.

Huiru's heartbeat kicked up another notch. "Are you a cop?"

At that moment, Fulai came out of the kitchen with Yan's noodles. He had a slight frown on his face as he set it down and turned to walk away.

Yan looked at Fulai and then spoke to Huiru. "No, I'm not."

Fulai stopped in his tracks.

"The police told me not to discuss details of the case with anyone besides police officers. Sorry."

"I'm terribly sorry," Yan said with a laugh. "I'm just a very curious person, that's all."

Fulai went towards the kitchen again.

Yan took a bite of the noodles and then said, "Sometimes when you try to help someone, it just leads to more trouble."

Huiru had already pulled out her phone and started playing a game.

"Isn't that right?" Yan said.

Huiru met his gaze with a vacant look. "If your friend thinks the dog is too much trouble, then I'll just take him back. I can find him another home."

"Luo is the kind of person who keeps his word. He would never back out on a promise," Yan said.

Huiru went back to playing with her phone.

After finishing his bowl of noodles, Yan left, satisfied that the number of unknowns were now more or less determined. The next step was to start checking answers when he plugged the suspects into his quintic equation.

Chapter 47

"I want to talk to you about the possibility that Ms. Zhu and Mr. Guo were involved in Xu Tianding's murder," Yan said, drinking a cup of water in Lin's office.

"Those two?" Lin looked confused. "They were eliminated as subjects very early on, Professor Yan."

"Could you list the reasons again?" Yan took out a piece of paper and a pen.

"Of course." Lin nodded. He opened the file, organizing his thoughts. Then he took a breath. "There are six reasons. One: their alibis. The time of death is 10:50 p.m., and they had left the park at that time, based on the surveillance cameras. The victim had fried rice in his stomach, which he would have only started to eat after the two of them left. There were shallow horizontal cuts found on the body which would have taken time to make, but Mr. Guo was in a convenience store—the staff working that night confirmed that. So their alibi is even stronger."

Yan's pen flew across the page as he took notes.

"Two: the killer spent tens of thousands of yuan to destroy the crime scene," Lin continued. "Mr. Guo and Ms. Zhu don't have that kind of money. Three: the murder weapon was likely a paring knife, but the knife in the noodle shop is brand new, and the nearby shops all said they didn't see either Ms. Zhu, Mr. Zhu, or Mr. Guo buying one like it. Four: there aren't any inconsistencies in their statements."

Yan nodded and continued writing.

Lin took a breath and said, "Five: a friend of the victim, Zhang Bing, received a threatening letter last Friday that was confirmed to be written by the killer. Both Mr. Guo and Ms. Zhu have alibis for the window of time in which the letter was delivered. Six: it has been proven that the person who committed this crime also committed serial murders. The first of these murders was committed before Mr. Zhu or Ms. Zhu were in Hangzhou, and Mr. Guo did not have any connections to the previous victim. On top of that, their fingerprints don't match the ones that we found at the scene of all six crimes."

Yan reviewed all six points in his notebook. "Impressive," he said to himself.

"What's impressive, Professor Yan?"

"It's impressive that a person would have so many different pieces of evidence to prove that they didn't commit the crime. Everything is perfectly airtight," Yan said, looking up.

Lin looked unconvinced. "But this is all hard evidence."

"Yes, but anyone in west Hangzhou could have committed the crime. And the only people who have the most evidence disproving their involvement are these two," Yan said with a smile.

Lin's mouth dropped open. "But even if they *did* do it, there is no way they could have fabricated all that evidence," he countered.

"You're right," Yan said, nodding. "But if you add one more condition to this assumption, then the whole thing unravels."

"What's that?" Lin said, breathless.

"A third person helped."

"A third person?" Lin said incredulously. "Like Zhu Fulai? At first I found him suspicious, but he has a lame leg and can't walk very well. He spends most of his time at the restaurant and also has an alibi for the threatening letter. He's successfully avoided investigation, but he's still not capable of doing all this, is he?"

"Your average person couldn't even do a fraction of it. Only a—" Yan stopped himself. "I want to discuss these points with you one at a time. First, the alibi."

Yan took a sip of water before beginning. "An alibi consists of evidence that proves that a suspect was not at the scene of the crime when it was committed. At 10:42 p.m. Guo Yu and Zhu Huiru were filmed by surveillance cameras. We can accept this as true because it would be impossible to fake the time, the place, or the people filmed."

He looked seriously at Lin, then continued. "The reason this video is thought to back up an alibi is because the time of death was determined to be 10:50 p.m. So the key to explaining why this alibi is fabricated is that the time of death was not in fact 10:50 p.m., but sometime *before* 10:42 p.m. I think the death occurred sometime between 10:20 p.m. and 10:40 p.m."

"That doesn't work," Lin said, shaking his head. "Zhang Bing got a phone call from Xu Tianding at 10:50 p.m. He heard his friend being attacked. Otherwise who would have made the phone call at 10:50 p.m.?"

"I think it was the third person, whoever was helping Mr. Guo and Ms. Zhu."

"Zhu Fulai?" Lin said, in an unconvinced voice.

"I said a third person," Yan said. "I didn't say that it was Mr. Zhu."

"OK," Lin said, his patience wearing thin. "But his friend Zhang was positive that it was Xu's voice. The two knew each other for almost their entire lives, and they hung out every single day. There's no way that Zhang would have mistaken someone else for Xu."

"Aren't there any other possibilities?" Yan asked.

"The killer might have forced Xu to record a few sentences into his own phone," Lin said thoughtfully. "But judging by the autopsy, the victim was stabbed three times in quick succession and hit in the back of the head. That means it was a sudden attack, not prolonged."

"Well, then it had to be recorded in advance. If Xu was already dead . . . what if the sentence 'Let's have lunch together tomorrow' was already in his phone?"

"I don't think we investigated that," Lin said.

"Where's the phone now?" Yan asked.

"Here in the district bureau," Lin answered.

"We need to check if that sentence is recorded on there. Could you get someone to do that?"

"Yeah, of course, it's just that—" Lin hesitated before continuing. "I think the conclusions you are making are, uh, problematic . . . in terms of procedure. It's not how you told us to handle an investigation."

"Why, what's wrong?" Yan asked.

"The Public Security Bureau wants us to look for evidence first and then identify suspects. But you're doing it backward," Lin said frankly. He coughed. "How should I put this? Some district cops in the country are so focused on the number of cases they've solved that they'll find a suspect, drag him into the station to give a confession, then find evidence by any means necessary to make it look like that suspect did it. A number of innocent people have been put behind bars this way. The provincial government has pardoned some of these innocents and disciplined the irresponsible investigators, but it's still a problem."

He paused and looked seriously at Yan. "And besides, when I took your class, your number-one rule was not to let your first impressions affect how you handle a case—you have to be as objective as you can. Otherwise the answer will be biased. Once you have all the evidence, you put it in the formula and you look at your answer."

Yan nodded. "That's true, and I still believe it," he admitted. "Cases are like equations, and most can be solved by applying knowledge from previous cases that are similar. It's almost like using a formula: you substitute the elements in the previous case with the elements of your case and then you'll get an answer. The thing is, even though that method works for most cases, it doesn't for all of them."

Lin looked a little alarmed.

"An extremely complicated case is more like a higher-order equation. It cannot be solved using theory. The only way to get a solution is to estimate numbers for your unknown variables and then check your answer. I think this case is a classic system of equations without a solution, which means you can't use the normal procedure to get your answer. You have to substitute a few numbers, or suspects, and then check your answer," Yan said.

Lin was silent for a while. Then he smiled. "Good thing I was a star math student! I actually understood what you were saying. I'll find someone to go through Xu's phone and give you an answer as soon as possible."

Chapter 48

Luo took his dog for a walk in the evening. He walked slowly on the path along the river.

Every time the dog arrived at a new tree, he stopped and sniffed for a long time. When he finished sniffing he left his mark and moved on. Luo was patient, lost in memories from eight years ago.

"Daddy, how long will it take before Doggie is all grown up?" His daughter tried to bring the dog closer to her father, but the dog wanted to sniff around the house and pulled against the leash.

"Hmm, a year, maybe two," he said absentmindedly. Luo didn't know very much about dogs, and he was trying to pack for a business trip.

"That's a long time!" she said.

"Your daddy doesn't know what he's talking about," his wife said with a smile. She placed a few more collared shirts in her husband's suitcase and gave her daughter a loving squeeze. "In a few months, he'll be all grown up!"

"Really? Just a few more months?" Luo opened a desk drawer and shuffled through a pile of papers.

"Most dogs are fully grown by twelve months. And they said you studied medicine," she teased.

"Huh." Luo grabbed some documents and put them in his bag. "Well, the dog will be all grown up by the time I get back," he said offhandedly.

His wife pouted in half-seriousness. "How long will you be gone this time?"

"The Ministry of Public Security invited me to attend a few meetings in Beijing, and then I've got to stay for a few courses designed for young forensic scientists. It should only be two or three months." He kept organizing papers as he spoke.

"You're always so busy." She sighed, a trace of resentment in her voice. Still, she went through her husband's things once more, making sure he didn't forget anything.

"There's nothing I can do about it. It's work."

"You got promoted to director of the Criminal Science department and then became a criminal investigation expert. I thought you would be able to delegate and spend more time with your family," she said, making a face. "But you are busier than you were before. You have so many titles! Director of Forensic Science, director of the Material Evidence department. Can't you quit one of them?"

Luo put the last pile of papers in his bag and zipped it shut. He sat on the edge of the bed next to his wife. "Which one?" he asked her with a smile.

She knew he wasn't serious, but she went along with it. "Let's see . . . Forensics. You can do everything for Material Evidence in the daytime. But when you're on a big case, Forensics calls you out in the middle of the night."

"But I studied medicine in college; that's what I do!"

"OK, then resign from the Material Evidence department," she said.

"But I have a doctorate in material evidence studies and patents in my name for micromeasurement. Only a handful of people can do that in this country," he said with a smile.

"I know you're proud. You probably remind yourself of those two doctorates every time you get up in the morning," she said, pushing him playfully.

Luo looked at his daughter and gave her a hug and a kiss. "Is Daddy awesome?"

"Daddy's not awesome, Mommy is," his little girl said stubbornly. "I want Doggie to grow up fast."

"It's OK. As soon as Daddy comes back from this business trip, he'll be all grown up."

"Remember to buy snacks for Doggie."

"I will; I promise. Should I buy you some snacks too?" Luo asked, taking his daughter gently by the shoulders.

"Yeah! I want juice! I want juice right now!" she said.

"That's not for me to decide; we have to ask Mommy." He spun his daughter around to face her mother.

"No, sweetie, it's bedtime. You can't have any juice before bedtime." Luo's wife was firm.

The girl ran to her mother and started using every trick she could think of to make her say yes.

Luo smiled.

"Another coincidence! Hi, Luo!" A familiar voice interrupted his memory.

Luo came back to reality as Yan smiled at him.

"We meet again, Professor Yan!" Luo approached Yan and shook his hand. "So are you visiting your friend who lives nearby again?"

"No, I'm working on a case and I happened to walk through this area."

"A case?" Luo was surprised.

"Yes, a case," Yan said, nodding. "I've decided to give old Zhao a hand and help him investigate that big case."

"So you're back in law enforcement?"

"No, no, no," Yan said. "I'm still at the university. I think I'll stick to it."

"Why did you suddenly change your mind about this?" Luo asked.

"Because of you, I think."

"Me?" Apart from his constricted pupils, Luo showed no sign of surprise.

"After we talked I thought of something you said several years ago. You said committing a crime is shameful, no matter the reason. I was really impressed by that idea."

Luo let out a hollow laugh. "It's good that you're giving back to society and helping with the case; I know you have a lot of free time as a professor."

Yan smiled again. "Does that mean you want to help?"

"Oh, well." Luo shook his head. "I haven't been keeping up with the news since I resigned. I just want to be an average citizen."

"That's fine too," Yan said. "Oh, by the way, you know that restaurant where we ate yesterday? Do you know the girl who works there? Zhu Huiru?"

Luo's heart beat faster. "I've had noodles at their restaurant many times, but I've never spoken much to the owners. Did something come up in the investigation?"

"That girl is considered a key suspect," Yan said, carefully watching Luo's face.

He remained perfectly calm. "Really? To me she looks like a regular girl, not like someone who would commit a crime. Huh, I haven't seen a case like that before."

"Yes, I know it sounds incredible. I'm not sure myself," Yan said with a laugh. "Anyway, I need to go. I'll see you later."

"See you later."

As Yan went off into the distance, Luo kept walking his dog slowly, making his way back to his apartment.

Chapter 49

Huiru received a phone call at 9:30 p.m. Luo wanted some noodles delivered to his house. She hurried to get it ready.

The man with the glasses who came in at lunch and asked a bunch of strange questions had made her feel extremely anxious.

Huiru had just reached the big gate that led to the man's apartment complex when she heard a voice beside her. "Are you making a delivery to your friend?"

Huiru stopped and looked for the source of the voice. It was him.

She wanted to panic, but she acted like she didn't see him and kept walking.

"Are you making a delivery to your friend?" Yan said again, this time so close that she couldn't avoid him. He smiled at her.

She hoped he couldn't hear her heart thudding and bit her lip. She nodded at Yan.

Yan nodded back at her, then left.

Huiru forced herself to act like nothing had happened and kept her pace just like it was before.

As soon as she reached Luo's apartment, she put the noodles down and told him everything, from the interrogation at lunchtime to the encounter at the gate of his neighborhood. When she finished, she burst into tears. "I'm so sorry! I'm not clever enough for this. I shouldn't have told him that I was going to deliver the noodles to you! Now you'll be in trouble too."

Luo patted her on the shoulder. "You did just fine," he said. "If you said it was for someone else, they would have gone and checked the phone records and seen that it was me who ordered the noodles. Then they would know that you had lied, and it would make both you and me look suspicious. You did the right thing. Remember, except for that one part of your testimony, you should always tell the truth. Always."

"I . . . did the right thing?" Huiru asked hesitantly. "He's not going to be suspicious of what I said just now? I can tell that he doesn't believe anything I say."

"Well, of course he will be suspicious; he just spotted you at the gate to my apartment," Luo said. "Do you think that was a coincidence? No, I think he was waiting for you. He might have even watched you all day long."

That sent a shiver down her spine. "Who is that guy?" she shouted. "He says he's not a cop; he says he's your friend . . . I don't get it!"

"He's not a cop," Luo said. "He's a mathematics professor. But don't let that fool you; he's more dangerous than any police officer you've met, and right now he's involved in the investigation. I'm not sure why exactly he thinks you should be a suspect, but I know him, and he wouldn't investigate something unless there was a good reason. That means that he has discovered something, some inconsistency."

"What? What happened? Why does he think I should be a suspect? I followed all of your instructions, didn't I?"

"Don't be nervous," Luo said calmly. "I'll admit that he is incredibly intelligent. He picks up on tiny details that most people never notice, then analyzes them in a brilliant way. But the police won't use anything except evidence. So even if he correctly guesses what happened, he won't be able to prove it."

"Really?" Huiru was still doubtful.

"Really. All you need to do is follow my advice to the letter. Remember, the police need evidence, witnesses, or a confession: if they don't have any of those things, they can't make an arrest," Luo said.

Huiru thought for a moment. Her eyes widened as she remembered something. "But you left fingerprints on one of the cans!"

Luo moistened his lips. He couldn't tell her the truth about the prints. "It's all part of the plan."

Huiru's anxiousness gradually melted away. "So what should I do now?"

"What we've been doing all along," Luo said. "In a few days he's bound to figure out that he can't find any evidence against you, and he'll stop asking questions, just like the other officers. No matter what he says, even if he describes exactly how the crime happened, don't trust him. He doesn't have evidence; he just has good guesses."

Chapter 50

"So what has Yan been up to lately?" Zhao asked Yang. It was early in the morning, and he held a large cup of coffee in his hand.

"At lunch yesterday, Yan went to that noodle restaurant and had a meal," Yang said. "He spoke to Ms. Zhu. In the afternoon he swung by the district bureau, then went to the university to teach a few lessons. After his last lesson, he had an early dinner on the university campus and then rushed over to the scene of the crime, where he met someone by chance who seemed to be a friend. This man here." Yang pointed at the screen of his digital camera.

"Luo Wen?" Zhao peered at the screen in disbelief.

In the picture, Luo was wearing a cross-body bag and holding a dog leash.

"That's Luo Wen?" Yang had heard of the brilliant forensic scientist, but he didn't know what he looked like.

"Yep. He wrote the book on collecting evidence for police investigations." Zhao looked at the screen again. "Is he walking a dog?"

"Yes," Yang answered.

"I see," Zhao said. "How long did Yan talk to Luo?"

"Not for long, just a few words. But after they said good-bye, Yan didn't go home."

"What did he do next?" Zhao asked.

"If I had to guess, he was following someone."

Zhao's eyes widened. "Luo?"

"No," Yang said, shaking his head. "He drove to the noodle restaurant, parked across the street, and stared at the entrance all night. Every time Ms. Zhu went out for a delivery, he got out of his car and followed her. The last delivery happened at about 10:00 p.m. Ms. Zhu was about to enter a neighborhood when Yan approached her and said something. Then he finally went home."

Zhao reviewed the case file in front of him. He thought quietly as he flipped to the section on Huiru and Guo Yu. He looked up. "Huh. I would say Yan is investigating Ms. Zhu."

"Definitely. He followed her for an entire evening," Yang said.

"But I've read that file plenty of times. There's no way Ms. Zhu is the killer."

"I read the file again after I got home last night," Yang agreed. "There is no way she is involved in the case; I'm sure of that. Do you think Yan didn't read the entire case file?"

"Impossible, in my opinion," Zhao said, shaking his head. "He's an incredibly meticulous person; now that he is unofficially involved in the investigation, I'm sure he knows every detail of the case backward and forward. Besides, he is actually a lazy investigator."

"Lazy?" Yang asked.

"That's right, lazy," Zhao said with a grin. "He used to say it was best to determine the direction of the case before starting. That's because he didn't want to do any unnecessary work. He prefers thinking over action. So his behavior confuses me. There's no way that Ms. Zhu could be the killer, but he's spending all this time and energy following her. What does he know that we don't?"

"Why don't you just ask him?"

"If he's not willing to talk, you won't get anything out of him. Otherwise why would I make you follow him?" Zhao shot a glance at Yang.

"So what are we supposed to do?" Yang asked.

"Just keep following him," Zhao said, closing the case file. "And let's focus on the fingerprinting. We have police protecting Zhang Bing and his family twenty-four seven right now, but we can't protect them forever. How many people have we fingerprinted in the past few days, Yang?"

"We've collected fifty-three thousand sets of prints, but none of them match our killer." Yang said.

"That's pretty fast. I'm still worried that the killer will go into hiding again," Zhao said, frowning slightly.

"I think we'll catch him, sir," Yang said. "As you instructed, we are comparing the prints of every adult male in the community. Everyone who answers the door gets printed, and if someone is not home, we get their details and come back. All the reserve forces and volunteers are pitching in—I think our work is even more thorough than the national census. Nothing is going overlooked. He won't get away, sir."

"I know you're doing a great job, but there's a huge floating population that we can't monitor very well. What if the killer is hiding in an apartment and making a friend answer the door? We aren't going to get warrants to search all the apartments," Zhao said.

"We can't control everything," Yang said helplessly.

"Keep up the good work, anyway. We'll get as many as we can," Zhao said with a sigh.

Chapter 51

Lieutenant Lin clicked a file on the computer screen. A voice said, "Let's have lunch tomorrow, OK?"

A smug smile appeared on Yan's lips. "Exactly as I predicted."

"You're a genius," Lin exclaimed. "We found that sentence recorded in Xu Tianding's phone on his messaging app, WeChat. People use it to send text and voices messages to each other. Mr. Xu was chatting with a girl on the afternoon before his death, and he sent that voice message to her."

"After Xu was killed, someone took his phone and found the message. He played it and recorded it with his own phone, then sometime after 10:50 p.m. called Zhang Bing and played it for him. He probably added the struggling sounds himself. The killer wanted us to pinpoint the time of death at 10:50 p.m., when in reality the time of death was earlier."

"What if that message hadn't been on Mr. Xu's phone?"

"Even if the victim didn't have WeChat, I think our killer would have thought of another way to falsify the time of death," Yan said confidently.

"But we have plenty of other evidence to prove that Mr. Guo and Ms. Zhu didn't commit the crime," Lin said.

"Well, let's take each reason one at a time. Let's assume that there is a third person helping Mr. Guo and Ms. Zhu. That person helped them fabricate multiple pieces of evidence. First, the killer spent a considerable amount of time making long incisions on Mr. Xu's body, and at that point in time, Mr. Guo and Ms. Zhu were already at home. Mr. Guo went to a convenience store, so a witness saw him there. So if there was a third person involved, that eliminates their alibi. Then the autopsy found fried rice in Mr. Xu's stomach and esophagus, which would suggest that he was attacked after the two young people left the park, in the middle of his meal. That's logical—Mr. Xu wouldn't start eating rice while Ms. Zhu was standing there. But according to the autopsy, he had had grilled meat with his friends and had had several beers before going to the park. He was already stuffed by the time he ordered the fried rice; why would he actually eat it?" Yan asked.

"But . . . what happened?" Lin asked, his eyebrows knitting together.

"I have a theory that Dr. Chen thinks is feasible. Mr. Xu was not eating at the time of his death. Someone forced food down his throat after he died. It's a disgusting process—the killer would have to stuff rice down the victim's throat, one bit at a time, push it down the victim's throat with his fingers, and then push it all the way down to his stomach using a stick or something else long and straight."

Lin grimaced—his throat hurt just thinking about it. "Well, that takes care of the alibis," he said.

Yan pulled out his notebook. "Reason number two. You said that in order to destroy the crime scene, the killer scattered tens of thousands of yuan on the ground. Neither Mr. Guo nor Ms. Zhu have the money to do that. But the third person is not only rich but fiendishly clever. He wouldn't mind throwing away twenty, thirty, even forty thousand yuan."

Yan didn't wait for Lin to answer. "Reason number three: the paring knife in the noodle restaurant was brand new. It was bought by the third person. Reason number four: there weren't any inconsistencies in

Mr. Guo's or Ms. Zhu's testimonies. The third person taught them how to deal with the police. Reason number five: Ms. Zhu, her brother, and Mr. Guo all have alibis for when the threatening letter was delivered to Zhang Bing. The letter was delivered by the third person. Finally, reason number six: the fingerprints found on the beer can at the park match the ones left by the serial killer. The third person is the one who killed the other five victims. So you see, if you add a third person to the mix, the evidence that proved Ms. Zhu's and Mr. Guo's innocence is no longer reliable."

Lin was flabbergasted. Still, after thinking about it for a while, he felt that something was not quite right. "Professor Yan, I . . . I think this is all based on educated guesses."

"That's true; technically it's all conjecture," Yan answered, without looking the least bit perturbed. "I can't find a shred of evidence to support my theory."

"What I don't understand is why are you determined to show that Xu's death was committed by three people and not just by the third person? Why do you think that Mr. Guo and Ms. Zhu have something to do with the case?"

"They killed Xu. The third person did not," Yan said seriously.

"But why?"

"Two reasons: first is the paring knife. Xu's wound perfectly matches the knife that we found at the noodle restaurant. Second, if that third person actually killed Mr. Xu, we wouldn't be racking our brains to try and crack the case."

"And why do you say that?" Lin asked.

Yan breathed in sharply. "Because that third person would never have left any evidence. We would have no way of solving it." Yan looked at Lin. He knew that it was not the time to mention Luo's name.

Instead he said, "Every time the serial killer committed a murder, the special task force was unable to find any clues. That crime scene was cleaned up by a pro. The serial killer didn't kill Xu, but he helped to clean up their mess. Mr. Guo and Ms. Zhu didn't know what they were doing; that's why he resorted to scattering money at the crime scene."

"If that's what really happened, the third person was taking a major risk on their behalf," Lin said.

Yan reflected on Lin's comment for a moment. "I'm not sure how the third person is related to Mr. Guo and Ms. Zhu. Perhaps they weren't close friends."

"Do you really think someone would help a stranger clean up a crime scene?"

Yan smiled wryly and shook his head. "I can't figure that part out. And I still don't know why the third person appeared in the park at the exact moment that Mr. Guo and Ms. Zhu attacked their victim."

"So what are you going to do now, Professor Yan?" Lin asked. "Your conjectures explain every point in the case, but you don't have any evidence to support them. There's no way of proving that Mr. Guo and Ms. Zhu were the killers or that a third person was involved."

"You're right, Lin," Yan said. "At the moment all I have is one solution to the difficult equation. I cannot prove that it is the only solution. If our equation is x squared equals four, one answer is two but we also have the answer of negative two. In other words, I can be sure that my solution is sufficient for this equation, but I can't prove that it is both necessary and sufficient," Yan said.

"How confident are you that you have the right answer?"

"One hundred percent. The only problem is that from a law-enforcement perspective, it looks like I'm inventing a story to explain what happened," Yan said with a smile.

"If you feel that confident, I'll get some guys to bring Ms. Zhu and Mr. Guo here immediately," Lin said.

"No, don't do that!" Yan said.

"Why not? Didn't you say that you couldn't prove your theory even though you're sure it's correct? We don't have physical evidence and we don't have witnesses, so we need confessions. If we can force a confession out of those two, we would definitely get the name of that third person and probably get more incriminating evidence too," Lin said.

"Interrogating them is our last resort. Don't use it unless you have to. Just think: if we don't have any evidence to show that they've committed a crime, we won't get an arrest warrant. We can summon them to the bureau, but what if they don't cooperate? I think the criminals involved in this case know that we don't have witnesses and we can't find any evidence. We'll be stuck," Yan said.

"What do you think we should do?" Lin asked.

"I'd start by listening to all the conversations between Ms. Zhu and Mr. Guo—and monitor any other messages or texts. They have probably been trained to avoid communicating by phone, but we might catch them being careless. Then let's go see Ms. Zhu and Mr. Guo together. I'm not a cop, so I can't force them to talk. But you can, and I want to see just how much those two have learned from their accomplice."

As he spoke, Yan looked out the window, his eyes distant.

Chapter 52

The next day, it was so hot you could fry an egg on the street. Nobody was willing to leave their house, so the noodle restaurant didn't have much business.

Fulai had taken off his shirt and was napping on a folding chair behind the cash register. The electric fan was on full blast. Huiru sat in a wicker chair, playing with her phone to pass the time.

At that moment, Professor Yan and Investigator Lin walked in. Lin was in uniform, but Huiru didn't notice either of them.

Lin saw that Huiru was totally absorbed in her phone, and he coughed to get her attention. "Ah, Ms. Zhu, we need to speak to you again."

When Huiru looked up, the color drained from her face.

Fulai woke up at the sound of Lin's voice. He hurried towards them. "Hello, officer. Can . . . can we help you?"

"It has to do with that murder," Lin said. "We need to ask Ms. Zhu some questions."

"My little sister has told you everything she knows, hasn't she? What—what else do you need?" Fulai said.

Lin was about to make up an excuse, but before he could speak, Yan smiled coldly and said, "Maybe she hasn't told us everything."

Fulai's expression changed but Huiru was prepared. She looked resigned and said, "Yes, I've told you everything, and several times already."

"Yes, you were very cooperative before," Yan said. "We'd like you to just clarify a few things."

"Cooperating with the police is the duty of every citizen," Lin added. "We specifically came in the afternoon so that you wouldn't be too busy in the restaurant. Believe me, we're also miserable in this heat. Would you please come with us, Ms. Zhu?"

"Where are you going?" Fulai asked, looking alarmed.

"Oh, we'll just go to one of the cafés around the corner. Somewhere with air conditioning, I think." Lin watched Fulai's reaction carefully.

"Just stay here. I'll turn on the air conditioning," Fulai said, turning it on.

"No, we don't want to trouble you. Anyway, we asked Mr. Guo to meet us there," Lin said.

While Fulai thought of an appropriate answer, Huiru acted as coolly as possible. "I wouldn't mind a free coffee. You're paying, right?" She stood up quickly and put her phone in her pocket.

Lin stared in surprise. She seemed totally at ease. Yan pulled him towards the door, and they all made their way to the café.

The three of them sat down at the table Lin had reserved. "What did you want to ask me?" Huiru asked.

"Let's wait until Guo Yu comes," Yan answered.

"OK," Huiru took out her phone and started playing a game.

Lin looked at Huiru and then at Yan. Yan had a slight smile on his lips as he watched Huiru. Lin decided it was best to keep his mouth shut.

Guo Yu arrived with tiny beads of sweat on his forehead. He saw Yan and Lin before he noticed Huiru. For a split second he looked unsure, but he quickly composed himself. "Good afternoon. Huiru, what are you doing here?" he said.

"The officer said he wanted to ask some more questions," Huiru answered casually.

"Have a seat, Mr. Guo," Lin said, indicating a chair. "We're sorry that we asked you to leave your office when the weather is so unbearably hot."

"It's fine. I asked for the rest of the day off," Guo Yu said, wiping his hands on his pants and sitting next to Huiru.

"Would you like something to drink or eat? Please get anything you like," Lin said, handing them each a menu.

"Maybe just something to drink, thanks," Guo Yu said.

The waitress promptly brought their order to the table: iced coffee, juice, and some snacks. Guo Yu nibbled self-consciously while Huiru took full advantage of the spread.

Yan smiled again. "Let's get started. On the night of Xu's accident, did you see a man wearing a cross-body bag?"

Guo Yu bent forward to take a drink.

Huiru scrunched her lips together and thought. "A man wearing a bag? No, I don't remember that. It happened a while ago, though. What about you, Guo Yu?"

"Hmm . . . I don't remember that either." Guo Yu had the kind of face that people tended to trust.

"Maybe if I describe him, you'll remember," Yan said. "He's between forty and fifty, he has short hair, and he wears this one bag a lot. Almost every day, in fact. He's very rich and he drives an Audi SUV. He lives in an expensive apartment, but it is not decorated very well because he lives on his own. There is only one photograph on the wall, a picture of him with his family. Should I go on?"

Huiru and Guo Yu knew not to admit to anything since the police were only guessing. They both acted very calmly, though they were worried about protecting their friend.

Lin, on the other hand, stared incredulously as Yan described the accomplice. Lin knew that the pervert had seen a man wearing a cross-body bag on the night that he assaulted a woman. But how did Yan know that? How did he know his age? How did he know about his nice car, his big apartment, and everything else?

Huiru looked confused. "Who are you talking about?"

"We know Xu's death was an accident," Yan said, avoiding her question. "You two aren't bad people. You're good, honest people, and if somebody humiliates you or takes advantage of you, or even smacks you on the back of the head, you'll just take it on the chin. You never wanted to kill Xu Tianding. But when an accident turns into a murder and you *lie* in order to avoid punishment, the situation changes. If you repent now, it's better than continuing to try to hide the evidence until everything gets totally out of hand."

"What do you mean?" Huiru asked, giving Yan a penetrating look.

Guo Yu coughed lightly. He kept his eyes fixed on Yan as he spoke in a soft voice. "Officer, do you mean . . . you think we did it?"

Yan let out a short, bitter laugh. "Some people might think that the man who wears the cross-body bag is a good man. That's because they don't know him—they don't know that this isn't the first crime he's committed. Have either of you been paying attention to the serial murders in west Hangzhou? It's been in the news for months. You know, the one who leaves a sign that says 'Come and get me'? He has killed at least five people. You can imagine what kind of trouble you'll be in if you keep hiding the identity of a violent killer." Yan's eyes flashed.

"I don't know what you're talking about," Guo Yu said, taking a sip of his drink.

"I don't understand either; you're not making any sense," Huiru said somewhat impolitely. She picked up her drink.

Yan sat and stared in the ensuing silence. Nobody moved until he finally pursed his lips. "Fine, then we have nothing else to ask you about. I'm very sorry for bothering you."

"Can we leave, then?" Huiru said, surprised that their meeting was so short.

"Yes," Yan said with a nod.

"OK then," Huiru stood, then sat down again. "Actually I think I'll finish my drink first. It's delicious. Just to check, are we paying or . . . ?"

"We're paying, of course," Lin answered.

"OK," Huiru said, focusing again on the food on the table. "You're not going to eat any of this?"

"I'm not very hungry. It's so hot outside," Yan said.

"Oh, that's great!" Huiru said. "I mean, if you don't want it, I'll ask the waitress to box it up and take it home. I don't want it to go to waste."

"Of course," Lin said, somewhat stunned. It was as if he had just met a Martian. He had worked in the force for years and had done countless interviews, but he had never seen anybody ask if they could take the food with them.

"No matter how you look at it, those two don't seem suspicious to me," Lin said later, gradually recovering from his initial surprise.

"I would give them full marks for their acting skills," Yan said, making a face. "The accomplice taught them some very effective tactics. Even when I made everything obvious, their expressions didn't change at all. If we brought them to the police station, it would be useless."

"But I think they're innocent," Lin said. "If anything I think Mr. Zhu is a bit suspicious. He looked apprehensive the minute we stepped into his restaurant."

"He's not even remotely related to the case," Yan said unequivocally.

"Why not? Ms. Zhu and Mr. Guo are calm and collected, but you think they are the ones who did it. Meanwhile Mr. Zhu seems to have a guilty conscience, but you say he doesn't have anything to do with the case. It doesn't make sense!"

"Do you remember when you asked about the knife, how Mr. Zhu said he had never seen it, but Ms. Zhu found it immediately and showed it to you? Ms. Zhu wanted to show you the knife to prove her innocence. I think Mr. Zhu was worried, and the fact that he was trying to cover up something as trivial as the knife shows that he's not very intelligent. I'm sure he's not involved," Yan concluded.

"By the way, how did you come up with so many specific details about the killer? It sounded like you had been to his house!" Lin asked.

"Oh, I was just guessing," Yan said with a smile.

"You *guessed* that he was in his forties, drove a luxury car, and lived in an expensive apartment? How?" Lin asked.

"I invented it. I just wanted to see how those youngsters would react. I told you already, I don't have evidence yet. When I do, you'll be the first to know," Yan said.

Lin raised his eyebrows at the professor.

Chapter 53

It was still light out, just past six, even though the sun had already set behind the mountains.

Luo wore his bag, his hands at his sides. He leaned slightly forward and walked along the river, calmly and slowly.

He was keenly aware of what the police were up to. Lots of people gossiped about the search for fingerprints in west Hangzhou. They were going to every house and ensuring that they didn't miss anyone. Still, they weren't going as fast as Luo had anticipated—at least, nobody in his neighborhood had been fingerprinted yet.

This wasn't very surprising, considering that over eight hundred thousand people lived in the district. On top of that, the police had to compare every fingerprint and keep track of the information. The workload was staggering. The Hangzhou census was easier, because the government hired an army of people to do it in a few days. But finger-printing was sensitive; only the police could do it.

Luo lifted his head and looked into the distance. "Hypothetically it wouldn't be difficult to avoid getting fingerprinted," he muttered. He pressed his lips into a line and kept walking.

Yan had invited him to meet at the park by the river today. That clever fox just wouldn't give up. But Luo wasn't the slightest bit nervous. He held all the aces. Even if Yan could guess some of the cards that Luo was holding, he couldn't predict what Luo's next move would be.

Then again, even if Yan would never beat him, did that necessarily make Luo the winner? Luo sighed and shook his head, a bitter smile on his face.

In a way, he was actually competing against himself.

How was it going to end?

He kept walking at his usual slow pace. A young woman walked past, probably on her way home from work. She wore an elegant platinum necklace with a sapphire pendant.

Luo stopped suddenly, his eyes fixed on the pendant as he was immediately dragged into the past.

He remembered that evening, one of the last nights he was in Beijing while his family was still in Ningbo. He couldn't recall the exact date because he had no idea that it would be the last conversation he would ever have with his wife.

"Did you have dinner already?" Luo had asked.

"Of course. It's nine o'clock. Did you just finish yours, then?" she asked.

"Yeah, just now," Luo said with a laugh.

"You only think to call us when you've had your dinner and you don't know what to do," she complained.

"I'm really busy; I couldn't call more even if I wanted to," Luo said sweetly.

"That's no excuse!" She raised her voice. "How many times have you called in the last two months? You're not even thinking of us."

"I'll try to be better, I will. I'll make sure to call you more and think of you more," Luo promised.

"You're so quick to apologize!" she said mockingly.

"It's good to humbly accept criticism."

She tutted. "Listen, our little angel isn't feeling very well," she said in a more serious tone.

"She's sick?"

"She's got a cold and a fever."

"Did you take her to the hospital?"

"I gave her a fever reducer and she felt better after that. Tomorrow I'll take her to the hospital—I'll need to take a day off work."

"Good," Luo said. "Try to get some medicine but not antibiotics. Taking too many antibiotics isn't good for her immune system—"

"I know, I know," she said, interrupting him. "Stop nagging! You've told me all this medical stuff ever since the baby was born. I know it backward and forward."

Luo laughed. "I'm getting old, honey; it makes me talk too much. Please forgive me."

"When are you coming home? Our little angel used to ask about you all the time, but lately she hasn't been talking about you at all." Her teasing was gentle, but it still hurt.

"Really?" Luo felt a bitter taste of guilt in his mouth. "I'm coming home next week, but I'm not sure which day. I'll call you as soon as I know. Talk about me to her, OK? I don't want her to forget who her father is."

"If you wait too long she really will forget. The puppy is all grown up and won't recognize you. He might even bite you when you come back!"

"Oh no! I'll be careful when I open the door, then," Luo said, feeling his heart grow warm.

"So have you bought a gift for her?"

"Not yet," Luo said, feeling guiltier. "Hmm, I could go shopping this weekend. Where do you think I should get presents in Beijing? People go to Wangfujing, right?"

"Why are you asking me? I've never even been to Beijing. Do you mean to say you haven't been out once during your two-month stay?"

"We all went to the Great Wall when we first arrived, but then I just spent all my free time in the hotel. You know how it is."

"Just go to Wangfujing. It's touristy, but you'll find what you're looking for." She knew that he was a hopeless shopper. There was no point sending him somewhere else.

"What should I get her?"

"You told her you were going to buy some snacks for her and the dog. Don't you remember? Get her a few toys too; you've been away for a long time."

"Should I get you something, honey?"

Luo's wife knew that it was unwise to pretend that she didn't want anything, because Luo would take her seriously. So she spoke frankly. "Yes, please. Get me a necklace."

"OK, I'll find something nice for you," he said.

That weekend he went to Wangfujing and followed his wife's instructions exactly. He bought snacks for his daughter, snacks for the dog, and three dolls. Then he bought a necklace made of platinum with a sapphire pendant. Just like the one that he would see eight years in the future on a young woman's neck.

The next week, on a Wednesday, he tried calling home but nobody answered. He didn't think anything of it. The next day, when his plane landed in Ningbo, he tried again but still got no answer. Something was not quite right. And when he opened the door to his apartment, nobody greeted him—even the dog was gone.

Chapter 54

Luo sighed and pulled himself back to the present. He pursed his lips and mustered up the energy to keep walking towards the park.

When he was almost there, he saw Yan standing on the metal disc where Xu Tianding had stood on the night of his death. Luo felt pangs of doubt. But as far as he could tell, everything was airtight.

"It's nice here, isn't it?" Luo said to Yan.

"Yes, it is," Yan said, twisting his body and looking at the parents pushing strollers and playing with their children in the park. "West Hangzhou is a wonderful place to live. Although I think if you lived here alone, it would be easy to get bored."

"Don't tell me you're going to introduce me to another one of your friends!"

"No, I'm not going to meddle in your personal affairs," Yan said with a laugh. "Although if you're interested in meeting some nice women your age, just say the word."

"Thanks again for the offer, but I'll pass. So why did you want to meet? Is it the case?"

"How did you know?" Yan's eyes grew wide, pretending to be surprised.

"Last night I ordered some takeout from the noodle restaurant. The girl who works there, Zhu Huiru, said she ran into you. I guessed that you were investigating her. And the spot where you're standing is very close to where I hear the body was found. Over there," Luo said, pointing towards the trees.

"Oh? What did Ms. Zhu say?" Yan asked.

"She said that you asked if she was delivering the noodles to me. She said you went to the noodle restaurant many times to speak to her," Luo explained.

"It's true; I'm suspicious of her and Mr. Guo," Yan said, clearing his throat. "I followed her last night, and this afternoon I spoke to both Ms. Zhu and Mr. Guo. One of the criminal investigators from the district bureau was there too. But those kids didn't tell me anything."

Luo shrugged with a smile. "I'm sure you suspect them for a good reason."

"You're absolutely right. They did it."

Then why haven't you arrested anyone? Luo thought. "Why don't you interview them in the bureau? You shouldn't need my help at all! I'm sure I'm not nearly as good as all the professional forensic scientists. Plus I don't have any of the equipment to do the job right."

"I just wanted you to confirm one thing," Yan said, with a look that seemed to cut right through all of his excuses. "Is there any way that a killer could get their victim to eat half a portion of fried rice after a person has died? Not only that, could the killer make most of that food go all the way into the stomach?"

Yan figured that one out too? Luo thought.

He pretended to think about the question. "Yeah, by forcing it down the victim's throat. Have you heard of a fish called the great croaker?"

"That's a popular fish in Ningbo, where you come from, isn't it? I hear it's very expensive."

"Yes. Wild great croaker costs about nine hundred yuan per pound. When I was still working in Ningbo, the vice director of criminal investigation gave us two fish as a gift just before New Year. My wife cut them open to cook them and found that they both had lead weights inside. Each one weighed two hundred grams. I was shocked."

"Hmm, it sounds like they were bought from an unscrupulous businessman. Are you sure you can do this with humans? Even if they are dead?"

"Of course. But a human esophagus is long. The killer would have to use a long stick to carefully push the food into the stomach. And if the killer wants to make things look even more realistic, he or she would have to move the victim's jaws to chew the food first."

"There's one more thing I wanted to ask you. I'm sure you saw the media reports on the serial killer in Hangzhou? The killer always leaves a Liqun cigarette in the victim's mouth. Why do you think that is?"

"Maybe the killer likes to smoke Liqun cigarettes," Luo suggested casually.

"Ha, ha, maybe. But what if the killer isn't a smoker?"

"Then I don't know," Luo said. "I think that's more your area. Even when I was working as a forensic scientist, I would find answers based on the facts. I don't know how to analyze the meaning behind things."

"That's OK. Sorry to bother you with all these questions," Yan said.

"Not at all," Luo answered. "I'm happy to help whenever I can. Although I don't think I'm as brilliant as the people still working in the force."

"Is that so? I'd say you're better than most of the forensic scientists in the bureau now. They couldn't have come up with those answers."

"That's what happens when you do the same job for a few decades, I guess."

"Well, thanks again. I'll take you out to dinner when you're free."

"I look forward to that."

Yan turned and walked away. After a few steps he turned back and called, "I still admire your motto. Committing a crime is shameful, no matter what the reason!"

Luo just nodded.

A chill went up his back as he watched Yan leave, freshly worried he would never get a chance to see his family again.

PART 7
THE UNAVOIDABLE TRAP

Chapter 55

Inspector Yang brought Professor Yan into Zhao's office, then turned and left when Zhao dismissed him with a wave of the hand. Zhao closed the door and poured a cup of water for Yan. Then he plopped down on the sofa. "You've been at it for a few days now," he said. "What have you got for me?"

"Nothing yet. I'll tell you as soon as I do," Yan said frankly.

"The police are going to every house and apartment in west Hangzhou to take the fingerprints of every adult male in the area. After one hundred thousand prints, they still haven't found the killer. Should we keep going?"

"Absolutely," Yan said. "Those fingerprints are the most solid evidence we have."

"But will it be effective?" Zhao asked doubtfully. "If the killer wanted to hide, he wouldn't have a hard time avoiding the police."

"Every investigation runs that risk. That doesn't mean we should stop."

Zhao frowned, pacing back and forth as he spoke. "Do you have any explanation for either the cigarettes or the word 'local' scratched in the pavement?"

"No," Yan said flatly.

"You can't figure *any* of this out?" Zhao said, his frown lines deepening.

"Of course not," Yan said with a scornful laugh. "I'm not a god; I can't know everything."

"I thought you were invincible," Zhao said.

"Over one thousand officers have pondered these homicides without coming up with an answer. I'm not nearly as intelligent as one thousand people," Yan reminded him. "We won't find the answers simply by guessing. I need to deduce things based on what I already know. Unfortunately, the information I have is limited, so I can't get very far."

"Do you think this is part of the killer's plan? Is he trying to mislead us?"

"No," Yan said. "I don't think he is the type to stoop so low as to plant false clues."

"But then what does it mean?" Zhao said, scratching his head.

"I don't know," Yan said.

"I heard you've been investigating Zhu Huiru and Guo Yu," Zhao said, lighting a cigarette and taking a puff.

"Did Lin tell you?"

"Yes, he did," Zhao said. "Word is that you are convinced that they did it. Can you tell me why?"

"I'm sorry, but I really don't have any proof," Yan said, making an apologetic gesture.

"But then why—"

"I have a hypothesis, but I can't confirm it."

"Making sweeping hypotheses and then slowly collecting evidence is great for solving a mathematical proof, but that doesn't work here," Zhao said.

"You know about mathematical proofs?" Yan said, deeply surprised.

"I'm not a total idiot, you know," Zhao said, scrunching his lips together.

Yan burst out laughing.

"But it doesn't seem like you are so sure that those two unlikely suspects are the killers. It would make sense to add a third accomplice—Luo Wen, perhaps?" Zhao said.

"What did you say?" Yan narrowed his eyes.

"Why does Luo carry that bag everywhere he goes?"

"You've seen him in Hangzhou?" Yan asked.

"When I saw him it reminded me of what that pervert said. The killer was wearing a cross-body bag," Zhao said.

"But you can find people with bags like that all over Hangzhou," Yan said.

"Of course, of course. And if the killer wore such a bag on the night of the killing, that doesn't mean that he wears one all the time. But still—" Zhao paused and looked more closely at Yan. "It wasn't a big deal when you went to see Luo once. But you've been visiting him an awful lot lately. And Lin tells me that when you two went to question Ms. Zhu and Mr. Guo, your description of the killer seemed strangely specific."

"You've been following me?" Yan asked quietly.

"I've just been investigating the case," Zhao said.

"So the reason you asked me to come today is to see if Luo is the killer?" Yan asked.

"I haven't had much interaction with Luo before," Zhao said, refilling his cup of water. "I don't know him as well as you do. He's capable of committing a murder and not leaving any tracks; he has experience as a forensic scientist. He wouldn't be afraid of a dead body; he's probably seen hundreds of them before. And he wouldn't have any trouble making those long, thin cuts. But . . . it's still strange because he was a cop. The director of the Ningbo Forensic Science and Material Evidence departments, no less. I just don't understand what his motive would be."

Yan exhaled. "Don't you think you're jumping to conclusions?"

"You tell me," Zhao countered.

"Do you have evidence?"

"I was going to ask you that question!" Zhao said, throwing his hands up.

"I don't have any evidence," Yan said with a wry smile.

"Then why do you suspect him in the first place? Just because he lives in west Hangzhou and could pull it off?" Zhao asked.

"All I have are logical pieces that fit together—nothing that would stand in court. But since you asked, I *do* suspect Luo. I have since the first time I met him in Hangzhou. He's the reason I asked to help out with your case," Yan said.

Zhao sat in stunned silence. He thought it was strange when Yan first asked to help, but he never expected the reason to be that he suspected his old friend Luo.

Zhao cleared his throat. "Based on what you know of Luo, why is he doing this? He kills ex-convicts every time. Does that mean he is taking the law into his own hands? Is he dissatisfied with the justice system?"

"No," Yan said quickly. "He always works within the framework of the law and loathes those who exact punishment outside of that framework."

"But then—"

"If he really did it, then he must have some other motive. Although to be honest, I have no idea what it could be."

"What about Xu Tianding's murder? Lin said that you think Ms. Zhu and Mr. Guo killed him, but a third person helped them to cover it up. But Luo doesn't seem to know either of them very well, so why would he go out of his way to help them?"

"I don't know," Yan said, shaking his head.

Zhao paced. He turned to look at Yan and said, "In other words, you suspect him, but you don't have any evidence whatsoever."

"That's right."

"Alright, I'll help you find evidence. I just hope that your guesses are on the mark."

"What are you going to do?" Yan said, a trace of alarm in his voice.

"Simple. I'll just get his fingerprints," Zhao said with a smile.

Yan shook his head. "Please, don't act rashly. The only thing you're going to do is let him know that you suspect him."

"You think he's the murderer, don't you?" Zhao said, looking confused. "Wouldn't we know for sure as soon as we check his prints?"

"If it were that easy, we wouldn't be going after a brilliant man like Luo," Yan said.

"Do you think the fingerprints at the crime scene belong to someone unrelated to the case?"

"If it were anyone else, I would say no. But this is Luo we're talking about. He's definitely clever enough to finish the job without leaving prints. He knows the police inside out. So if he actually did it, then the clues you have found thus far are clues that he wanted you to find. To use a university metaphor, not only did he write up a test for you, but he printed out the model answer. He's just waiting for you to fill it out."

A look of pure terror flickered across Zhao's face. Then he shook his head. "I'm going to verify this. We have more than just the fingerprints; we have the electric baton and the jump rope. Maybe there's something in his bag right now!"

"I'm telling you, don't act rashly," Yan said, raising his voice.

"I don't need someone to teach me how to solve a case! If he's the one, I'll get that evidence, come hell or high water!" Zhao looked furious.

Yan looked Zhao directly in the eyes and took a deep breath. "Have it your way. Maybe you can provoke him into doing something. Either way, I need your help."

"Well? Spit it out!"

Yan couldn't help but smile. "I'd like you to write me a letter of introduction for the Ningbo Bureau. I need to look into a few things."

"This is about Luo, isn't it?"

"Yes, it is."

"Are you going to Ningbo by yourself?"

"I would prefer if people didn't know who my primary suspect was until after I have cleared a few things up."

"OK," Zhao said, nodding.

Chapter 56

Luo was enjoying his regular Saturday routine: breakfast at one of the restaurants downstairs, then a lazy day of watching television.

He didn't have many hobbies. When he was working in Ningbo, he rarely had free time, and when he did, he would just read forensics textbooks. But in the past few years he had cultivated at least one new hobby: stretching out on the sofa and watching television.

He often thought that it would be much more enjoyable if he found his wife and daughter again. All he had now were his idle day-dreams and the photo on the wall.

In three years he would be fifty, an old man.

His memories of his wife and his daughter were crystallized in time—his daughter didn't grow older and his wife looked exactly the same. He was the only one who changed. He felt so different from the man in the picture that he sometimes felt like he was no longer his daughter's father or his wife's husband.

The doorbell rang. Luo stood, curious.

Apart from maintenance workers and the occasional takeout delivery, people never rang his doorbell. Not since he moved into this place anyway.

Who was at the door, then?

He peered through the peephole.

An old man was standing outside. He looked vaguely familiar. Luo guessed that he was one of the apartment management staff.

"Can I help you?" Luo called through the door.

"Good afternoon. The tenant below you says there is water leaking from their ceiling. We would like to come in and check your apartment."

The tenant below me?

Luo's mind raced through the possibilities. He never saw someone standing on the balcony below. In fact, nobody even put chairs out. He never cooked, so the kitchen sink wasn't the answer. The bathroom was working properly; he showered yesterday without any problems. It hadn't rained recently, so that was an unlikely explanation. How on earth would there be a leak downstairs?

He had worked as a police officer long enough to know the ways to get a suspect to open the door. Yan had moved on from guessing to collecting evidence. What did they find out? Where were Zhu Huiru and Guo Yu?

A knot of anxiety grew in his stomach. There was no point in hiding.

As he turned the latch, he heard someone running. The door thumped loudly as someone crashed against it.

He was surprised by the force even though he was partly expecting it.

"What the—?" a voice said. It was Investigator Yang, wearing his police uniform. He rubbed his right shoulder, and his three colleagues stood awkwardly next to him. Yang frowned.

They had planned to rush into Luo's apartment the moment he opened the door so they could subdue Luo and collect evidence without interference. It was an effective way to frighten a suspect from the moment the police arrived—sometimes it even resulted in the suspect confessing on the spot.

Yang didn't expect Luo to keep the chain on when he opened the door. Instead of bursting into the apartment and scaring his suspect, Yang was still stuck outside, worried that he might have broken a bone.

Luo sighed. If he hadn't put on the chain, Yang's attack would have sent him flying. He glared at them through the partially opened door. "What the hell do you think you're doing?"

The policemen all looked awkward now. Their plan had seemed perfect; they hadn't expected that a tiny chain lock would scupper it.

Yang tried to look serious again and coughed. "We're part of the Narcotics Division. We received a report suggesting that there are drugs hidden in your apartment. We need to search it."

He couldn't believe they could get away with such a flimsy excuse. *Yan didn't teach them to say that,* Luo thought. Luo didn't drink or smoke; why would he take drugs? Only a novice would use that excuse to conduct a search without a warrant.

Then he realized that this was probably a good sign. If they had to make up lame excuses, it meant they were trying to leave an out for themselves. That meant that they didn't have any evidence, which meant that Huiru and Guo Yu were safe.

Luo frowned slightly, sizing them up. "The Narcotics Division usually operates undercover. Why are you wearing your uniforms?"

Yang was taken aback. But he had no choice but to continue the charade. "That's enough from you. Open the door!" he growled.

"There must be some mistake. Perhaps the tipoff was wrong? It might even be a prank," Luo said calmly as he undid the chain. He made sure to stand to the side so that he wouldn't be pinned against the wall.

Yang was surprised again. Here was Luo, opening the door and allowing them to search his apartment!

A serial killer wouldn't do that in a million years. This couldn't be the right person. There must have been some mistake.

He still looked serious, but his demeanor was much politer. "We have to follow our investigation procedures, sir. We would appreciate your cooperation."

"Of course, of course." Luo nodded.

"Now, according to regulations, we need to search the entire premises. Would you please take us through all the rooms in your apartment?" Yang asked.

"If you must. Where would you like to begin?" Luo said kindly.

Luo followed the police through the bare rooms of his apartment. He noticed that they spent extra time on the walls, as if they hoped to discover a secret compartment.

Half an hour later, the search was over. Yang's gaze fell on the cross-body bag that was sitting on a table. "May I look through your bag?"

"Of course," Luo said, handing it over.

Yang removed all of the bag's contents. He found a pile of cash, multiple debit cards, a driver's license, and resident identity card.

Yang scrunched his lips in displeasure. "And your car?"

"Yes. It's in the parking garage. Come with me."

All they found were a few papers and some gifts given to him by a client.

Yang felt very embarrassed. "I'm sorry, it looks like our tip was completely off base."

"That's perfectly alright. It's important to cooperate with police investigations. You must be exhausted, working outside in this heat!" Luo said.

Yang smiled weakly. "Finally I need to take your fingerprints for our file."

"OK," Luo said. "I was wondering if you could do me a favor. Now that we all know you came here in error, could you please let the property management staff know that it was a mistake? Otherwise they will suspect that I'm involved in a narcotics case."

"Of course we will," Yang answered. The four officers left.

Luo sighed as he closed the door to his apartment and looked out the window. "Well, Yan, I hope you've given up now," he said quietly to himself.

Chapter 57

"You're sure they're not a match?" Zhao asked, looking first at Yang and then at Professor Yan, who was seated across from him.

"Yes. They were completely different than the killer's prints."

"Did you find anything else there?" Zhao asked.

"We searched his apartment and his car from top to bottom, but we didn't find any suspicious items. I'm not sure we could think of a reason to search his office," Yang answered.

"No jump ropes?" Zhao asked.

"No jump ropes, no electric baton," Yang said.

"Did you check his bag?" Yan asked.

"Yes. He had a lot of cash, some cards, and his ID," Yang said.

"How much cash?" Yan asked.

"A couple thousand."

"Only a couple thousand yuan? Did he have cash anywhere else in his house?"

"Yes, he had about twenty or thirty thousand yuan in a nightstand in his bedroom."

Yan considered the figure, then nodded.

Zhao stroked his chin and dismissed Yang. He looked at Yan. "See? We didn't find anything."

"I told you if you did this, it would just tip him off. You're not going to get evidence this way."

"So how do you explain the prints?"

"Fake," Yan said, as if this was obvious.

"His *fingerprints* are fake?" Zhao scowled. "Impossible."

"It's quite easy. Employees who are required to scan their fingerprints at work will order a mold of their print so their colleagues can clock in for them. You can get them online now."

"I know all that," Zhao said. "But the employees are using real fingerprints, aren't they? They can't just be pulled out of thin air. If Luo is the killer and the fingerprints aren't his, whose are they?"

"Some stranger, probably," Yan said, pursing his lips. "Or maybe they are prints from a previous case."

"So you're saying sending all those officers out to collect fingerprints was a complete waste of time?"

"That's standard protocol for an investigation; I had no reason to object to it," Yan said primly.

"Why do you suspect Luo anyway?" Zhao asked impatiently. "I don't believe it, and that means other people aren't going to believe it either."

"I'm sorry, but this is the answer that my educated guess has outputted. Checking my work is taking a lot longer than I expected," Yan said helplessly.

"Well, what if your educated guess is wrong? What if Luo has nothing to do with this case?"

"I haven't wasted any of your resources, have I?" Yan asked. "You were the one who decided to send men to Luo's apartment; I was firmly against that. You probably wasted a lot of manpower following me around, but you shouldn't blame me for that."

"You're affecting the way I approach the case and make judgments, Yan!"

"I don't think you ever had a real approach to the case," Yan shot back.

"You, you—" Zhao had half a mind to kick him out. But soon he smiled. Yan had a point. It didn't really matter how Yan conducted his investigation: if he got more leads, that was a good thing, and if he didn't, Zhao shouldn't blame him for it.

Zhao stretched and sat down again. "What are you going to do next?"

"Tomorrow I'll bring your letter of introduction to the Ningbo Bureau," Yan said. He paused, "But since you've already started investigating Luo, please continue."

"What else is there? His office?" Zhao said, surprised. "Keep in mind he knows a lot of people at the provincial level and could file a complaint against me for affecting his work and daily life."

"No, don't go to his office," Yan said. "It would be too risky to hide anything there. Check the video surveillance for Luo's apartment block on the night of Xu Tianding's murder. There are cameras at the entrance, in the parking lot, and even in the elevator. I'm sure that he came back very late, if at all."

"Piece of cake," Zhao said.

"Excellent. See you in a few days."

Chapter 58

"Luo got back around midnight on September 8. He was alone and on foot." Investigator Yang played the surveillance footage from Luo's apartment building.

Zhao stared at the screen. The video was very dark, but the camera in Luo's expensive apartment building showed more pixels than most models. The two lights at the entrance to the apartment complex gave just enough light for Zhao to make out the face of each person who walked past.

"There isn't any sign of blood or anything else out of the ordinary. Although he did come home pretty late for someone who doesn't party," Zhao said.

"There's more," Yang answered. He closed that section of video and opened a different file. "A few hours later, at about ten minutes to two, Luo drove his car out of the apartment block. The light is not perfect, and we can't see the face of the driver, but the license plate is his. Twenty minutes later he returns. It seems odd."

Zhao frowned and nodded. "Just as Yan suspected. Can you confirm whether there is anyone in the car when he returns?"

"We can tell that there is no one in the front passenger seat, but there could be someone in the back," Yang said, shaking his head. "That's not enough information, is it?"

Yang opened a third file. "At 3:35 a.m. he drove his car out of the apartment complex again and did not return until about 9:00 a.m."

"Yan thinks that Zhu Huiru and Guo Yu killed Xu Tianding, that Luo was the one who cleaned up the mess." Zhao sighed. "He also thinks Luo taught them how to give airtight statements, which takes time. Twenty minutes wouldn't be enough. Unless he . . . unless he picked them up and brought them back to his apartment?"

"No big deal, we'll just ask Luo what he was doing. Then we will check up on whatever he says. See how he responds to that, eh?" Yang said.

"That will be harder than you think," Zhao answered. "What if he says he couldn't sleep and he took a walk? Nobody would have seen him or remembered him walking around."

"Umm . . ."

"That isn't enough to prove he's guilty; it just raises a few suspicions for us," Zhao said.

"What are our options, sir?" Yang said, sounding dispirited.

"What floor does he live on?" Zhao asked.

"The seventh."

"Let's check if the elevator has a camera." Zhao's face lit up. "If Ms. Zhu and Mr. Guo are with him in the elevator at that time of night, he'll have to admit that he was involved!"

Yang left to find the footage, but came running back less than five minutes later. "We caught him! We caught the killer!" he panted.

"What?!" Zhao said, confused.

"They just got him," Yang said, catching his breath. "Squad 2 was collecting fingerprints in an apartment. They confirmed that it was a perfect match in the lab and arrested the guy. His name is Li Fengtian, he's thirty-two, and he's a local Hangzhou resident. He's a lefty and he smokes Liqun cigarettes. It all fits! All that stuff about Luo Wen was just paranoia, I guess."

Zhao stood up and paced his office excitedly. "OK, interrogate him immediately and make sure to get a video and audio recording."

The Hangzhou and the Zhejiang Bureaus had both made the serial case a top priority, but Zhao never expected to get the answers in just a few weeks. And as for all of Yan's speculations, it turned out that they were just a distraction with no bearing on the case.

Chapter 59

Yan approached Zhao's door and knocked. He heard Zhao shout, "Come in."

"I hear you caught the killer?" Yan said, coming straight to the point.

Something was not quite right. He looked more closely at Zhao, who was looking down and smoking a cigarette.

"What is it? He won't talk?" Yan said.

Zhao sucked in a breath and extinguished his cigarette in the ashtray. "That bastard has an alibi."

"Have you confirmed it?"

"Li Fengtian has a stall at a market that specializes in construction materials. He sells paint," Zhao said. "He traveled to Jiangsu province on September 7 to replenish his stock and didn't return until September 9. His wife managed the stall while he was there. On September 8, the night of Mr. Xu's death, he was having a meal with a factory owner there. He couldn't have possibly come back to Hangzhou in time to commit the crime. And that's not all! He only came back to his hometown of Hangzhou last year. He has no relationship with any of the victims, and we've searched his apartment but didn't find murder weapons or anything else to connect him to the crime."

"Apart from the murders, has he admitted to any other crimes?" Yan asked.

"What other crimes?" Zhao asked, looking confused.

Yan smiled and shook his head sadly. "That would be a no."

"What are you trying to say? Do you still think that Luo, Zhu, and Guo are the killers?"

"No, I still think that Li Fengtian is also culpable," Yan explained. "But he's the secondary killer and Luo is the main killer."

"There is no evidence pointing to Luo!" Zhao said, exasperated. "Everything points towards Li Fengtian. The prints, the fact that he's a lefty from Hangzhou, even his preference for Liqun cigarettes. It all fits."

"That's it, then," Yan said, nodding to himself.

"What did you learn in Ningbo?" Zhao asked anxiously.

Yan stood and stretched, then refilled his cup of water. "Do remember how we speculated why the killer would use a rope and not a knife?"

Zhao answered after giving the question some thought. "We don't have an answer to that question, as far as I know."

"Why didn't the killer leave Sun Hongyun's body on the grass? Why did he drag it to the concrete and go through all that hassle of faking the footprints?"

"To make our jobs harder?" Zhao guessed.

"That only makes it harder for the criminal to execute the crime," Yan said, shaking his head.

"Well, do you have the answers?"

Yan asked another question. "Why did the killer make it look like his victim wrote the word 'local' just before he died?"

Zhao shrugged and shook his head.

"Why did he leave a Liqun cigarette after killing his victims?"

Zhao frowned at Yan.

"Why did he leave a sign that said 'Come and get me' at every crime scene?"

"Get to the point, Yan!"

"Why were all of the victims ex-convicts?"

"It sounds like you already know the answer," Zhao said.

"You're right. One reason explains it all."

Zhao gaped at Yan. "You're telling me this because—"

"My guesses can explain everything, but they would be worthless in a court of law. There is no evidence," Yan said earnestly.

Zhao scratched his chin. "I'll get someone to drag Luo in here, and we'll interrogate him for three days straight. I think he'll crack if he's not allowed to sleep for seventy-two hours."

"Not everyone gives in under pressure, you know," Yan said with disdain.

Zhao looked up—Yan had gotten his attention.

"Tough interrogations can grind people down, and a lot of people crack. But then why do tough guys still confess in the end? It's because the police present some evidence and describe the crime as it actually happened, making the tough guys think that the police know exactly what happened and they have the evidence to back it up. They confess because they think their conviction is inevitable. But this case is different! Luo knows that we don't have witnesses or physical evidence. As long as he doesn't confess, he's in the clear. If he does crack, he would get the death penalty. What do you think he will do?"

"What can we do?" Zhao said, pacing his office. "We can't just let him go when we know he should be behind bars!"

"One thing that I haven't figured out is why Luo helped those young people when they seem to have met by chance," Yan said.

"If he doesn't tell us, we'll never know. We haven't found anything to indicate a special relationship. I don't think we'll find out suddenly that Luo is Zhu Huiru's real father!" Zhao laughed loudly in an attempt to clear the cloud of frustration that had settled in the room.

"I have a plan," Yan said quietly.

"What is it?"

"Li Fengtian has solid alibis and we should let him go. You aren't allowed to keep him for any longer unless you find incriminating evidence anyway."

"Just let him go?"

"Yes, then I want to lay a trap for Luo."

Yan explained the details of his plan.

Zhao looked anxious. "Luo is very clever. Don't you think he'll see through this?"

"He's been waiting so many years for this. He'll do it," Yan said confidently.

Zhao was uncertain. "We can make him see this document without you personally delivering it. I'm afraid once he finds out that you know everything, he might try to hurt you."

"No! I have to do this myself," Yan said, his face flush with anger. "I want to see what he's really made of!"

Zhao watched Yan without speaking. He had never seen him like this before. "Alright, go see him."

PART 8

THE MAGNETIC PULL OF THE TRUTH

Chapter 60

Luo watched TV on the sofa. His dog slept on the floor next to his slippers.

It was early evening. Neither the police nor Yan had come by in the past few days.

Luo had avoided eating at Chongqing Noodles—he didn't even order takeout. But he saw Huiru earlier that day, and she had said that everything was fine.

Just then, the doorbell rang. The dog ran towards the door, barking loudly.

Luo stood up, immediately alert. *Not this again.* Would they ask to see his temporary residence permit? He owned this apartment, but his household registration still tied him to Ningbo, and he didn't have a temporary residence permit. That might give them just enough legal cause to come into his property unannounced. He looked through the peephole in his door.

Yan Liang? Again?

Luo frowned slightly, took a breath, and opened the door.

His dog backed away, barking at the visitor. Luo scolded the dog and shooed him away.

Yan grinned. "He didn't bark this much last time I came. It looks like he already knows who the master of the house is."

"He would be a pretty ungrateful dog if he didn't recognize his owner by now," Luo said, smiling back. "He's been here for a long time. He's almost finished with the bag of treats you gave him."

Yan picked up a rawhide bone and threw it to the dog, who picked it up in his mouth and went to chew it in the corner. "You really like this dog, don't you?" Yan asked.

Luo nodded.

"Is it because the dog looks like the one your daughter used to play with?"

Luo nodded.

"It was worth it for Huiru to give you this dog, then," Yan said, sighing.

"Pardon me?" Luo said, giving him a sidelong glance.

"Zhu Huiru picked up this dog off the street, but she had to give it away. Perhaps if she had given him to someone else, they wouldn't have taken such a liking to him."

"Hmm, I guess so," Luo said in a flat tone.

"You watch TV?" Yan said, commenting on one of the few things Luo had in his living room.

Luo pretended to be confused. "Is it strange that I watch television?"

"You never used to have so much free time," Yan answered.

"I usually spend my evenings watching television now and I like it."

"Oh, really," Yan said, still smiling.

"Would you like something to drink? I only have tea," Luo said as he got a mug.

"Water is fine," Yan said.

"OK," Luo said, handing him a mug of water.

"Thank you," Yan said, and sat down on the sofa. "I came looking for you today because I wanted to ask you about something important."

"Oh? What's that?" Luo said, sitting on the other side of the sofa.

"In your professional opinion, is there such a thing as a perfect crime?" Yan asked. He looked at Luo as he spoke.

"What do you mean? A criminal who is never caught?" Luo asked.

"No, plenty of criminals are never caught. In a perfect crime, the criminal is capable of tampering or removing all the evidence in the crime scene."

"Theoretically it's possible." Luo's expression did not change in the slightest. "The police have lots of technology at their disposal, but there is still a finite list of tools to catch a criminal: fingerprints, footprints, DNA, fiber analysis, and a few other kinds of evidence analysis. If the criminal can eliminate any evidence associated with those tools, he or she would never be caught."

"So let's say we have this kind of case, and all the clues that the police could possibly find have been eliminated. Can the case be solved?"

"In other words, the forensic scientist didn't manage to get any information, so the only possible option is your logical deduction?" Luo laughed.

"But logical deduction is based on the investigative work carried out by forensic scientists!" Yan protested.

"It's a paradox," Luo said. "If there isn't any physical evidence, the case would depend on logical deduction, but logical deduction depends on physical evidence. The case couldn't be solved."

"I think you're right. Hey, I left the house in a hurry. Do you think I could use your bathroom?"

"Of course," Luo answered.

Yan picked up his bag and the envelope concealed underneath it. He went to the bathroom. One minute later he shouted in pain. Luo rushed over. "Is everything OK in there?"

"Oh, I'm fine. I almost slipped," Yan said and flushed the toilet. He then walked out with his bag and closed the bathroom door. "I need to take care of a few things. Let's catch up again soon."

Luo said good-bye to Yan and closed the door. Then he went back to the sofa to lie down.

Yan seemed to be convinced that the case couldn't be solved. He must be giving up by now.

One hour later, Luo's phone rang. It was Yan.

"Luo, can you check if I left an envelope in your house?" Yan said.

Luo looked around the sofa. "No, I don't think so."

"What about in the bathroom? I almost slipped, so it might have slid on the floor."

Sure enough, when Luo looked in the bathroom he found an envelope under the sink. "Yeah. Are you going to come by and pick it up?"

"No, it's late. I'll come by tomorrow," Yan said, and hung up.

Luo eyed the envelope warily, not wanting to touch it. His eyebrows knitted as he thought.

The front was printed with the words "Zhejiang Public Security Bureau." It wasn't sealed.

Luo turned and went to get his toolbox in the study. He turned off the lights in the bathroom and turned on an ultraviolet flashlight. He didn't see anything strange around the letter. He put on gloves and opened the envelope with a pair of tweezers. He stared inside the envelope for a long time, trying to figure out if Yan left it there to trick him. Once he was absolutely sure that there wasn't some way that Yan would know if Luo read the contents of the letter, he carefully took out the contents and examined them. Then he finally unfolded the papers inside.

They seemed to be official documents.

As he read the contents, Luo's hands clenched into fists. He was shaking.

He was absolutely sure that Yan left it on purpose.

Yan had managed to find his weakness.

It was clearly a trap! But could he resist it?

Chapter 61

Yang entered the room that had been temporarily designated as head-quarters for all major cases. "We reviewed the surveillance cameras in Luo's apartment building and made a spreadsheet of the times when he typically arrives home," Yang said, reporting to Zhao and Yan. "Sometimes he is home as early as 6:00 p.m. and other times it's after 9:00 p.m. Occasionally he doesn't get home until the middle of the night. On the night that Sun Hongyun was killed, he arrived in the early hours of the morning. On the night that Xu Tianding was killed, he got home at midnight. In other words, he wasn't home at the time of either of the two latest murders. But he has such an irregular schedule that I don't think we can threaten him with that information," Yang said.

"He is so meticulous," Yan said to Zhao. "He deliberately goes home late every once in a while so that these nights don't stand out."

"We also checked the surveillance of the parking lot elevator on the night of Xu's murder. Luo was alone. We did not see any sign of Zhu Huiru or Guo Yu," Yang added.

"He thought of everything!" Yan said angrily. "I bet he made those kids take the stairs."

"Is there anything else we can do?" Zhao asked, frowning.

"No. All we can do is wait," Yan replied.

"Are you sure he'll fall for this?"

"Absolutely."

"But what if he didn't see the document? Yesterday when you got the envelope back, the fingerprint detectors only found the prints of other cops," Zhao said.

"If he had wanted to read the contents of that envelope, he wouldn't have touched it with his bare hands," Yan said impatiently.

"Yesterday we had men watching him all day long and nothing happened. He just stayed at home!" Zhao said, feeling frustrated.

"I think he's waiting until we are off guard before taking any action," Yan said. "We don't need someone watching Luo's house all day; as long as we catch him, in the end it will be fine."

"No way. What if something goes wrong? I can't afford to have another death on my hands. We have already invested so much time and energy in these murders," Zhao said firmly.

"Fine. Then we wait."

"And you're sure that he will fall for this?" Zhao said doubtfully.

"He has to!" Yan cried. Everything was riding on his plan.

The major-cases hotline rang. It was one of the officers assigned to follow Luo.

From his computer display, Zhao saw that the caller was standing on a corner close to the noodle restaurant.

"The target crossed the street and turned north. He's taking something out of his bag. It's wrapped in a black plastic bag," the investigator reported. "He's checking his surroundings . . . OK, he just threw it away in a trash can."

"Get someone to pick it up, now!" Zhao ordered. Then, quietly to Yan, he said, "Maybe it's a weapon."

"I don't think so," Yan said, shaking his head. "There are a lot of ways to dispose of a murder weapon. I think Luo would be the type to burn it."

"We got the bag. What the—?" the voice on the other end said.

"What's in the bag?" Zhao asked immediately.

"It's a piece of meat."

Another investigator at the scene spoke. "Yeah, it's meat alright," he agreed.

"Meat? Is it . . . human flesh?" Zhao asked, his face draining of color.

"No," the investigator responded. "It looks like a chicken breast."

"It's definitely a chicken breast. It feels like it was just taken out of the freezer," the other investigator said.

Zhao and Yan exchanged confused looks.

Zhao and the two investigators got another call from an investigator watching from a different vantage point. "The target is walking back to the trash can! I repeat! The target is walking back to the trash can!"

Yan leaned forward and said, "Hurry! Put the plastic bag back in the trash can! Try to make it look like you didn't move it!"

Zhao realized what was going on. "Do it!" he ordered.

"Copy that! It is in the trash can," the investigators said. They went back to their stations.

Two minutes later, Zhao heard another report. "The target is walking to the trash can. He took the plastic bag . . . He's walking back in the direction of his apartment!"

"Looks like he's doing some countersurveillance," Zhao said, exhaling loudly. "Good thing we put it back in time, otherwise we might have been found out."

Yan didn't respond, his eyebrows knitted in concentration. "Was there anything special about that chicken breast, in your opinion?" he asked them.

"Only that it was frozen."

"Did either of you touch the meat itself?"

"No, just the bag."

"Can you and the other officer return to the lab? *Don't* wash your hands or touch anything. I want the lab technicians to find out if there was anything special on that bag."

"Why do you want to do that?" Zhao asked.

"Luo returned to check up on the bag. That should have been the end of it. Why did he take the bag out of the trash can and bring it home?"

"You're right; that seems a little unnecessary. He should have been happy to see that the bag was exactly where he left it."

"He knows police tactics. He'll be expecting our tricks, every last one of them," Yan said.

Chapter 62

As soon as Luo returned to his apartment, he went straight to the bathroom. He left the light off and closed the door, shining his ultraviolet flashlight on the bag and the chicken breast. Then he turned off the flashlight and sat in the dark, without making a sound.

Before he left the apartment, he had put a fine fluorescent powder on both. The chicken breast had not been touched, but the black plastic bag had someone else's prints. He was being followed.

It was definitely a trap. Yan left that document so that Luo would read it and be taken in.

He had acted casual when he left the apartment, still paying close attention to his surroundings. He didn't see anyone suspicious at all. So the police were using experienced staff members.

Yan was no longer in the police force; he didn't have the authority to order so many investigators to follow him. Zhao Tiemin must suspect him.

One thing was certain: they didn't have any evidence. Otherwise they would simply arrest him.

He was at a crossroads. He could continue to pretend he was not involved and stick to his normal routines, living as he had for the past three years. What did he care if the cops followed him around for a few weeks or even months? When they saw that his daily routine was not in the least bit suspicious, they would be forced to give up the investigation. As for Zhu Huiru and Guo Yu, they could keep living their lives too. The three of them would be safe for a very long time.

The other option was simply to step into Yan's trap. He couldn't predict what would happen, but wasn't this exactly what he had been waiting for all these years?

He knew he was facing a major dilemma.

Luo thought about it all afternoon. Finally, at dusk, he put some things in his bag and poured several days' worth of food into the dog's bowl before walking out the door.

He knew from the moment he stepped into the elevator, several pairs of eyes would be on him. There was no way to avoid it. He walked confidently to the entrance of Chongqing Noodles and went inside.

He stared at the menu.

Huiru hurried over to Luo. "Would you like something to eat?"

"Yes . . . What should I get?" He made a show of scratching his head and spoke quickly. "I just wanted to tell you that if the police tell you I've been caught, or if they seem to know about many details of the case, don't believe them. They're just trying to trick you. Be strong! As long as you don't confess, they can't arrest you. They don't have any evidence."

"Oh, uh . . . but why are you . . . ?" Huiru didn't know what to do. She had never seen Luo so intense.

"Try to act natural, Huiru; you have to remember what I taught you. As long as we don't confess, we'll all be safe. If one person confesses, then all three of us are in trouble. I'll have noodles with beef, please. Oh, and a cucumber salad. That's it."

"OK, have a seat." Huiru turned and went into the kitchen.

After he finished his meal, Luo paid and left. Then he entered another small restaurant close by.

Chapter 63

Zhao and Yan were in Dr. Chen's lab, examining a microscope slide.

"We found some particulate matter on Zhou's hand. It's a fluorescent powder."

"Fluorescent powder?" Zhao and Yan asked.

"And not just any fluorescent powder. This powder is exclusively used by forensic scientists to examine evidence. Each individual particle is so small that it cannot be seen by the naked eye. Look at this slide. It looks perfectly transparent, doesn't it? Zhou told me he only touched the outside of the bag, which means it was more or less covered in this powder. I assume Luo took the bag home and saw the investigators' fingerprints when he shone an ultraviolet light on it."

"So that means Luo knows that we're following him?" Yan asked.

"Most likely," Chen said, nodding.

Zhao let out a frustrated sigh.

"If he figures it out, he figures it out; it doesn't change much. I would be surprised if Luo *didn't* notice us. It might even be a good thing." Yan shrugged.

"A good thing?" Zhao said incredulously. "Do you think he would knowingly step into the trap?"

"Yes. Think about it: if Luo doesn't commit another crime, can we catch him with the evidence we have now?"

Zhao grunted. Of course not.

"Not only are we powerless against Luo, we can't get Zhu Huiru or Guo Yu either. Their statements are flawless. We can't touch them without any evidence."

Zhao clenched his teeth and remained silent.

"Clearly Luo knows that I'm testing him. If he wanted to continue his normal life, he would not take any action. But right now he's on the offensive, testing our surveillance," Yan continued.

"That's true," Zhao said with a nod.

"And doesn't that give the police more reason to believe that he did the crime? The police will latch on to him and refuse to let go, like a terrier," Yan said.

"Ahem," Zhao said. "Be careful what words you use to describe the police."

Yan smiled apologetically. "I mean that the police would follow him even more closely and not give up. But more to the point, why would he go on the offensive now? Why would he take on that risk? I think it's because he wants to step into the trap."

"But now that he has confirmed that the police are following him, will he?"

"Yes," Yan said confidently. "He's been waiting many years. He knows the risks. I'm just worried that he might wait until the police have let down their guard before he does anything drastic."

"We can't let anything like that happen," Zhao said sternly.

"He's extremely patient."

"So are we," Zhao said.

"You're determined. That's good."

With that, Zhao and Yan went out for a quick dinner before returning to the police station.

"Any news?" Zhao asked the investigator who had just returned to headquarters.

"The target went to a noodle restaurant and ordered. When he finished his meal, he went into another restaurant just down the street."

"Was it Chongqing Noodles?" Yan asked, frowning.

"Yes. He sat alone without speaking to anyone."

"And then he went to a different restaurant?" Yan asked.

"Yes, sir," the investigator answered.

"How long has he been there?"

"About twenty minutes, sir."

"Is he eating?"

"Yes, sir. It's strange."

Zhao looked dissatisfied.

"Get a plainclothes officer to go in and check on him," Yan suggested.

Minutes later the officer reported back. "The target left the restaurant! I spoke to the owner, who said he claimed to have forgotten his phone and borrowed the restaurant's to call a taxi. He left from a side door!"

"You guys are a bunch of—" Zhao said, but Yan intervened, tapping Zhao on the arm.

"It's fine. There's someone watching on that street; they'll see him," Yan said.

Zhao hung up in a huff and called the officer by the side door. He had been there all day but never saw Luo. Zhao quickly got the taxi company on the line. They confirmed that Luo asked to be picked up at the front gate of his apartment complex. The plainclothes officer there was focused on the restaurants, so he didn't see Luo either. The taxi driver said that Luo told him to drive east for a few minutes, and after five or six intersections he got out again. He had no idea where Luo was going.

Zhao's face blanched. Luo had somehow given them the slip.

How were they going to find him again? They could check the surveillance cameras and ask people, but that would take time.

"It's a race to see who can get to Li Fengtian first," Yan said.

Zhao cracked a smile. "We have police at the entrance to his building. He's walking right into the trap."

"Exactly. Once he gets to Mr. Li's house, the officers can arrest him. But we need good timing," Yan said.

"I know," Zhao said.

Chapter 64

The taxi stopped at Luo's destination. He stepped out and looked around.

He was in a suburb of west Hangzhou, not far from his apartment.

He had waited eight years and lived in Hangzhou for three just so he could find the answer to one question. It was shockingly close now.

So close and yet so far. Suddenly he felt nervous.

He was finally going to get his answer.

But did he want it?

He took a deep breath.

The sky darkened. Luo knew that the police must have realized that he wasn't in the restaurant anymore. He needed to act.

He made a fist, then relaxed, forcing his feet to move towards the shabby apartment complex that housed mostly migrant families.

The address was seared into his memory. He found the correct building and went straight to Apartment 302.

He stood at the door for a moment, hesitated, and took another deep breath. Finally he rang the doorbell.

"Who is it?" A woman in her thirties answered the door. A four- or five-year-old girl stood close behind her. She mimicked her mother. "Who are you looking for?"

For a split second, Luo almost thought that this was his wife and daughter.

But it was a fleeting thought. "I'm looking for Mr. Li Fengtian. Does he live here?"

"Fengtian, someone's here for you," the woman shouted.

"Who is it?" a thirty-something man said as he came to the door. He was lean and stared hard at Luo before concluding that he did not know him. "Who—?" he said in a confused tone.

"We're investigating a matter and I need to ask you a few questions," Luo said with perfect composure. He walked inside and closed the door.

Mr. and Mrs. Li were dumbfounded. He turned to his wife and said, "Go and watch television in the bedroom. This won't take long."

The woman took her daughter away, but not before giving Luo a hateful look.

Luo was disgusted by how easy it was to convince them that he was a police officer.

"What are you investigating, Officer?" the man asked.

"This is part of the fingerprinting project. Please let me see your hand," Luo said.

Li Fengtian's eyes flashed with alarm. Finally he acquiesced, slowly extending his right hand.

Luo took the man's hand. Within seconds, his face turned white and he was frozen to the spot. He stared intently at Li's hand without loosening his grip, finally asking the question he had been waiting to ask. "Eight years ago, a mother and child living in Apartment 201, Unit 1, Building 2, Heavenly Apartments, 186 Pingkang Road, Haishu District, Ningbo, went missing. Where are they now?"

A look of fear spread across Li Fengtian's face.

"Where are they?" Luo kept a tight grip on Li's hand and looked sharply at him. His stillness was terrifying.

"What are you talking about? I don't understand," Li said, pulling his hand free and stepping back.

Luo repeated his question, this time with less power in his voice. "Eight years ago, a mother and child living in Apartment 201, Unit 1, Building 2, Heavenly Apartments, 186 Pingkang Road, Haishu District, Ningbo, went missing. Where are they now?"

"I don't know what you're talking about. Eight years ago? Ningbo? I've lived in Jiangsu province for all that time," Li protested, afraid to look Luo in the eyes. Li took another step back.

"Tell me. Where are they?" Luo said, approaching Li.

"What are you talking about? What are you doing here?"

"You know perfectly well. Where are they?" Luo continued to approach slowly. In one swift movement, he grabbed Li's neck.

"What are you doing?!" Li said, struggling to loosen Luo's grip.

Mrs. Li ran into the living room. "What are you doing? Stop it!" she screamed. "Keke, go back to Mommy and Daddy's room." She closed the door between the living room and her bedroom and turned back to Luo. "You're scaring my daughter! What do you want? Police aren't allowed to rough up people like that!"

"I never said I was a police officer," Luo said disdainfully.

"Then who the hell are you?" Mrs. Li snapped.

"I'm the man who used to live in that apartment," Luo answered, never taking his eyes off Li.

"What is this?" Li shouted. "You're out of your mind!"

Mrs. Li pulled Luo off of her husband and pushed him towards the door. "Get out of my house, you madman! Now!"

Luo pushed her away and glared at Li. "I'm going to ask you one last time. Where are they?"

Mrs. Li grabbed Luo's hair to drag him away. In a fit of rage, Luo kicked Mrs. Li to the ground, grabbed a chair, and smashed it into pieces on the floor. He cut his hand, but he didn't notice the blood. "Where are they?" his voice boomed.

Just at that moment, someone knocked loudly at the door. "Open the door! This is the police!"

Li and his wife each gave Luo a few more punches before Mrs. Li opened the door. Eight or nine plainclothes officers stood outside.

The leader of the squad flashed his badge at Mrs. Li. "We're with the Hangzhou Police. What's going on here?"

Mrs. Li was shocked. She had no idea how so many of them got to her apartment in such a short time, but she didn't dwell on it. "Officer, this deranged man attacked us. Arrest him!"

The officers all streamed into the room and restrained the now-bloody Luo, while the other officers confiscated his bag. The leader of the squad frowned and handed the bag to another officer so he could call his superiors. "Yes, sir. He doesn't seem to have any weapons. Copy that. We will wait at Mr. Li's apartment."

He hung up and turned back towards Luo and the Lis. "Wait here, please." The officer heard the child crying and said to Mrs. Li, "You can go to your child."

After Mrs. Li left the room, the plainclothes officers stood next to the door, silent.

"What—what happens now?" Li said, looking panicked.

"We are waiting for my superior," the officer said brusquely. He turned to stare at the wall.

Luo stood still, staring into empty space, as if time had lost all meaning.

It was twenty minutes before the doorbell rang.

A grim-faced Captain Zhao entered the apartment. First he looked at Li Fengtian, and then he turned and appraised Luo.

Luo looked right back at Zhao with a neutral expression on his face.

Zhao nodded hello and said, "Luo Wen. Why don't you come with me to the bureau?"

"OK," Luo said, without the slightest trace of panic in his voice.

"Take him away," Zhao said abruptly.

An officer handcuffed him on the spot.

"What's the meaning of this?" Luo asked in a challenging tone.

"You know what this is about," Zhao said. He gave Luo a cold look.

"I think there has been some mistake."

"We'll work that out at the bureau."

The arresting officer escorted Luo to the car.

Zhao pointed to Li. "Take him away too."

"But why do you want to arrest me? You interviewed me a few days ago!" he protested.

The officer handcuffed Li.

Mrs. Li rushed into the room just as her husband was being handcuffed. She pulled Zhao's arm and shouted, "What are you doing now?"

Zhao pushed her firmly away and quickly exited the apartment, followed by the crowd of policemen. Both wife and child were crying, refusing to let go. Li had to be pulled away.

Luo was already on the street when he heard the mother and child shouting and crying. He stopped and turned his head towards the sound, a tiny smile on his lips.

PART 9

REACHING THE SAME END BY DIFFERENT MEANS

Chapter 65

Luo had been at the Criminal Investigation Division of the Zhejiang Public Security Bureau for two days.

Yan walked into Zhao's office early in the morning and found Zhao in his chair, smoking a cigarette. "Has he confessed?" Yan asked.

Zhao stubbed out his cigarette and grunted. "I haven't let him sleep for the past two days. He looks exhausted—but he keeps repeating that he's innocent."

Yan had the vague feeling that something wasn't right. "Have you officially arrested him?"

"No, I don't have any evidence. How do you expect me to get an arrest warrant?"

"So right now, you're . . ."

"I've summoned him here to help with the investigation."

"You can only restrict his freedom for a maximum of twenty-four hours. You've kept him for at least thirty hours now . . . That's against bureau policy, isn't it?"

"I know the policies better than you do, Yan," Zhao said in an irritated tone.

"You can't just extort confessions like this!" Yan said angrily.

He stood to leave.

"Wait, where are you going?" Zhao said, standing up.

"Back to the university. I don't want to be involved any longer. Good luck."

"Yan, hey, wait!" Zhao ran to the door and pulled his arm. "Who said that I am extorting a confession from Luo?"

"You've already violated bureau policy by keeping him for more than thirty hours and not even letting him sleep. Isn't that—"

"I'll admit, in the past, a lot of bureaus bent the rules in order to get confessions," Zhao said, interrupting him. "But we don't do that anymore, at least not in Hangzhou. I believe that extorting confessions is morally wrong. Besides, in a case as important as this one, I wouldn't dare try a tactic like that—it could get me in a load of trouble. If Luo retracts his statement or he complains to a former colleague from the Ningbo PSB, I could be charged."

"So what are you doing?" Yan said, unconvinced.

"Relax." Zhao patted Yan's shoulder and gave him an easy smile. "Last night, when we had almost reached the twenty-four-hour limit, I got one of my men to take Luo out to the entrance gate of the bureau. We let him get out of the car, then gave him a new summons to bring him back in."

"So that's how you're handling this?" Yan was dumbstruck.

"That's right," Zhao said proudly. "The law has never determined exactly how many summons in a row constitutes a consecutive summons. To be honest, I wouldn't use this if I didn't have to, but I can't think of any other way to crack Luo Wen."

Yan gaped at Zhao. "You . . . you're . . . you're just going to take him in and out of the bureau every day? You could detain him indefinitely!"

"Well, in theory, yes," Zhao said uncomfortably. "But he can't keep this up forever, can he? He has to confess."

Yan looked down and thought for a moment. Then he looked at Zhao. "Can I interrogate him?"

"Of course," Zhao answered, without hesitation. "This is a local-level police station; I'm the boss of everyone here. I've spoken to my subordinates and told them you're a criminal investigation expert, and anyway, the older officers know you. As long as nobody tells the Public Security Bureau, we'll be fine."

"Thanks," Yan said, nodding gratefully.

"No, I should be thanking you. If you weren't here, I wouldn't even have a primary suspect. How confident are you that you'll get him to talk?"

"I don't know, but I have to try. I just never expected him to go to Li's apartment completely unarmed," Yan said.

"The good news is that Mr. Li has already admitted to his crimes," Zhao said, waving a stack of papers. "We're just investigating the details now."

Yan took the papers from Zhao and scanned them briefly. He then handed them back to Zhao and turned to the door, sighing quietly at the difficult job ahead.

Chapter 66

The moment Yan walked into the interview room he saw Luo's weary face.

Luo was in the prime of his health—he wasn't even fifty yet. But two straight days of interrogation was testing his limits.

A coffee and a box of cigarettes were in front of him. Luo had already gulped down countless cups of coffee, but he hadn't touched the cigarettes. That didn't surprise Yan. There was also another officer in the room taking notes.

At the sight of Yan, Luo tried to muster up some energy, sitting up straight and smiling serenely. "The police have got it all wrong. I've repeated myself many times already: this has nothing to do with me."

Yan sat down slowly, without taking his eyes off Luo. He finally said softly, "So you're not admitting to it?"

"I don't know what I'm supposed to be admitting to," Luo said, taking a deep breath and shaking his head slowly.

"Well, I do: you committed five murders and abetted a sixth."

"Five murders? Abetted a sixth?" Luo said. "I didn't realize that a math professor could make so many counting mistakes."

Yan narrowed his eyes. "I know you didn't kill Xu Tianding, but if it weren't for your involvement, the police would have found the killers within a few days."

Luo shook his head, as if everything Yan said was completely inconceivable.

"I have to hand it to you: you are a very talented criminal," Yan said.

"Like I said before, none of those murders have anything to do with me," Luo said with a frustrated sigh. "Do you have any proof? And besides, if I committed those murders, don't you think I could finish the job without leaving any clues? I used to work in criminal investigations. Hypothetically I would make it impossible to recover the victim's body."

"Yes, I know that you could eliminate every last hair follicle and fingerprint at the crime scene. But you wanted to accomplish something else," Yan said.

Luo rubbed his nose.

"As soon as I suspected you, I was plagued by questions. Why did you leave a Liqun cigarette in the victims' mouths when you didn't even smoke? I went to Ningbo to learn more about your past. That's when I finally understood why you left those clues. You *wanted* the police to discover them."

Yan paused to take a sip of water. "It's easiest to explain in chronological order. You rejected a more effective weapon like a knife in favor of a jump rope. The jump rope had two important advantages. First, it had two handles, which made it easier for you to leave fingerprints and easier for the police to lift them. Second, it made it easier to show that the killer was left-handed. A knife would not make Li Fengtian's left-handedness so obvious."

Luo couldn't help but smile. "Why would I make things so complicated for myself? If I failed, wouldn't that make it easier for the police to catch me?"

"You wouldn't fail. You're Luo Wen, the brilliant forensic scientist," Yan said, looking Luo directly in his eyes.

Luo shook his head before downing the rest of his coffee.

"After you killed your victim, you put a Liqun cigarette in his mouth. The killer smoked Liqun cigarettes."

"I don't smoke," Luo said bluntly.

"Yes, but you wanted the police to think the killer did."

"And why would I do that?" Luo asked.

Yan didn't answer. "One of your victims was from Shandong province. You wrote the word 'local' next to his body but made it look like his work. You wanted the police to think the killer was a Hangzhou local. Finally, you left a piece of white paper with the provocative phrase 'Come and get me.' In a city as big as Hangzhou, murders happen every single day."

"I know that Hangzhou is a big city," Luo said calmly.

"The district PSB would pay attention to the case and assign someone to investigate it, but one or two officers was not enough for you," Yan continued. "You needed a massive response, and you could only achieve that by provoking the police into putting a lot of resources into the case. The sign was effective: the media loved it. The police made the case a high priority."

"So let me get this straight: in your opinion, I committed the crimes, but I wanted to get caught as soon as possible?"

"Exactly," Yan said, nodding.

"Then you don't need to interrogate me, just put me in a mental hospital!" Luo said with a laugh.

"Your motive was for the police to find and catch a different killer."

Luo sneered but fell silent.

"Eight years ago, you came back from a business trip. When you opened the door you found it empty. No wife, no daughter, no dog. The floor had been wiped clean. Something very wrong had happened."

Luo looked at Yan and clenched his teeth. It still felt like yesterday.

The fear had started at the bottom of his stomach and spread throughout his body. For eight years, the same nightmare woke him in the night. All the furniture was carefully arranged and the room was spotless.

"You calmly stood in the threshold and called your office to ask one of your best junior officers to bring a forensic toolkit to your house. Then you investigated every last inch of that apartment. You both went over every room several times, working through the night. You wrote a case file reporting a lack of evidence at the site. Someone had clearly put a lot of effort into making the floors spotless, because there were no footprints. Looking at the way the rag was pushed, you determined that the person must have been left-handed. But your wife was right-handed," Yan said.

Luo was still.

"You also did blood-analysis tests, but you didn't find anything. In the bathroom, underneath the sink, you found a small pile of ash. The lab test results indicated that it was cigarette ash. You bought and tested every cigarette brand at the supermarket and finally determined that it came from a Liqun cigarette. Finally, after looking all over the house, you found one perfect print. It wasn't yours or your wife's—it belonged to someone you didn't know. All you had was the one fingerprint. I'm sure you remember all of this."

"Yes, I remember," Luo said.

"Thanks to your rank at the Ningbo PSB, your case was made a top priority. Someone discovered that a young garbage collector went missing soon after your family did. You went to the room that he rented in Ningbo and got more fingerprints, which matched the one you found in your house. You also confirmed that the garbage collector was left-handed and smoked Liqun cigarettes. Liqun is a mid-market brand, but people working in low-income jobs usually prefer cheap cigarettes. The garbage collector became the primary suspect."

Yan continued without waiting for a response from Luo. "His land-lord only remembered that he was about five feet six inches tall, rather slim, and came from west Hangzhou. Unfortunately he didn't even have a number for his tenant. Otherwise you could have gotten his identification information very quickly. A lot of deaths would have been avoided."

Luo remained silent.

"That's when you asked the bureau to contact the police in Hangzhou to help track him down," Yan continued. "But there weren't enough clues: a man in his twenties living in west Hangzhou with aver-age height and body type. The fact that he smoked Liqun cigarettes and was left-handed was not enough to narrow down the search. You had a perfect set of fingerprints and nothing else to work with. And since there was no sign of forced entry or blood, the case was labeled a missing-person case instead of a homicide."

Luo clenched his teeth harder.

"Your objective wasn't to kill criminals, but to find the one suspect that mattered to you."

When Luo didn't react, Yan lost it. "I worked in the police force for most of my life. I've come across all kinds of motives. Sometimes it's an accident. Some do it for money or revenge; some are blinded by love or jealousy. Some are trying to frame others. But I never would have dreamed of someone killing multiple innocent people just to mobilize the police!"

"You didn't know the truth about what happened to your family, and you knew very little about the man who was inside your apartment that day," Yan continued. "You wanted to do everything in your power to find him. So you moved to west Hangzhou to commit murders. Apart from leaving a few strange clues, you left your crime scenes totally clean. You knew that the police would be compelled to collect a huge amount of fingerprints to solve the murders. Unfortunately the garbage collector wasn't found after the first murder, or the second. The scope of the search was too big, and the police were only checking residents close to the crime. So you kept changing the location in the hopes that the police would gradually collect fingerprints of people all over west Hangzhou."

Luo didn't even bother looking at Yan.

Yan continued. "You knew that after a number of years, the garbage collector's weight could change drastically, so you made sure to remove any footprints from your crime scenes. Otherwise the police might narrow down the investigation to people of a certain height and weight and overlook the person you were after. After the fourth murder, you started to get nervous. You wanted to give the police another clue, so when you killed your fifth victim, Sun Hongyun, you dragged him all the way to the concrete just so you could write the word 'local' next to him. You wanted the police to know that the person you were looking for was from Hangzhou. But you didn't want to leave footprints, so you wore your victim's shoes and made it look like he struggled."

Yan took a deep breath. "Actually I still saw a trace of goodness in your heart. You didn't want to hurt others. You used to say that committing a crime was shameful, but you were desperate to know who broke into your apartment. You told yourself it would be better if you killed people who had committed crimes before. So you logged on to the internal database and identified ex-convicts living in west Hangzhou. I checked in Ningbo: you resigned three years ago, but your account was never deactivated."

"I was just interested in keeping up to date with the latest developments at the Public Security Bureau. That's not a crime, is it? You can deactivate my account at any time," Luo said calmly.

"You're still not admitting to what you've done?" Yan asked with a frown.

"I think your story is fascinating, but no part of it is true," Luo said with a smile.

Someone knocked and the officer went to open the door.

It was Zhao. His gaze rested on Luo for a few seconds before he finally spoke to Yan. "Are you finished?"

"He's admitted to almost everything," Yan said loudly.

Zhao smiled and stepped aside so that two young people could get a closer look. It was Huiru and Guo Yu. Both were surprised to see Luo but covered up their shocked expressions very quickly.

"Professor Yan, your story is certainly interesting, but do you have any evidence to back it up?" Luo said quickly.

"Alright, you can have him for a little longer," Zhao said through his teeth. He closed the door, taking Huiru and Guo Yu with him.

"You saw Zhu Huiru and Guo Yu, didn't you? Now that they've seen you here, they're going to have a hard time keeping it together. Zhao will get the truth out of them soon enough. It doesn't matter if you won't confess to the first five murders. Their confession is tantamount to yours."

"Oh really?" Luo said, with a calm expression. "I know Ms. Zhu; she's from the noodle restaurant I like to eat at. But who is that young man? I've seen him a few times, but I don't know his name. What do those two have to do with me?"

"They killed Xu Tianding. You helped them remove evidence from the crime scene. You also taught them how to handle interrogations."

"Oh? Am I supposed to be connected to that case too?" Luo said contemptuously.

"Yes. We found the same fingerprints at the scene of the crime," Yan retorted.

"Are they my fingerprints?"

"Do you want me to go over what happened that night? I shouldn't have to—you and I both know," Yan said.

Luo pursed his lips. "Hmm. Are you sure I know those two young people? Why would I go out of my way to help strangers cover up a serious crime?"

"I asked myself that same question: Why would you take on such an enormous risk for two people you had just met? At first I thought you were in love with Ms. Zhu—"

Luo scoffed.

"But that wasn't your style. I investigated the area by the canal many times. It was impossible to see the outdoor gym from the sidewalk. Otherwise someone would have noticed you. According to my timeline, you must have come across Ms. Zhu and Mr. Guo the moment after the crime was committed. The timing seemed too perfect to be a coincidence. On that night, I think *you* had planned to kill Xu Tianding. Otherwise why would you have carried the mold of Li Fengtian's fingerprints in your bag? I don't think you would be so brazen as to carry your special toolkit on your person at all times."

Luo said nothing.

"You wanted to kill Mr. Xu for two reasons: first, because he was a terror to the community, and second, because after the first four murders, the police worked too slowly for your liking," Yan said. "You wanted this one to be more dramatic so you would get more resources allocated to finding the garbage collector. Sun Hongyun, your fifth victim, was killed a few days before. If you killed both Mr. Sun and Mr. Xu within the span of a week, the shock would resonate throughout the Zhejiang PSB. They would use as many resources as possible to collect fingerprints. Crucially you planned to attack Mr. Xu in a different area, so the scope of the project would cover all of west Hangzhou. But Ms. Zhu and Mr. Guo accidentally killed Mr. Xu before you could get to him. You thought the best plan was to help them cover it up. You thought that you could save their lives and carry out your own plan simultaneously. Unfortunately the crime scene was a total mess.

So you left Li Fengtian's fingerprints and didn't use any of your other signature clues."

"Your story is really interesting, but it still has nothing to do with me," Luo said.

"I never imagined that an idealist like you could kill five people and not show the slightest bit of remorse!"

"The law cares about the evidence, not elaborate stories. I'm sure I could modify your script to fit anyone in Hangzhou," Luo said.

"Why did you return to your apartment in the middle of the night on September 8?" Yan said vehemently.

"I often come home late," Luo answered.

"Where did you go on September 8, and can anyone corroborate your story?"

"Let me think. Usually I just go for walks at night," Luo said. "I go by myself; nobody can corroborate my story. I live by myself and sometimes I get bored stiff, so I go out to relax."

"Why did you leave and then return to your apartment at 2:00 a.m. on September 9?"

"Let me think. Oh, I know, I was very hungry and I didn't have anything to eat, so I went out. But everything was closed, so I went back home."

"Then why did you leave again sometime around 3:00 a.m. on the same day?"

"I was so hungry I couldn't stand it. I tried to look for a snack shop or something."

"You didn't leave your apartment to scatter tens of thousands of yuan onto the crime scene?"

"No, of course not," Luo said with a laugh. "I would have to go to the bank to take out that much cash. The police can check my withdrawal records at the bank."

"We found a lot of cash in your bedroom when we searched your apartment. You wouldn't need to go to the bank," Yan said coldly.

"So how am I supposed to prove my innocence then?" Luo asked with a sigh.

"Where did you have breakfast?" Yan asked tersely.

"I couldn't find anything open in the morning, so I went for a hike. I just wanted to kill time. After my hike I drove to the closest KFC. Maybe that KFC has a surveillance camera." Luo said.

"Nobody saw you hiking?"

"I saw some people but I didn't know them. I don't know if they'll still remember me," Luo said.

"In other words, the police have no way of checking if you're telling the truth."

"To put it another way, I have no way of proving that I'm innocent."

"Why did you go to Li Fengtian's apartment?" Yan asked.

"If there's one thing we can agree on, it's that I want to know who came into my apartment eight years ago. A few days ago you came to visit me and left a letter in the bathroom. I accidentally read the contents of that letter—it said the police had compared fingerprints and found the primary suspect for the case involving my family. But the suspect was released because there wasn't enough evidence to convict him. When I saw the fingerprint—by accident, mind you—I could tell it was the same one that I found eight years ago, because that fingerprint has left a very deep impression on me. I knew that Li Fengtian was the person I had been looking for over the past eight years."

"But why didn't you tell me? Why did you go straight to his house?"

"I'm sorry I didn't contact you, but I had to see the person for myself. The case file said that the police compared the fingerprints, and they matched the fingerprints of the serial killer. But he had plenty of alibis for each murder. So after you questioned him, you let him go. I just looked up Li's address and went to his apartment," Luo explained.

"Right. A few days ago you were walking on the street, and you threw away a chicken breast in a trash can. Then you picked it back up. Why?"

"I had a feeling that someone was following me. It's just a little countersurveillance. I already told the other officer who was questioning me earlier. I didn't know that you were following me because you suspected I was the killer," Luo said.

"All of your answers are perfectly airtight!" Yan said, letting out a sigh of frustration.

"I'm just telling the truth."

Yan fixed his gaze on Luo. "You've been searching for the truth about what happened to your family. Have you found it yet?"

Chapter 67

Luo's eyes flickered. He leaned forward, speaking deliberately and locking eyes with Yan's. "Tell me what happened."

Yan spoke slowly. "Li Fengtian grew up in a village close to Hangzhou. His wife was from Jiangsu, so he lived there for many years. He had a business selling construction materials. When farmland owned by Li's family was taken by the government, they compensated the family by giving them six houses in another area. So Li decided to move back to Zhejiang province. He moved his construction business with him. But do you know why he spent so many years in Jiangsu?"

Luo didn't answer. He simply watched Yan.

Yan couldn't bear to meet his gaze. "Eight years ago, Li Fengtian lost a lot of money gambling. He moved to Ningbo to avoid paying his debts. He didn't have a job or the ambition to get one. He decided to see if he could make a quick buck robbing people if he dressed up as a garbage collector. On his third night in Ningbo, he stopped in front of Heavenly Apartments, 186 Pingkang Road."

Yan hesitated, but he felt like Luo had a right to know and pushed himself to continue. "He saw that one of the windows next to the balcony of Apartment 201 was open. It was winter, and there weren't many people on the street at night. Li sat and waited until everyone turned their lights off and climbed up to the second story along the water pipe, pushed the window open, and jumped into the room."

The corners of Luo's mouth twitched. He always knew that his worst fear might eventually be confirmed, but hearing the truth aloud was almost too much. He had a sudden desire to cover his ears.

"The balcony was connected to the master bedroom. Li, a burglary novice, assumed that the occupants of the house would all be asleep. But on that particular night, the little girl had wet the bed, and her mother got up to clean the mess. She was just going back to bed when Li slipped in the room. Their eyes locked and Li panicked. His first thought was to grab the mother and overpower her."

Luo's mind went blank. The world suddenly became hollow. He saw Yan's lips moving, but the words felt like they were coming from another world.

"He throttled her to death."

Luo felt like he had been bludgeoned in the head. The room was humming loudly. Over the years, he told himself not to lose hope. He banished the thought of her death because it was just too awful to think about. Now he finally knew the truth. It hurt much more than he ever dreamed it would.

His wife was dead.

He throttled her to death. The words clanged again and again, like a terrible bell.   .

He gazed blankly at the two faces in the interview room, now totally unfamiliar to him.

Yan watched Luo for a long time. Finally he continued. "The family owned a dog, and he barked loudly as his mistress struggled against the intruder. That woke up the daughter, who came to the master bedroom. The scene before her was so terrifying that she couldn't speak or cry. She stood perfectly still. Once Li realized that he had killed the woman, he knew that the situation was out of control. He couldn't think of any other way out. He ruthlessly strangled the puppy. The girl . . . was killed in the same fashion."

Luo slipped out of his chair and fell to the bare floor.

The other officer hurried to help him back into the chair. Luo stayed put.

Opening his mouth, Luo tried to speak, but no sound came out.

"You can probably guess how it ends," Yan said, holding his head in his hands. "The killer put the mother in one bag and the dog and child in another. He carefully wiped down everything he touched. The only two things he missed were a bit of ash from a cigarette that he nervously smoked in the bathroom, and a single fingerprint that he forgot to wipe clean. He fled to Jiangsu province and only came back to Hangzhou when he thought the whole thing had blown over."

Luo sat woodenly on the floor, not making a sound for five minutes. Then suddenly he spoke. "Where are my wife and daughter?" His voice was flat.

"According to Li's statement, he put the bags in the back of a tricycle built to haul garbage. He then pedaled to an artificial lake about two hundred yards away from your apartment. He filled the bags with rocks and then tossed them in the lake."

Suddenly Luo screamed twice as if in extreme pain. He opened his mouth a third time but no sound came out. Tears started streaming down his face.

Neither the officer nor Yan said anything.

When his tears finally dried, Luo spoke in a shaky voice. "That lake—that lake has already been filled. An apartment building was built on top of it. I'll never . . . never see them again."

It was hard enough knowing that he would never see them alive again. Now he had to cope with the reality that he would never even give them a proper burial.

Yan covered his eyes with his hand.

Almost half an hour later, Luo was still staring at the wall with a stony expression.

Yan sighed lightly. He tried to be delicate with Luo. "Now that you know the truth, can you give me the answers I'm looking for?"

Luo slowly turned to look at Yan. "What sentence is Li Fengtian going to get?"

"He'll get the death penalty."

"Good. That's good," Luo said, nodding slowly.

"So do you have anything to say?" Yan asked.

Luo let out a long exhale and looked back at Yan. "I'm not involved in this case in any way."

"Luo!" Yan shouted. "Why won't you confess?"

"You can arrest me right now, if you have sufficient evidence." Luo's voice was hard.

"All this time I thought you had principles! But you have none whatsoever!"

"I'm very tired. I would like to go home and rest," Luo said.

Yan stood up and left without a word.

Chapter 68

"You want to let Luo go home? Did I hear you correctly?" Zhao shook his head emphatically. "No. Absolutely not. Zhu Huiru and Guo Yu aren't giving in either. Now would be the worst time to let him go."

"They're not confessing?" Yan was surprised.

"We interviewed them separately and even let them see Luo in custody. But they say the same thing every time. I can't just walk them to the main entrance and then summon them back every twenty-four hours, can I?"

Yan thought for a minute. "Luo taught them exactly what to say. It would be hard to get them to slip up in the short term, but if we kept at it long enough, I'm sure they would confess eventually. Luo is another story; there's no way we would get it out of him unless he wants to cooperate. How about we let him go home and rest?"

"You want me to be nice to him because he's your friend!" Zhao said, looking betrayed.

"Well, yes, but I just told him the truth about his wife and daughter. I think if we keep him here for much longer, he would really suffer."

Zhao looked Yan up and down. Finally he nodded reluctantly. "If Ms. Zhu and Mr. Guo haven't confessed by tomorrow, I'm going to bring Luo back in. And I'm going to have my men follow him."

"Thank you."

Zhao looked up impatiently. "I'm not doing it as a favor to you, and I'm not going easy on that criminal. I'm sticking to the law," he said, stretching back.

Ten minutes later, Yan saw Luo to the main entrance.

"Thanks," Luo said with a nod.

"You killed so many people just to bring one person to justice. I understand it, but at the same time I can't accept it," Yan said.

Luo looked at the ground before turning to leave. After a few steps, he turned back to Yan. "You were right about everything—except one thing."

"What's that?" Yan said, frowning.

"I still have principles. When Li Fengtian is formally sentenced I'll voluntarily come back here and tell you everything."

Yan looked at Luo for a long time. He smiled and nodded. Luo needed to be sure that Li Fengtian was brought to justice. He needed to do this for his wife and daughter.

"I'd like to ask you something, Professor," Luo said, with the tiniest hint of a smile. "How did you know it was me?"

"I knew that you were the answer, and then I worked backward from there," Yan said honestly.

"Really?"

"It was just like a quintic equation. Not even the world's most brilliant logician could find the answer with the regular methods. I knew that the killer left all the clues on purpose and that the victims were killed in order to mobilize the police to find one particular person. Now where would I find someone with such a unique motive? In this situation, mathematics recommends using substitution. So I came up with a possible solution, and calculated all the details to see if they would fit. I was lucky enough to guess correctly on the first try. Do you remember when we met a few weeks ago?"

"Did I give something away?" Luo asked.

"You didn't, but your car did."

"My car?"

"You bought your own apartment in an upmarket area, which made sense. You can certainly afford it. But you completely neglected furnishing it."

"But why does that matter? I've never cared about any of that."

"Exactly. Your house was the way I expected it to be—you were still the same person who didn't care what others thought. But then you told me that you bought a fancy car and took the bus to work. You claimed you liked having a car to cruise around. That highlighted two contradictions. First, not decorating your house and buying a luxury car are polar-opposite actions. Second, you told me you didn't care whether others saw you driving it, because you just wanted to enjoy it for yourself. The only reason you bought it was to commit crimes. Most people don't think the driver of a luxury car would be suspicious. The pervert who saw you on the night you killed Sun Hongyun wasn't caught by the police for a long time, and that was partially because he drove a BMW. After I knew it was you, I put all the details into the equation, and the truth gradually became clear."

"Well, that goes to show that logic is better than physical evidence," Luo said with a sigh.

"But if you never helped Ms. Zhu and Mr. Guo, I wouldn't have met you or suspected you either. You probably regret helping them now," Yan said, looking at Luo.

"Five years ago, you helped a young person destroy evidence that proved he killed his own father. Eventually the truth came out. Do you regret helping that boy?" Luo asked.

Luo turned to leave as Yan stood there, shocked.

Two brilliant men with totally different personalities had made the same decision when they came across an innocent on the wrong side of the justice system.

Chapter 69

Luo watched the scenery glide past the window as the taxi drove him home. It felt like he was reliving the past eight years all over again.

From the moment his wife and daughter went missing, he spent every waking minute looking for them or thinking of them, holding on to the hope that they were still alive.

Now his tiny flame of hope had been extinguished.

For eight years, he had gone back and forth between Hangzhou and Ningbo, begging the Hangzhou PSB, the Ningbo PSB, and the Zhejiang PSB to investigate the case.

But without the bodies or any traces of blood, the case could not be classified as a homicide. It was still treated as a missing-person case— not even Luo's special connections could change that. The head of the Ningbo PSB wanted to help and ordered a major investigation, but nothing was found. In Hangzhou, the head of the Zhejiang PSB called for his officers to find the culprit, but there simply weren't enough clues. The Hangzhou PSB couldn't collect the fingerprints of everyone in west Hangzhou for a missing-person case.

For five years, he didn't receive any new information about his wife and daughter.

Three years ago he had handed in his resignation, gravely resorting to his last hope for finding the man.

He committed serious, shocking crimes to mobilize the Hangzhou police to help him find the garbage collector, the man he would later learn was named Li Fengtian. Every crime was committed with the express purpose of transferring the information he knew about that man to the crime scene so the police would pick it up.

Even though he was successful, he regretted all the things he did to get his answer.

The taxi slowed to a stop at the end of a street, not far from Chongqing Noodles. "What's going on up there? The road is blocked. I need to turn around," the driver said.

"Mmm," Luo said absentmindedly.

The driver looked carefully at Luo. This was one of his strangest customers.

The taxi driver made a U-turn in the middle of the street.

Suddenly Luo's attention returned to the present. He saw people all over the sidewalk and police tape cordoning off some of the restaurants. Uniformed offices were pointing and shouting. Luo's favorite noodle restaurant seemed to be in the center of the mess.

Luo couldn't believe his eyes. He asked the driver to let him out and stepped into the crowd, listening to what people around him were saying.

"The guy who owns the noodle restaurant says that he killed Little Gangster."

"Yeah, I heard that the police brought his sister and some other guy into the station to investigate a case. Nobody expected that cook to run out and take Little Gangster's friend hostage—he rushed at him with a knife and then dragged him into the restaurant."

"So wait, is he lame or not?"

"He's got a lame leg, but he acted so unexpectedly that the other guy was afraid to fight back."

"What does he want?"

"He says he's the one who killed Little Gangster and his sister has nothing to do with it. He wants the police to let her go and arrest him."

"Did he do it?"

"Dunno. If he did, then why did the police arrest his sister? But if he didn't kill anyone, that tactic is useless. The police are going to find the person who's really responsible, aren't they?"

Luo's heart sank. *Zhu Fulai, what are you trying to do? Your sister and Guo Yu were just summoned to the station. They knew not to confess. You've turned everything into such a mess!*

Luo pushed through the crowd until he finally reached the police tape. The officers weren't letting anyone past.

Fulai held a knife to Zhang Bing's throat. He stood behind the cash register at the very back of the restaurant. Two officers were trying to reason with him.

The crowd outside made way for police cars.

Captain Zhao and Professor Yan stepped out of the first car, and Zhu Huiru and Guo Yu came out of the second. Neither of them wore handcuffs, immediately proving that they were still free. More police stepped out of the last two cars, including one carrying a long, thin black box. Luo recognized it as the case of a sniper rifle.

"What are you doing, Fulai?" Huiru shouted to her brother. She wanted to run towards him, but Captain Zhao held her back.

Yan had a few words with Zhao, and Zhao said something to his subordinates. Finally Yan walked towards the entrance of the noodle restaurant. He asked the police officer on site to step away so he could have a chat with Zhu Fulai.

Zhao stood near the car, looking calm. He watched the sniper place a mat and a shooting rest on the hood of the police car.

Seeing the sniper in action, many onlookers took photos with their phones.

Zhao got a few of the police officers to move the police tape so the sniper would have more room. He turned to speak to Huiru. "Xu Tianding wasn't killed by your brother; there was no evidence that the killer had a lame leg. Now that you see him in such a desperate position, don't you think it's time to confess?"

"I . . ." Huiru swallowed and resolutely shook her head. "You have made some mistake."

"Is that so?" Zhao glanced at the sniper, his face showing no trace of compassion. "In a situation like this, if the police accidentally shoot your brother, I'm afraid that—"

Suddenly he was interrupted by a loud voice. "I killed Little Gangster! My sister has nothing to do with this! A life for a life is fair, isn't it?"

Luo's heart tightened. Even though Fulai was slow-witted, he should have understood that the police might free his sister but ultimately would still get to the bottom of the investigation. His tactic of taking a hostage served no purpose whatsoever.

If he wasn't going to kill the hostage, what was he doing?

He was going to commit suicide!

Fulai reckoned that if he claimed to have killed Little Gangster and then killed himself, the police would only have his word to go on. He could protect his sister and get the police to release her.

If he had just waited, his sister would have been perfectly safe.

Luo's heart filled with regret.

Fulai's love for his sister was the same as Luo's love for his wife and daughter: unconditional.

"Stop!" Two voices shouted in unison. Both Yan and Luo were trying to intervene.

"I killed him!" Luo added.

Everyone looked at Luo. Fulai was holding his knife at his own throat, but he moved it back to Zhang Bing's throat.

A smile crept across Zhao's face. Luo had finally confessed.

Yan looked at Luo, who was battling conflicting emotions.

Luo walked towards the restaurant. An officer tried to stop him. "Let him through," Zhao ordered.

Luo nodded at Zhao and walked straight to the entrance to the noodle restaurant. He took one look at Yan and then entered the restaurant.

Luo's eyes shifted from Zhu Fulai, now trembling uncontrollably, to Zhang Bing, who had lost all color in his face and already had a few cuts on his neck from the knife. He swiveled to look outside, where Zhu Huiru was crying. "Did you really think your little sister killed Xu Tianding? Did you think you could get her out of trouble by taking her place in prison?" Luo said, loud enough so everyone could hear. "I killed him, got it? Your hostage tactic really screwed it all up!"

Yan, Zhao, Guo Yu, Huiru, Fulai, and even Zhang Bing stared at him in surprise.

"Why did I kill him, you ask? Because he was cruel to dogs. You got a threatening letter, right, Zhang Bing? You tortured that dog too. You almost killed him, dragging him back and forth like that. Luckily I adopted him and took care of him, but from that moment I decided that I would not have mercy on you two."

Yan watched Luo's performance in awe. Was he . . . ?

"You are very lucky, Zhang Bing. I was ready to kill you, but I didn't have the chance because the police caught me. Before I killed Xu, I killed five other people. I am the serial killer that the police have been searching for! The evidence all points to me. In fact, the evidence is in my car right now: two jump ropes, an electric baton, the paring knife, and special gloves that I made with fingerprints molded on them. It's taped to the inside of the right front wheel. I used a printer in my office to make the 'Come and get me' signs. The printer is in a meeting room."

The officers looked at each other. They hadn't checked the wheels. Once they had that evidence, it would be so easy to prove he was the one who did it! Guo Yu and Zhu Huiru were just kids—they couldn't have been the killer. Luo was responsible for everything.

Luo paused and flashed a chilling smile at Fulai. "I've admitted to everything; do you still want to take the blame for the murder? Hurry up and let go of that hostage!"

Fulai felt dizzy. Was it possible that Huiru never killed Xu Tianding? Suddenly the knife fell out of his hand. Zhang Bing jumped at the opportunity and pushed Fulai down as he ran out of the restaurant.

The police began to swarm the restaurant, until Luo picked up the knife and held it against his own neck. He positioned himself in a corner.

"Luo! Don't be such a coward!" Yan shouted with all his might.

Luo gave him a strange smile as the color left his face. He settled his gaze on Yan. "I really did kill him," Luo said. "This has to do with me, not anyone else, and the evidence in my car proves that. Take care of my dog, will you? He's going to run out of food." He took a breath. "I used to have a dog that looked a lot like that one, only . . . he went missing . . ."

With that, Luo slit his throat. Bright red blood sprayed everywhere.

The police officers ran towards him as they shouted for an ambulance. Someone tried to stop the bleeding.

Yan covered his face and sank to his knees, paying no attention to the officers that hurried around him.

"He's dead. Captain Zhao, he's dead."

"What do we do now?"

"I guess the case is over?"

"He committed suicide to avoid punishment."

"We should get the evidence from the inside of his car wheel."

When the noise subsided, Yan felt someone patting his shoulder. He looked up and saw Zhao.

Zhao tried to speak, but there was nothing to say. He helped Yan to his feet.

Fulai was taken away by the police. Taking someone hostage and threatening to kill them was a criminal offense, after all.

Huiru shouted but couldn't get closer because of all the police cars. "Fulai! Fulai!" Guo Yu followed her.

Zhao looked at Yan. "So they—"

"I killed him! Please, let my brother go! Please!" Huiru cried, running over to Zhao and kneeling at his feet.

"Don't listen to her! I killed him!" Guo Yu said, swiftly stepping in front of Huiru.

Yan rushed forward and slapped both of them in the face. "What, have you never seen that much blood before?" he shouted. "You're inventing stories. We all know that Luo killed him. Now go home. Huiru, your brother took someone hostage and there's nothing you can do. Go!"

He straightened up and tried to pull Zhao away from Huiru and Guo Yu.

"Do you want to repeat the mistake you made five years ago?" Zhao said to Yan.

Zhao stayed next to Huiru and Guo Yu.

Yan was shocked, but he relented and made his way through the crowd.

Zhao stared at Huiru and Guo Yu, pursing his lips. He pulled out a cigarette and turned his body as he lit it. "Hurry up and clean up the scene. I want you to take Fulai to the station for now, and don't let any of these bystanders get too close to the restaurant. Now, Luo's evidence—"

Huiru called after Captain Zhao. "No, really, I killed Xu Tianding! Luo helped me hide the evidence! I did it!"

"No! It was both of us!" Guo Yu said.

Zhao stopped. All the other officers were watching them now. He clenched his teeth and called to Investigator Yang. "Yang, take these two suspects to the station."

Yang put handcuffs on Huiru and Guo Yu—they were formally arrested.

Huiru and Guo Yu both looked terribly afraid.

After all of Luo's efforts, it still ended in tragedy.

But for the first time, as they walked towards the police car, her hand brushed against his.

ABOUT THE AUTHOR

Photo © 2015 Zijin Chen

Zijin Chen is a bestselling author of suspense fiction. His critically acclaimed books include *The High IQ Crime* and *The Forbidden Place*.

ABOUT THE TRANSLATOR

Photo © 2014 Alex Deeter

Michelle Deeter is a translator based in the United Kingdom. She holds a bachelor's degree in international relations from Carleton College and a master's degree in translation and interpreting from Newcastle University. She translates and interprets both technical texts and works of fiction.